He looked at her from hooded eyes.

"Tell me, lady, is it true that you have not met your future husband, the heir of Montefiore?"

"That is true, yes, but what is that to you?"

Niccolo appeared to consider for a moment. "Does the fact that Leonardo di Montefiore is the heir to a duchy mean nothing to you?"

"Only that by marrying him I obey those who made the match for me. In any case, it is as the Lord God wills, not I." Marina folded her hands and looked at him with a composure she did not feel.

The blue eyes were blazing at her now. "You show a singular meekness in action, lady, which contrasts with the fieriness of your language. I would enjoy making the one match the other."

Paula Marshall
The Lost Princess

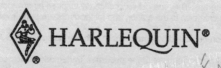

HARLEQUIN®

TORONTO • NEW YORK • LONDON
AMSTERDAM • PARIS • SYDNEY • HAMBURG
STOCKHOLM • ATHENS • TOKYO • MILAN • MADRID
PRAGUE • WARSAW • BUDAPEST • AUCKLAND

ISBN 0-373-30337-8

THE LOST PRINCESS

First North American Publication 1999

PAULA MARSHALL,

married with three children, has had a varied life. She began her career in a large library and ended it as a senior academic in charge of history in a polytechnic. She has traveled widely, has been a swimming coach and has appeared on *University Challenge* and *Mastermind*. She has always wanted to write, and likes her novels to be full of adventure and humor.

Chapter One

She was lost in a forest, at night. But she was not alone. Her hand was in someone else's. A man's hand. Large and strong and warm. He was urging her along, almost running her through the trees. What man was this? Why was he being so urgent with her? There had been other men with them once, but they had been sent away some days ago. How did she know that?

Did she know the man whose hand she held—or, more accurately, whose hand grasped hers? More importantly, did she trust him?

She stopped suddenly, so suddenly that he stopped too—and spoke to her.

For some reason she could not see his face, but she could hear his voice.

"Do you trust me, Marina?" he asked her urgently.

"With my life!" she told him. "With my life."

Even as she said the last word everything swirled away into the dark—the moon, the forest, and the man—and she was awake again, remembering everything which had happened to her since the morning when her uncle Ugo, the Marchese of Novera, had unexpectedly sent for her to end for ever the peaceful life which she had been living as Novera's lady...

"Marina, my child, the lord your uncle wishes to see you at once."

The lady Marina Bordoni, princess of Novera, looked up with a sigh. She was seated in front of a tapestry depicting the rape of the Sabine woman, which she had designed and was stitching for the great hall of the Castle in which she lived. She might be almost twenty years old, the nominal lady of the city state which her uncle ruled, but to her middle-aged companion, Lucia Capponi, she was still the child whom she had come to serve fifteen years ago.

"Immediately, he said," murmured Lucia anxiously; the lord always frightened her, if he did not frighten his niece.

"It is always immediately with my uncle," remarked Marina with a smile, "but his bark is worse than his bite. You should know that by now, Lucia."

Lucia looked her disbelief. Ugo Bordoni, now in his middle sixties, had been a *condottiero* of note, a mercenary captain of great panache and ruthlessness in his long-gone youth, and Lucia could never forget that.

"So you say," she muttered, as Marina rose gracefully from the tall stool on which she had been sitting.

Lucia noted with approval that however urgent the lord's commands, Marina always did everything gracefully. She invariably moved slowly with great confidence, possessing a natural dignity and a graceful stately walk. The whole charming effect was heightened by her calm golden beauty, that of a Madonna painted by Fra Lippo Lippi. Her hair was caught behind in a large knot, her eyebrows were dark and fine, her eyes a translucent grey, her nose was straight, and only a beautifully shaped, generous mouth hinted that there might be a passionate nature beneath her lovely placidity.

Even the knowledge of why her uncle was so wishful to speak to her on the instant was not allowed to disturb Marina's perfect self-control. He had returned from a short trip to Florence, Novera's great and powerful neighbour, the day before, an expression of extreme self-satisfaction on his face.

Marina knew only too well what had put it there. The one thing which she did not know was to what decision concerning her future her uncle had finally come. But her walk was as stately as ever, and when she entered the great hall of the Castle where Ugo sat in state in a high-backed chair, Father Anselmo beside him, and old Benedetto Spano, his one-time lieutenant, now the Captain of his Guards, standing at his back, no-one could have guessed at her inward misgivings.

She leaned forward to kiss Ugo's wrinkled old cheek, a surge of affection running through her. Whatever he had done, or was about to do, was being done with her best interests in mind, she was sure.

He had gone to Florence to find her a husband—he had not told her so directly, but he had spoken often enough of his desire for her to marry, and now the time had come: he had made his decision.

He had done so without consulting her—and that, she told herself ruefully, was because she had so often refused to discuss her marriage with him.

"I would wish," she had told him, "to be the lady of Novera, the Marchesa without a Marchese. You have taught me the art of governance, why am I not to be allowed to practice it? You know as well as I do that any husband whom you find for me will see me only as the mother of my children, his superior chattel. I would wish to be more than that. I thought that *you* wished it, too. There have been other great ladies who ruled fiefs, and ruled them well."

"Oh, Marina," her uncle had sighed at her. "Those days are gone, if they ever existed. I was wrong to raise your hopes. You need a husband, not only to protect you, but to protect Novera from the greedy claws of Florence, or even of Milan. And not only from them: you must know that every lordship left in the hands of a woman is also at the mercy of every ambitious rogue who sees a way to ennoble himself by conquering the lordship and marrying its lady.

"No, do not argue with me, child. Events have determined this, not I. I should have seen you married long ago, but, alas, I did not want to lose you, as I lost my brother—your father—when he died fighting for Milan. You are the last of the Bordonis of Novera, and the future hopes of the lordship rest on you and your husband.''

And that had been that. Marina had hoped that he might have heeded her wishes. But shortly afterwards he had gone without her to Florence with the most magnificent train he could summon to stay with their distant relatives there, leaving only old Benedetto behind to guard the lordship until he returned.

Now he was back to tell her whom he had chosen, what plans he had made for Marina Bordoni, who could make none for herself. But however much she might have wished to argue with him, Marina knew only too well the truth of what her uncle had said to her. She also knew that it was true that he did not wish to part with her. Childless himself, his own wife long-dead, and her father gone, too, he had treated Marina more as a grand-daughter than a niece.

She straightened up, and as she did so, he snatched at her hand. ''Sit, sit, my child.'' He hooked a stool towards them with his right foot. ''Sit here, where I may hold your hand as I speak.''

To do as he bid was a small thing, for he was showing his affection for her, where many a man would have made his arrangements without any thought for her, would have roughly shouted at her to do as she was told, or get herself to a nunnery, whilst he found a young mercenary captain of promise whom he could trust, in order to adopt him as a son to be lord of Novera when he died.

Once she was comfortable, her small soft hand in his rough large one, he told her his news.

''Dear child, you know whereof I am about to

speak. I went to Florence to find you a husband, determined that whoever I chose would be one to treat you kindly. There I met, as arranged, my old friend and companion in arms, the Duke of Montefiore, who has a son, Leonardo, in need of a wife—as you need a husband. He is a man of good repute. We arranged the marriage on the spot, for such an alliance is most propitious. It means that not only will Novera's future be assured, but by adding to Montefiore's lands and riches, you will enable that duchy to hold off the Florentines when they turn covetous eyes on Montefiore itself—"

Marina could not prevent herself from interrupting him. Usually hard-headed, and prepared to agree to her uncle's wishes, and fully understanding the politics of the matter, there was one question which needed to be asked, for something was missing in her uncle's story.

"You have met my future husband, then?"

"Alas, no." Her uncle shook his head a trifle ruefully. "He did not accompany his father to Florence, but he assured me that Leonardo is a fine young man, learned as well as brave, and most fit to be the husband of a Bordoni."

"It is hardly likely that his father would say anything else," returned Marina quietly. Her happy life at Novera was at an end, she was to be married to a man whom she did not know, go to live in a place which she had never visited and Novera would become an appendage to another family's duchy. However expedient this was, however necessary to secure Novera's future, it was all to be done at her expense.

She released her uncle's hand, rose, and walked to the narrow window which overlooked the beautiful valley below the rock on which the Castle of Novera stood.

"You know, uncle, that you promised that you would never do this to me. You said that you would never marry me, sight unseen, but that I should have the privilege of meeting my proposed husband, and having the right to refuse him if he did not please me. Besides, I might not please him!"

"No likelihood of that, my dear," exclaimed her uncle fondly, looking at her golden beauty, enhanced by the deep blue and white of the gown which she wore. He thought that she resembled one of the statues of beautiful women left behind by the old Romans who had conquered Tuscany long ago. They had been dug up recently when the town of Novera was being enlarged. "A man would be a fool not to wish you for his wife, and I firmly believe that Leo di Montefiore is a man whom you can respect."

Marina shrugged. "That is for me to find out on the day I am married—but, no, uncle," she cried, impulsively for once, as she went on her knees before him. "Do not look at me like that. Of course I will do as you wish. I must remember that I am a Bordoni of Novera, and what I do must be done for the lordship, not myself."

Ugo Bordoni smiled in relief. "There, my niece, I always knew that you would do your duty. You will not regret it, I am sure. Duty done leaves one fit to meet one's Maker when the time comes to do so.

I have told the Duke that we shall travel to Montefiore for the wedding. It must be done in fine style.''

Well, she would have to be content with that but, in an unusual burst of inward rebelliousness, Marina could not help but think that the Lord God was asking too much of her, to give her to a man who, for all she knew, would mistreat her for the rest of her life.

She must hope that what his father had said of Leo di Montefiore was true.

This thought buoyed Marina up in the days which followed as the preparations for her to travel to Montefiore for the wedding went ahead. Dresses were fetched from the great painted chest in Marina's bedroom, and the jewellery which had last been worn by Marina's mother was taken from the strong box in which it had long been kept. At the last moment, a few days before they were due to set out, when she was stitching at the great tapestry, so soon to be left behind for one of the sempstresses to finish, Lucia came running into her room.

''Oh, lady, the lord is ill. They say that he fell after he came from the chapel, and could not rise again. Father Anselmo is with him, and a physician, and he is asking for you.''

Her uncle ill! On the one hand Marina felt sick at the very thought, on the other a treacherous voice in her brain was saying to her, Perhaps this will mean that the wedding will be put off. She silenced the treacherous voice, and made her way to her uncle's bedroom.

For the first time, seeing him there, propped up

against cushions, she realised how frail he had become, and why he was so insistent that she should marry. She felt ashamed that she had temporised with him for so long. He gave her a weak smile, murmured painfully, "Oh, Marina, do not be distressed. This is nothing, a passing malaise…"

At the bedside, unseen by him, the Castle's physician shook his head at both of them. "No, lord," he intoned repressively, "for while your illness does not as yet threaten your life, it is imperative that you rest."

Ugo sat up, for a moment completely the lord, before he sank back again, exhausted on his pillows. "Silence, man. I have a duty to perform. I must escort my lady niece to Montefiore for her wedding."

The physician shook his head again, his face severe. "Set out for Montefiore in your present condition, lord, and you will die on the way. My life on it, if you do."

"The journey and the wedding can be delayed until you are fit to travel, uncle." Marina's voice was as tender and loving as she could make it. "I know how much it means to you and to Novera, but…"

This time when Ugo sat up, he remained upright, although the effort cost him dear.

"No," he commanded. "Listen carefully, Marina. It comes to me that I might never be able to make such a journey again, and this wedding must go ahead without me, if the Lord God so wills. I wish to live until it is accomplished. The journey will be made. Benedetto and Father Anselmo shall escort you—your worldly and spiritual guides as they have been mine.''

"But, uncle," Marina began to remonstrate with him, although she knew that the matter was hopeless.

"But me no buts, girl. I have spoken, and so it shall be done. You shall be Montefiore's bride before the month is out. This is no time to delay."

Marina could not argue with him. She could see the effort that he was making, even to speak to her in a low and broken voice. To oppose him might be to kill him. She saw by the physician's expression that he wished her away. She must agree, and endure—for was not that woman's lot?

"Come, lady," ordered the physician as Ugo's eyes closed, the effort of speech having almost exhausted him. "The lord your uncle needs to rest. You may see him later when he is a little recovered."

And later on, thanks be to the Lord God, he was somewhat better, though still insistent that Marina should set out for Montefiore without delay—"so that I may know that you are safely married before death claims me."

His counsellors, grave and reverend men all, supported him in his wish. Indeed, the most senior of them, Cola da Rimini, insisted that he would lead the party so that Novera's heiress should be supported with all due ceremony and solemnity when she arrived in Montefiore.

Ugo, against his physician's orders, had himself carried down to the courtyard in a chair mounted on poles to see his niece begin her journey. Marina clung to him, as she bade him farewell, hoping against hope that it was not for the last time. Ugo was almost as much affected and, kissing her on the cheek, he murmured, "Go with God, dear niece, and the blessings of an old man who loves you."

Pain on his grey face, he watched her enter her sumptuous litter, beautifully gilded and painted, with curtains to protect her from the sun of early summer. For her to travel in this fashion rather than on horseback would slow the party down, but Ugo had insisted that she must in order to demonstrate to all the world that she was a lady of high degree. Afterwards Marina was to wonder how different her life might have been if she had travelled on horseback as she had wished.

At the time it seemed little enough to do for him to agree to her uncle's orders without argument. After they had travelled beyond Novera's walls, she opened the curtains to look out at the smiling countryside, and to wave to the occasional staring peasant who rarely saw such a prosperous and splendid cavalcade. Opposite to her, Lucia fanned herself and complained vigorously of the heat, of having to go to Montefiore at all. "I am growing too old for such jaunting," she told Marina. "The lord should have sent a younger woman with you."

Later when they sat eating in a shady copse, just off the crude road, she changed her tune. "The lord said that your future husband is noted as a handsome young man, a soldier and a scholar, too." She gave an arch giggle. "Such a man should be an excellent bedmate for you, lady. You are blessed among women.''

Marina, who was eating good bread, butter and cheese vigorously, for the fresh air had made her hungry, shivered a little at Lucia's words. A bedmate! For the first time she forced herself to contemplate the realities of marriage. For the first time, also, she acknowledged that her opposition to marriage was because she was strangely fearful of the whole business of getting into bed with a man, and the love or lust, call it what you will, which went with it.

Living as she had done, the favoured child of an elderly uncle, she had had little to do with any young man, and now was frightened of all men. They were strange brutal beings who laughed and belched and swore and stared frankly at one's breasts with hot eyes. They might say that they obeyed and feared the Lord God, but their actions certainly didn't support any such belief.

And now she was going to belong to one of them. The only way in which she could have avoided such a fate was to have declared that she had a vocation and wished to become a nun, renounced the world, and retired to a nunnery. That, however, would have been a lie, and Marina prided herself that she never lied—and besides, one should never try to cheat the Lord God.

Perhaps her uncle and Lucia were right. She would have the good fortune to marry a handsome, meek and kind young man, who was more of a scholar than a soldier, and she would live happily ever after with him. Well, she would soon know the truth of the matter for each slow day was bringing her nearer and nearer to her fate.

But the fate which was awaiting her as they left Noveran lands, and entered the great forest which covered much of the territory of the neighbouring state of Verdato, was not the one which she was anticipating. Her party was not expecting any trouble when they passed through Verdato since its tyrant, Gentile da Cortona, had recently visited Novera, and had made a pact with Ugo that neither should attack the other. He had been a *condottiero*, a one-time friend of Ugo's, but his reputation, unlike Ugo's, had not been good.

It had been rumoured that, more than once, Gentile had sold the lord who had hired him to the lord's enemy, because that enemy had secretly offered him a large sum to betray his master. Nothing had ever been proved, and finally, in early middle age, he had won his lordship and settled down into something resembling respectability.

Marina remembered him as a large man, middle-aged, running to fat, with a blowsy wife who had died suddenly, shortly after his visit to Novera. She remembered, too, that he had been another of those lecherous men who had looked at her with hot eyes, and that those eyes had made her shudder.

They were halfway through the forest, their speed still at the same steady pace which they had kept up since leaving Novera, several days earlier, when disaster struck. The forest had become broken, with clumps of trees alternating with scrub through which the wild boar roamed, so the rider leading the way was keeping a look out for danger, when danger of an entirely different kind was upon them.

Marina and her companions had heard the steady approach of thundering hooves for some time, the noise of a large party of men riding towards them. Their small column drew to a halt, Benedetto turned in his saddle to speak to Cola da Rimini when a crossbow bolt struck him in the chest so that he fell, dying, to the ground. da Rimini, a peacable man who had never seen war, wrenched his horse's head around to flee from what was now apparently a body of heavily armed men, intent on attacking the Noverans. He had only galloped a few paces when the bolt which killed him struck him in the back.

A crossbow needed to be rewound each time that it was used, and that was only possible on foot, so the oncoming cavalry were restricted to loosing off one bolt each but, owing to the advantage of surprise, these bolts were deadly enough to deprive Marina's escort of any chance of defending themselves. That the attack was carefully planned became clear when Father Anselmo was the only male member of the party to be left alive, apart from those underlings who had managed to ride off into the forest.

At the sound of men shouting and cursing, of galloping hooves, of neighing horses, Marina pulled back the curtains of her litter—to reveal a scene of carnage as their attackers mercilessly slaughtered those of her party who had not had the time, or the good fortune, to escape on horseback.

Marina, in the grip of a desperate belief that she might somehow escape, although how she could not imagine, climbed out of the litter, Lucia following, crying and wailing at the dreadful sights around them. Any hope that Marina might have entertained of salvation was dashed when the leader of the assassins, a big man accoutred in splendidly chased armour, and wearing a steel helmet with a beak like a swan's, dismounted, removing his helmet once he had done so.

She recognised him at once. This was no leader of rogues who haunted the badlands of the lonely borders between the city states, preying on hapless travellers, but the lord and tyrant of Verdato himself, Gentile da Cortona in all his monstrous glory.

He ignored the wailings of Lucia and the remonstrances of Father Anselmo, who had been pulled from his horse, and pushed roughly to his knees before him, to say with dreadful jocularity to Marina, who was trying to control her fear at the sight of him, and the massacre he had perpetrated, "Welcome to Verdato, lady of Novera. We are well met. Allow me to escort you to my humble home, which shall be yours for a space—or perhaps for ever, the Lord God willing."

Chapter Two

From the window of the turret room in which she had been confined Marina could see the road leading from the small town of Verdato towards the forest where she had been captured. The view was beautiful, but she was in no condition to enjoy it.

She had expected immediate rape, or worse, but Gentile had proved far more subtle than that. She had been thrown up on to a horse behind one of the men-at-arms, her litter left behind, and a wailing Lucia was compelled to ride pillion behind yet another grinning soldier. Father Anselmo had been treated equally roughly whilst protesting his priestly station and his noble rank. All he earned was a buffet for his pains from the tyrant himself.

"Be quiet, shaven-head! Did I not need you to take a message to the lord of Novera, I would have left you dead with your companions. Be thankful that you have been left alive and cease trying me with your puling." He followed these unkind words with yet another blow.

To Marina he had been grotesquely polite, after a manner which made her skin crawl. He had walked towards her once they were in the great hall of his stronghold and he had laughed to see her shrink away from him.

"Have no fear, lady. I am of no mind to take your maidenhead yet. You are worth more to me as a virgin, if that is what you are, than as damaged goods. The priestly sniveller who accompanied you, and the noisy shrew who is your woman shall take my demand for your ransom to your uncle and through him to the Duke, whose son you are marrying. A refusal will mean that I marry you myself, although I would prefer the treasure your ransom would bring me, for I have no wish to provoke a war with Novera and Montefiore."

"Oh," blazed Marina at him, showing open emotion for the first time in her life, to the astonishment of Lucia who was cowering behind her. "But I would prefer that they went to war to rescue me, if only to disoblige you!"

She had thrown her head back and spoke to her captor in as arrogant a manner as she would have used to discipline a grossly disobedient servant. Far from annoying him, Gentile seemed to be pleased by such a show of defiance.

"Oh, the pretty princess who looked at me so loftily when I visited Novera has spirit, has she? I thought you were made of milk and water, lady, more fit for a convent than a palace. I see that I was wrong. I am of a mind to hope that your uncle refuses me a ransom so that I may marry you, if only to have the pleasure of taming such a vixen." He put out a hand to her and Marina dashed it away.

Afterwards she was to wonder at her own daring in baiting and defying such a monster, but anger at her treatment and at the cruel deaths of so many whom she had known since childhood overcame her fear. Once alone in the room he had assigned her in the tower she had wept bitter tears, but she would not show fear before him, even though she quaked inwardly.

Because he said that he admired her spirit, Gentile had allowed her to make her farewells to Lucia, who accompanied Father Anselmo on his journey to Novera carrying the letter containing the demand for her ransom. "I don't wish you to have any allies whilst you are in my castle, lady," he told her. Instead for a tirewoman and companion, almost a gaoler, he gave her a grim-faced woman, Letizia, who was barely polite to her.

All that she had to do was wait. Each evening Letizia escorted her to the great hall to eat dinner with Gentile and his companions. He treated her with a politeness which was almost grotesque, and when one of his minions spoke a little disrespectfully to her, knocked him from his stool with a blow which half-stunned him.

"Due deference to the lady," he bawled, when the man slowly rose from the floor. "She may yet be the mistress of this castle." He favoured her with a smile which was meant to be kind, but which had Marina shivering in her shoes. She, who was used to having everyone obey her lightest command, had never felt so helpless.

But as time slipped by, Gentile began to lose his deference to her. One afternoon, seated before the window, an illuminated missal on her knee, her only reading matter, the door opened, and Letizia entered, delighted to be the bearer of bad news.

"Up, my girl, up on your feet—at once! The lord wishes to see you immediately." When Marina moved a little slowly she was treated to a buffet on the ear. "I said at once, girl, the lord is in no mind to wait for you."

This time Gentile greeted her with a frown. He was pacing up and down the long hall, and his chamberlain, who was his chief adviser, was running after him, attempting to placate him. As he had dealt with the unfortunate henchman earlier, so Gentile did with him. He silenced the poor wretch with a blow which set his ears ringing, and caused him to stand back, alarmed and silenced, after stammering, "I had not meant to offend, lord. Your pardon."

Gentile waved him on one side and advanced on Marina. This time his anger was written so sharply on his face that she retreated before him.

"You do well to fear me," he told her, his voice high and furious. "It seems that your uncle, and your future husband's father, set so little store by you that not only do they palter with me by informing me that they are *still* debating whether to pay me a ransom, but they have offered a reward to any chance-met reckless fool who might be stupid enough to try to reft you from me! They are demanding more time whilst they consider the conditions in my letter. Well, *my* demands have changed, and they shall pay the price of their folly. I shall marry you tomorrow and then advance on Novera to wrest from that old fool your uncle, not a ransom, but Novera itself, which I shall claim in your name—he being incapable of ruling it.''

''I cannot believe that my uncle would leave me to your tender mercy, Lord Gentile, knowing that you have none.''

Marina heard Letizia give a great gasp behind her as she came out with these brave words, and no wonder, for Gentile advanced on her, his huge fist raised, ready to chastise her. And then, as he drew it back for the blow, he checked and smiled a cruel smile.

''No, lady. You must wait for your just punishment for your insolence until after we are wed. You may spend the time between now and our wedding night pondering on what exactly it will be. I want a wife, but I require a meek one, not a termagant. It will be a pleasure to tame your haughty spirit, lady.''

Marina had never felt less haughty in her life, but as before, she would not show her fear. Instead she simply bowed her head before him and turned to leave. He caught her by the arm and swung her round to face him, his eyes shooting fire and his teeth showing. He looked like a wild animal, ready to attack.

''By God, lady. I have a mind to take you here and now, on the floor before all my court. You will not leave my presence until I bid you go. Understand me, by the time I have finished with you you will crawl before me to lick my feet, if I so will.''

From whence came the courage which enabled her to stare back at him, even as he threatened her, Marina never knew. She was discovering in herself reserves of strength and determination which until now she was unaware that she possessed. All the same, by the time that she was back in her room, she found herself shaking at the very memory of what she had risked.

But before then Gentile had roared at her that he would have her robed on the morrow as befitted the bride of the lord of Verdato. "Letizia shall dress you in finery suitable for a princess, and you will be ready by morning to wed me in Verdato's cathedral. I am determined to celebrate our union with nuptials fit for a Prince."

By cathedral Gentile meant the small church which stood in Verdato's main square, but he made it sound as though she were going to be married in the superb confines of Florence's Duomo at the very least! No-one could say that Gentile da Cortona was other than grandiose in his pretensions. As Marina had half-expected, the "suitable finery" turned out to be the beautiful dress which had been pillaged from the baggage which she and her party had been carrying with them for her wedding in Montefiore to the Duke's son.

Letizia brought it to her room, together with the headdress, slippers, and cloak which had been made to go with it, as proudly as though she had stitched them herself, and laid them reverently on the painted chest at the end of Marina's bed, ready for the morning.

"Sleep well, lady," she bade Marina as she prepared her for the night, slipping one of Marina's bedgowns, made for her wedding over her head: yet another garment from her baggage. "It is not every woman who has the privilege of wedding the lord Gentile." And then, she added with a sly wink, "Oh, he is a lion in bed, is the lord, as well I know. Oh, the lucky girl that you are!" She blew out the candle and Marina could hear her laughing all the way down the tower's winding stair.

Sleep well! Marina could not sleep at all. Fear had her in its grip. She would, she knew, have been a little apprehensive on the night before her wedding to Leonardo di Montefiore, but the very thought of being Gentile's unwilling bedmate had her sitting up and gasping for breath.

"May the Lord God give me strength," she murmured at last, "and may the sweet Virgin bless me by saving me from such a fate." It only seemed fair to give the Deity and His mother the chance to save her, but how? She was trapped in Gentile's eyrie and from what he had said no-one, not even her uncle, seemed anxious to save her. But to give up hope seemed as bad as to surrender life, and at length Marina slept.

Her dreams were strange and uneasy. Waking, she could not remember them, only that at the very end she had been in a glade in a forest, like the one in which she had been captured by Gentile. There was a man with her. She could not see his face. She knew that he was speaking to her, but she could not hear his voice. He seemed to be encouraging her. He took her hand and began to run with her, and when she felt that she could run no more, he stopped, swung her towards him, and bent his face towards hers.

In her fear Marina still could not make out his features: she was not even sure whether or no it was Gentile who was with her. She was only aware that the man was about to kiss her, but as his mouth neared hers, she was suddenly sharp awake, panting, sweat pouring down her face, although whether from fear of the unknown stranger in her dream, or of Gentile, she could not be sure.

Dawn was breaking. There was a lovely apricot light in the sky, making long lines across the deep blue of the dying night. Her wedding day! Like all young women Marina had often wondered what her husband would be like, but never, in any of her dreams of the future, could she have imagined herself marrying such a one as Gentile, and after such a hugger mugger fashion, far from family and friends, and everything she knew.

She found a sad amusement in the fact that three weeks ago she had baulked at the very thought of marrying Leo di Montefiore because he was unknown to her, even though he was supposed to be a handsome young man from a noble family. Yet here she was preparing to be married to a monster who was famed throughout all Italy for the cruelties which he had committed.

Perhaps the Lord God was trying to teach her a lesson. Marina could almost hear Father Anselmo telling her that God's ways are mysterious, and that what He does for and to us, is always for our own good. "We may be sure," he was fond of saying, "that if He is harsh to us, it is meant to be a punishment for our sins." But if so, surely the lesson was a harsher one than any sin of hers deserved!

But what can't be cured must be endured, and whilst Letizia was dressing her, and exclaiming how lovely the lady looked in her cream silk dress, embroidered with carnations, with a silk wreath of them set on her blonde head, Marina was telling herself that endure she must and would. So much so that when she arrived in his great hall Gentile was almost awed by the lovely calm with which she greeted him and took his hand. He bowed low to her and kissed it, saying "Come, lady, we must away to the church, the priest awaits us, and all Verdato is in the streets to see us go by and cheer our union."

Letizia was nodding and bowing beside her, before standing back to take her place immediately behind her, level with Gentile's chamberlain whose face still bore the evidence of the great blow which Gentile had given him the day before.

It was as though she were living in a dream from which at any moment she might wake up to find herself back in her bed in Novera. But it was no dream, it was harsh reality. Still holding Gentile's hand, a few members of his guard and a herald preceding them, Marina walked out of the castle and into the main street lined with Verdato's citizenry.

Gentile had proclaimed the day a holiday and all had been bidden to be present to cheer their lord on his wedding day. The herald, brilliant in his particoloured clothing—one of his legs was green and the other yellow—was blowing his small trumpet, and between blasts was shouting, "Make way, make way for the most noble lord, Gentile da Cortona and his most noble lady, the princess Marina Bordoni."

Calling him a great lord was a bit much, Marina thought, trying not to giggle hysterically. It was said that like Francesco Bussone, the great *condottiero* known as Carmagnola, whom the Venetians had put to death for treachery, Gentile had started life as a swineherd. But he would not, she knew, be the first mercenary captain to begin life as a peasant and end it by ruling a great state, as now looked likely once he had married her and could claim Novera because he was her husband. And as for calling her a princess, well, that too was something of an exaggeration: nobility she could claim, but little more.

Still as in a dream, she and Gentile walked up the steep street until they stood before the steps of Verdato's "cathedral". At the top of them, immediately before the open doors, the herald was intoning something which, at first, she could not properly hear because of the noise of the crowd assembled in the large square which fronted the "cathedral".

He was reading from a scroll, and presently she grasped that it was Gentile's military victories which he was celebrating. The crowd cheered as each battle and siege was named. Then he read out her name and the roll of honour of her ancestors so that all might know what a noble wife the lord Gentile da Cortona was acquiring. The crowd cheered again, but somewhat less loudly than they had applauded Gentile.

The press of people was so great that Marina began to feel overwhelmed by them. Fortunately, after a few more moments of vainglory from the herald, he at last stood aside, bowed low, and allowed them to enter the blessed cool of the church away from the cheering throng.

Inside, after the golden splendour of the sun, it was as dim as though dusk had fallen. There were a few candles already lit, whose flickerings cast giant shadows on them as they processed in. A party of boys was lighting more, so that by the time they reached the waiting priest, standing before the altar, she and Gentile were in the centre of a great pool of yellow light. The congregation standing behind them was a small one, consisting mostly of the leading citizens of the town. Letizia had told Marina before she left her room that Gentile had summoned them there to bear witness to the coup he had brought off in marrying such a great heiress.

In a few moments she would be Gentile's wife. The priest was bowing to the altar, Gentile was turning to face her, and now that the irrevocable moment had come, Marina found that her unnatural composure was about to crack. She was on the verge of falling on her knees before him and begging him for mercy, begging him to send her back to Novera, or forward to Montefiore.

Whether she would have done so, she would never know, for even as the priest began to speak, the great doors of the church were thrown open again, and a small party of armed men advanced up the aisle towards them. They were dressed in the uniform of mercenary soldiers, leather jerkins and woollen hose, heavy boots, and steel caps. Some of them were armed with broadswords which they unsheathed as they walked up the aisle; others held crossbows wound up and at the ready as though they were about to do battle at the sounding of a trumpet.

They were led by their captain, a tall, broad-shouldered man, also in military uniform, but wearing a steel helmet with a nasal, a broad bar which covered and protected the nose, but which also hid the features of whoever wore it. He was carrying not a sword but a long dagger, which he swung negligently at his side. The whole party resembled nothing so much as a group of *banditti*, mercenary soldiers who had left their *condotta* to prey on everyone and everything which they came across.

At the sight of them, the priest began loudly objecting to naked swords and other weapons being displayed in church. Behind him Gentile's chamberlain was bleating, "What's this, then? What's this?" while Letizia confined herself to wringing her hands and wailing.

Gentile, forgetting he was on holy ground, roared at the sight of them, "In hell's name, what have we here?" Turning to the captain of his guard, he asked, "What in the name of Satan, Cecco, were your men outside thinking of to let this armed rabble in?"

"Armed rabble!" exclaimed the leader of the *banditti* reproachfully. "Oh, I do object to that. We're a very well disciplined body as you are about to find out."

With the speed of a striking panther, before anyone could stop him, he launched himself on Gentile, seizing him by the neck and holding his dagger to his throat. So sudden was the attack that neither Cecco nor any of his men, let alone Gentile, was expecting it.

He was now so near to Marina that she could see that his eyes were a brilliant, blazing blue, although the rest of his face was shadowed by the nasal and the side of his helmet.

Cecco bellowed orders at the guards behind him, at which they began to draw their swords, which had the captain saying, still in the same reproachfully mocking voice, "Oh, I shouldn't do that, Cecco, for if you do I shall be compelled to cut Gentile's throat for him, and order my crossbowmen to shoot your men down—starting with you. And what would the survivors do for pay day then? Besides, we outnumber you, the citizenry in the church are unarmed, and I've been looking forward to committing a massacre for days—life's been damnably dull lately."

As Cecco hesitated, he pulled the dagger across Gentile's throat so that a thin line of blood ran from it, before continuing conversationally, "Tell them to behave themselves, Gentile mine, or I shall finish you off before the high altar, and enjoy doing it."

Gentile, caught in a death grip, croaked, "Do as he says, Cecco. We'll kill him later—slowly."

"Oh, bravo," drawled his captor. "Now, Marco," speaking to the leading crossbowman who appeared to be his lieutenant, "escort the lady of Novera to the church door, while I follow you with Gentile here, and remember, Cecco, a false move from any of you, and he's butcher's meat.''

Marina, who had been silent and motionless from the moment the armed men appeared, and who had been trying to work out how they could have entered the church so easily that they were able to surprise Gentile, allowed Marco to take her arm. If she was going from one ruthless captor to another, then so be it. At least this one seemed to be younger and leaner than Gentile, if equally as bloodthirsty. Looking forward to a massacre, indeed! Could he possibly have meant it?

The whole party, Marina included, retreated to the church door behind Gentile's captor, who was still holding Gentile, the dagger to his throat, and was crooning in his ear, "The lady is an even better prize than I thought. I shall enjoy relieving you of her."

This had Marina quaking inwardly all over again. Any hope that her new captor might be a mercenary trying to claim the reward which her uncle had offered for her return was beginning to fade. More likely that he was imitating Gentile and was either going to marry her forcibly, or was going to hand her back only after a much bigger ransom had been paid than the one offered.

By now they had reached the church door, and she and Marco and the men in front of them, swords and crossbows at the ready, were through the door and beginning to walk down the steps—and what would happen once they were in the open again?

Having merely exchanged one monster for another—and a more efficient one than Gentile at that—there was still the problem of how this new monster thought that he could get away without a pitched battle in Verdato itself. When Gentile's men outside the church and at the castle realised what had happened, they would surely attack him and his followers with all the strength at their command. And if these were all the men whom he had brought with him, how could he hope to escape with her?

No time to think of anything more, for as he reached the top of the steps the man holding Gentile flung him into the church and banged the doors shut behind him, shouting, "Key, Dino, quickly!" Whereupon one of the burly rogues produced a key and locked Gentile, his men and the congregation in the church. Other men trotted up with a stout piece of timber which they ran through the door handles to imprison the lord of Verdato and his men more securely. They could hear Cecco's guards hurling themselves unavailingly at the doors.

In the square a further line of *banditti* was holding the townsfolk back without much difficulty. For the first time Marina realised that if Gentile ruled Verdato with such careless brutality as she had seen him display, then its citizens would not enthusiastically defend him against any man or group of men who proved that they could defy him. They might, indeed, see such a band of men as saviours—a new master might prove kinder than the old—or so they could always hope.

Even when the invading banditti began to retreat they made no effort to remove the timber from the doors.

"To horse," shouted the captain briskly. Without more ado he took Marina by the hand, and shouting, "Hurry, lady, hurry, before the doors give way," he ran her down the street so that Marina thought that she was back in her dream again. She saw the remnants of Gentile's small bodyguard which had been left outside the church lying dead and wounded in the steep roadway.

Unhindered by the townsfolk they tore through the great arch which led out of the town, and there, beyond it, were a few more men who were guarding the horses which belonged to her rescuers.

Marina was panting with the unaccustomed effort of running. She felt as though her legs were giving way even before they reached the horses. Her captor, ignoring her gasping cries, flung her up on to the first horse which they came to, and shouted, "Astride, lady, astride," before he mounted the one beside it.

Once astride her horse—something which she had not been since she was a child—Marina struggled to pull her incongruous wedding finery down to hide her legs.

Ignoring her futile efforts at modesty, her new captor cut his whip across her horse's flanks so that it bounded forward, almost unseating her. Shouting, "Follow me!" he galloped his party down the cobbled road beyond the gate, which soon turned into a track which they left to make for the forest in which Marina had been captured.

Even as she struggled to control her horse, Marina noticed that not all of the men with them had horses, and that some of them, once they were through the gate, had disappeared into the scrub which lined the road. They took the opposite direction from their captain's party which was now reduced to some ten in number.

Well, she was escaping from Gentile, whose very touch had revolted her, but she was now at the mercy of an arrogant swine who bawled peremptory orders at her as though she were her own waiting woman. The sooner she found out who he was and what his intentions towards her were, the better. She had a horrid feeling that they were not benevolent, but for the moment all that she could do was follow him, and hope not to fall off her lively horse...

Behind them, in the town, the church doors burst open when Gentile's maltreated citizenry belatedly pulled out the timber which held them. Cecco, Gentile and his men streamed after Marina and the *banditti*, to find horses and to take up the pursuit.

Chapter Three

"Well, lady," drawled the mercenary captain, offering her his hand to help her dismount. "The forest is not as comfortable as Gentile's castle, but at least you don't have to share it with him."

Hot, tired and sore, Marina made him no answer. She could barely think, let alone speak. As her feet touched the ground her knees gave way and she would have fallen through sheer exhaustion had not her captor caught her to him to steady her. For a moment, before he released her, she could feel the hard strength of his long and shapely body, the strength with which he had held and controlled the massive Gentile so easily. It came to her that she ought to fear him even more than she had feared Gentile.

"No need to assist me," she told him haughtily; it was time to put him in his place. "It was a mere passing weakness, that's all."

He smiled at her for the first time, showing excellent white teeth. "If you say so, lady, but I thought that you might be tired after your unaccustomed ride.

I doubt me that you often venture out of Novera's castle, wearing a wedding dress, and riding astride— but perhaps I am mistaken.''

Oh, the insolence of him! Marina had never been rude or unkind to her inferiors, or those who served her, but she had hardly spoken to this man, or he to her, and she already resented him, resented most of all his air of effortless superiority.

''No mistake,'' she informed him coldly, grey eyes frosty. ''But the lady of Novera would be a poor thing if she allowed such a trifle to discommode her.''

His helmet hid the look of admiration which he unwillingly threw her. Exhausted by having been kidnapped, not once but twice, having ridden hard across country and then wound her way painfully through that part of Verdato's forest which climbed into the mountain beyond it, she was still showing a haughty, froward spirit. Unable to see his expression, Marina mistakenly thought that he held her in despite as a useless great lady, fit only to be coddled.

So she walked away from him to sit on a fallen tree, her legs trembling and her whole body vibrating after the rigours of her ride. She wondered why he had chosen to take them all so high that she could look across the valley which divided Verdato from them, and see it on a hill below them, blue in the distance. His men were too absorbed in looking after their horses, in unstrapping their saddle bags, in making a small fire, and preparing themselves to remain for a time where they were, to take any notice of views, however beautiful.

Not that Marina was registering its beauty, either.

She was too engaged in watching her captor. He had taken off his helmet to hang it from his saddle, beside the broadsword which he had not taken with him into the church, so that she saw his face for the first time—and it surprised her.

By his easy command and his tone of ruthless, effortless impudence she had not thought him to be young, but she could see at once that he had barely thirty years to his name. And he was handsome also, after a fashion which she had not expected. His blazing blue eyes she had already seen, but not the curling waves of his black hair worn long, nor the perfect oval of his strong face with its straight nose and shapely, amused mouth. It was not by any means the face of a coarse and brutal bandit. The only thing which kept him from being an absolute Apollo was a scar beneath his eye on the right side of his face. It was not large enough to mar it: in an odd way it enhanced the general impression he gave off of careless assurance, based on the kind of superb athleticism which she thought that her uncle Ugo must have possessed as a young man.

His men were obedient without being servile. He gave them orders which he obviously expected to be carried out on the instant—as they were—but now that the urgency of their escape was over, he neither bellowed at nor struck them, as Gentile had so often done. He saw her watching him—did he see everything?—and called to her, "Lady, we are about to eat. We have not done so since dawn, and I doubt that you have, either. Afterwards, we will talk, but not before. Decisions taken on an empty stomach are rarely wise. I advise you to join us.''

Marina's answer was a brief nod. Speech, for the moment, seemed beyond her. Too much had happened to her since morning, but yes, astonishingly, she was hungry for the first time since Gentile had captured her. The wretched man was right again.

He ordered two of the men to reconnoitre the neighbourhood. Marco cooked their meal. Another looked after and fed the horses. Two of them set up a small improvised tent. When the reconnoitring men returned he spoke swiftly and certainly to them after they had made their report to him, gesturing with hands which were as long and shapely as the rest of him.

In some odd way, he was beginning to fascinate her. She had never met anyone quite like him before. The men around Ugo had been old and grave; such smiling insouciance as he was displaying was foreign to them—and to her. A stately gravity had been the order of the day in the court of Novera and she had been a willing party to it.

How would that serve her here? Were all the lessons she had so painstakingly learned to be of any use to her? No doubt she would soon find out!

His lieutenant, Marco, a burly man nearing middle-age, who reminded her a little of poor Benedetto came over to her with water in a small pewter cup. ''Drink, lady, drink. Your day has been hard and long.''

She was drinking it gratefully when *he*, for so she was beginning to think of him, still having no knowledge of his name or rank, walked towards her. She looked at him over the rim of her cup, murmured

"Yes?" and managed to make the brief word a haughty command as much as a question. She must never forget that she was the lady of Novera and that he was some nobody who had rescued her. Worse, she was not yet certain whether she ought to be grateful to him for that—he might be a worse master than Gentile.

He sat beside her on the log, and looked frankly at her as—apart from Gentile—no man had ever done before. She had become used to deference, but it seemed that there was little of that on the mountain beyond Verdato.

"My men tell me," he said, "that there is a waterfall and a small pool some hundred yards from here where you might be able to refresh yourself after your hard ride. I have some clothes in my saddle bags which are more suitable to your present condition than the frippery which you are wearing. You could take them with you and change into them. I guarantee that neither my men nor I will molest you while you do so."

He hesitated, and then with a wicked smile, added, "And, of course, you will do nothing so foolish as to try to run away. You have no notion of how to survive in such conditions as these, and there is always the possibility that Gentile's men might find you. You will behave yourself, I trust, and save us all a deal of trouble."

Marina flushed angrily. "I am not a fool," she informed him frostily. "You have no need to bully me. I have no intention of trying to escape, the mere idea is ridiculous." In reality, she was grateful to him for his suggestions, but she was not about to tell him so. Not only did the notion of exchanging her soiled and sweat-dampened clothing for something cleaner and warmer attract her, for it was cold here, high in the thin air, but he was also solving another problem for her, which she had been fearful of mentioning through very modesty.

''So happy to learn that we understand one another, lady,'' was his only reply to that, before he went over to his horse to collect the clothing which he had promised her from his saddlebags. He had obviously thought of everything which might be needed when he had set out to capture her, and the knowledge infuriated rather than pleased her. It added to his air of infallibilty, and made her feel even more helpless before him.

The clothes he handed to her were of a rough coarse frieze, brown in colour, and the dress was so made that she would be able to ride astride without the loss of modesty which her light wedding gown with its tight skirt had forced on her. There was also a length of black ribbon with which she could tie up her hair which had fallen down. A pair of scuffed heavy boots completed the unlikely ensemble.

Nevertheless, it was with real gratitude that she carried them all to the waterfall, laid them on the ground, and retreated into the scrub where she was at last able to answer the call of nature. After that she washed herself, took off her tattered and stained wedding dress, and changed into the rough and ready garments which meant that no-one looking at her could conceivably imagine that she was the missing lady of

Novera. Her long blonde hair she arranged into two plaits which she wound round and round her head, trying to see herself in the troubled waters of the pool to check that she was as neat and tidy as a woman could be who had endured the kind of day which she could not have dreamed of before she left Novera.

Her reward when she returned was to have *him* stare hard at her, and remark, "Excellent, lady—you have exactly the look of the miller's wife at Monreale. We have a chance of escaping alive if only the rest of us are able to appear as harmless. Marco, hand the lady her share of the rabbit, and a piece of bread to eat it on."

Beforehand Marina would have sworn that she could never have sat at the end of a day spent in the open, wearing rough clothing and enjoy eating coarse yellow bread and rabbit's meat tinged with the smoke of the camp fire over which it had been cooked. But the meat tasted like manna, and the rough red wine which Marco poured into her pewter cup from a skin which had hung from his saddle, tasted even better.

She found that she was so hungry that she licked her sticky fingers in appreciation. She caught Marco looking approvingly at her. "You enjoyed my cooking, lady?" he asked her with the kind of directness which told of the camp rather than the court.

"Delicious," she told him truthfully, and he rewarded her with another joint which she attacked as hungrily as the first. His master was seated opposite to her, cross legged on the ground, hardly distinguishable from his men. His gaze on her was sardonic, but he was eating his share of the food as greedily as she was, and had he said a word of criticism to her she would have told him so. Perhaps, she thought, as she stared aggressively at him, it was the change of clothing which was making her assertive after a different fashion from that of the lady of Novera.

"We need to talk," she told him abruptly once the meal was over, and the fire had been extinguished so that it might not give their presence away.

"Indeed, we must." He smiled at her, and came to sit closely by her on her log.

Marina, avoiding his impudent eyes, moved away from him and went straight to the point. "I do not yet know your name, ser captain, or whether I ought to thank you."

He showed his excellent white teeth again. "Very wise, lady. I am not sure whether you ought to thank me, either."

"That is a matter of opinion," she returned, "on which I shall make up my mind when I not only know who you are, but what your intentions are towards me. Am I to suppose that you will escort me safely to Montefiore and claim the reward from the Duke and my uncle, the Marchese?"

She said this with all the arrogance which she could summon up to remind him who she was—and who he was.

He was not in the least put out, but said lazily, "I am a mercenary captain, Niccolo da Stresa by name. I heard of the reward offered for your return, but now that I have met you I am not sure that I want to hand you back to Montefiore and Novera." Having thrown this dart at her, his smile grew more brilliant still.

"Why should I not make my fortune as well as another, by marrying the heiress of Novera? Tell me that."

He put his head on one side, and said, still in that lazy impudent voice, "You are passably good looking, have a haughty temper—but that is of no moment, marriage to me would soon cure it. I shall need to keep my options open, lady, and shall put off any decision until we are safely out of Gentile's clutches. Does that satisfy your haughtiness?"

Marina tried not to betray her agitation and dismay as he justified her suspicion of his motives. "You must know that it does not," she told him, trying not to provoke him in any way, for she had been right over one thing, if nothing else: he was as dangerous, if not more so, than Gentile. "I will make sure that you will be well rewarded if you take me to Montefiore, and I am sure that my future husband, Leonardo di Montefiore, will also reward you highly, too."

He looked at her from under hooded eyes. "Tell me, lady, is it true that you have not met your future husband, the heir of Montefiore?"

"That is true, yes, but what is that to you?" Marina was rather proud of the coolness of this answer, and the sentence which followed it. "Between the three of you, you, Gentile and Leonardo, there is little to choose, for I am being taken against my will by all of you, and in the end what matters it but that you are men, and I but a hapless woman?"

Niccolo appeared to consider for a moment, then said gravely, "Very true, lady, but does that mean that you have no care for which of us you wed? Does the fact that Leonardo di Montefiore is the heir to a duchy mean nothing to you?''

''Only that he offers me a more settled life than either you or Gentile can, and that by marrying him I obey those who made the match for me. In any case, it is as the Lord God wills, not I.'' She folded her hands and looked at him with a composure which she did not feel.

The blue eyes were blazing at her now. ''You show a singular meekness in action, lady, which contrasts with the fieriness of your language. I would enjoy making the one match the other.''

Now this was a two-faced statement. For what did he mean—that he wanted her fiery in action, or meek? And in any case, did what he meant matter to her? He was certainly looking as grave as Father Anselmo had done when discussing a problem in logic with her. But this was no problem in logic: they were discussing the disposal of her body.

And then Marina made her mistake. She said, as grandly as she could, ''Seeing that I am indifferent towards all men, whether they be dukes or bandits, it means little to me personally whom I marry, so to please both God and my uncle I must do my duty and marry Leonardo di Montefiore.''

The blue eyes blazed at her harder than ever. He leaned forward and said softly, ''Say you so, lady, say you so. I pity the poor devil whom you do marry. Indifferent to all men, eh?'' His fine black brows rose. ''I shall test that one day, not here, not now, but soon,'' and his hard stare was for her and no-one else.

Marina did her best not to quail before it. She might

be at his mercy, but she would neither shrink before him, nor beg anything of him. She would be as cool and distant with him as she had been with Gentile. Her dignity was all that was left to her, and she was determined not to lose it.

His eyes hooded again, Niccolo rose in one swift and supple movement. He was like a great cat, stretching and enjoying the power and grace of his superb body. He was done with her for the moment, having made his none too veiled threat. He was once again the soldier and organiser, urgently calling Marco to him, saying so that all might hear him, "We must have a counsel of war, and make plans for the morrow before we sleep."

Marina watched him as he talked, watched him listen also to what Marco had to say. Again there was the contrast with Gentile, who went his own way without consulting others. There was something formidable about him. He reminded her of a young *condottiero* who had visited Ugo when she was still little more than a child. The Leopard he had been called, and he had possessed the same leashed power which Niccolo unthinkingly displayed.

Marina shivered. Handsome he might be, and young, but where she was concerned he was only Gentile writ large, after all, and she was more in his power than she had ever been in Gentile's. For who would rescue her now—from him?

"The devil is in it," raved Gentile da Cortona at Cecco Fioravanti, his captain of the guard. "And who the devil was he?"

Cecco shook his head. "I know him not, lord. One of his men, yes. Marco Despini. He was with Gattemelata in his youth. A sound man in a tight corner, I do know that."

"Which is more than I can say of you," snarled Gentile, still raving, "after yesterday's bungling. Half of my personal guard dead or wounded, and my bride snatched away from me while some nobody treats me like a bale of rotten goods. I have a mind to send you to the stranglers were it not that I have none fit to put in your place until Braccio returns from his errand. Though God knows, my youngest page might have done better by me than you have done. One more mistake like that and I'll have you gutted on the instant!"

"But who could have guessed at such impudence?" returned Cecco desperately—he knew his master's wicked temper. "To come into the church—and with so few men—and to disappear so quickly."

"The devil was in that, too." Gentile ceased raving. "Before I do aught else I'll round up a few of those who stood in the square and took so long to open the doors for us, and hang them up in the church for all to see what the reward for treason is."

"But the church is holy ground, is sanctuary," yammered Cecco, who was beginning to wonder whether the pay he was getting from Gentile was worth what he was being asked to do for him.

His reward was a blow in the face from Gentile's mailed fist which sent him reeling. "By the living God, man, did the fiend who stole my bride away and cut my throat for me care about holy ground or sanctuary? If it were not that he has done me a mortal harm, I had better find him to make *him* my captain rather than carry on paying such a bleating sheep as you have proved to be.''

He swung about to bellow at his chamberlain, who cowered at the very sight of his scarlet, angry face. ''Send out heralds and messengers to offer a reward to any who will either capture the foul fiend who has my bride, or will give us news of where he is. I'll have him on the rack to entertain us all before the week is out. He cannot have gone far—wherever he has gone.''

Gentile had just returned empty-handed from a fruitless chase after Marina and her new abuctor— fruitless because the trail was lost shortly after Verdato's limits had been reached. Pounding far into the night along the track which ran northwards had brought them nothing but tired horses and repeated cursings against fate from Gentile himself.

There he had been, decked out like a bullock for slaughter, standing in the church, one of Italy's richest heiresses by his side, his future seemingly assured, and the next minute she was gone, snatched away by God knows who, gone God knows where, his throat and body aching and his guard half massacred. He would be the joke of all Italy—as he suspected he was the joke of the townsfolk who lived under his brutal and tyrannous heel. Well, some of them would pay a nasty price for their laughter, he would make sure of that before the day was over.

Meantime he set in train the further pursuit which would surely net the man who had humiliated him, and return the woman who, having gone meekly with him to church, had left equally meekly with her new owner.

"When and how did they arrive?" he snarled at Cecco, who was nursing his bruised mouth which would no longer allow him to speak clearly.

"Yesterday, lord," he lisped. "Half of them put up at the inn, and said that they were a small company making for Florence where they had been hired by the Signoria. The other half slept in the open. When they saw that the day was given over to carnival by reason of your wedding, their leader said that they might as well stay to see the fun before they left for Florence."

"See the fun!" Gentile was raving again. "I shall teach Messer bandit what fun is before I have done with him."

Cecco said nothing, for he was thinking of the old French maxim regarding the killing of a flea... "First catch your flea..." Wisely he said nothing, but began to organise the search for the lady of Novera and those who had spirited her away. To spirit himself away from Gentile once this unfortunate episode was over was an even better idea—but that would have to wait until he had recovered the lady. To desert Gentile now would mean that Gentile would hunt him to his death with all the savagery of which he was capable.

Cecco called his lieutenants to him and began to give them orders urgently. After all, his own pride was at stake here, too.

"They will be after us, no doubt of that," Niccolo was telling his remaining men and Marina, who had just breakfasted, and were seated before him. "And if I know Gentile, he will have sent messengers, heralds and envoys to every quarter of Verdato telling everyone to be on the look out for us—and offering rewards for information which proves fruitful as large as the one which Montefiore offered for the lady and which brought me here."

He paused. "And, mark this, we shall not be safe even when we're out of Verdato's territory until we reach Montefiore's lands—if that is where I decide to go. What I *have* decided is this. Gentile will be looking for a large party and it was for that reason that I paid off most of my company *before* snatching the lady away, and told them to make for safety at once, once the raid on Verdato was over. The rest of you, who have served me in the past, I retained until we were safely out of Verdato's immediate bounds.

"Marco will pay you off—handsomely—for the excellent way in which you backed me up. I know that I can trust you not to run to Gentile and betray me—but if you do, no matter, you have no idea where Marco, the lady and I, are going, nor in what guise we shall travel. And I would advise you to trust Gentile even less than you might trust me!"

There was a general laugh at this, which Niccolo joined in. Men! thought Marina disgustedly, there was no knowing what they might find amusing. Niccolo had not finished.

"If any of you wish further employment, then make for Florence and the house of Giannini Belforte. Tell him that you have been serving under me—show him as proof the paper which Marco will give you, and he will find a captain for you to serve under. Never let it be said that da Stresa neglected the fortunes of those who served him well.''

One of the men said, ''I would rather stay with you, Captain. I have served you before, and know you to be a fair man—if hard. I may not be so lucky in my Captain again.'' Several of his companions nodded as he finished speaking.

Niccolo said gravely, ''What you say pleases me, Enzo, but if the lady and I are to avoid Gentile's traps, then we must travel light. Perhaps in the future we may be comrades in arms again?''

The man was clearly disappointed. What he had said had thrown a new light on Niccolo, confirming her belief that, for all his ruthlessness, he was not simply another brute like Gentile. But she was going to be alone with him and Marco. The thought troubled her. But the thought that Gentile might recapture her troubled her even more.

''Ser Niccolo.'' She spoke a little peremptorily to him after the meeting had broken up and Marco had begun to hand the men their money and their papers.

''Lady?''

''Ser Niccolo. You said, if I mistake not, that you had not yet decided whether you would take me to Montefiore. Did you mean that? Remember that Montefiore and Bordoni will reward you well for my return, and I should beg them to raise the reward as a bonus for returning me when you were tempted to do otherwise.''

Niccolo looked steadily at her. She stood straight and tall, not quailing before him, quite emotionless.

He had not once seen her display emotion. She was like a beautiful living statue which was more stone than woman. What would it take to break that lovely calm? Even when she was a little fierce with him the fierceness was measured, controlled.

Would passion ever rule her? If she were in a man's arms, in the throes of love, would she still resist love's pangs and be as cool, as measured, as she was now? Was she essentially cold, or was the coldness a mask beneath which the currents of passion swirled and boiled? For no reason at all, Niccolo thought that the mask existed and was there to be torn away.

What if *he* were to tear it away? What transports would reward him? His eyes dilated at the very thought. His expression changed.

The woman before him knew that something had happened, some balance which had lain between them had been tipped in a direction which she might not like. How she knew was a mystery. She said, "You heard me, Ser?" because he was as still and silent as an animal which had scented danger.

"I heard you, lady, and I will say this. I have not yet made up my mind what I shall do with you. I shall make no decision until we are safe out of Gentile's clutches—and then—" he smiled tantalisingly at her.

Marina could not stop herself. "And then?" she queried almost despairingly.

"And then," he told her gaily, "why, lady, you will have to wait—until then!"

Chapter Four

"Where are we going, Ser Niccolo? Or do you not intend to tell me?"

Niccolo looked up from his work. He and Marco were busy erasing all traces of their overnight stay from the small glade where his party had camped. They had restored ruffled grass as much as possible, and had just begun to drag fallen branches and other debris over the fire and the disturbed ground where the tent had been erected so that none might know that anyone had camped there. Marina had slept in it, sheltered a little from the full rigours of spending a night in the open. He had been considerate about that, if nothing else.

He straightened up, stretched himself frankly, and remarked, "You would learn little if I told you, lady, for it is no place you have ever heard of, or would be likely to visit. We are heading for a small farm some few miles from here, off the road to Verdato—"

"Off the road to Verdato! How far from Verdato?'' Interrupting him, Marina was trying not to betray her agitation. "Why should we go anywhere near Verdato at all? I thought that we were trying to *escape* from Gentile's territory, not making it easy for him to find us."

He was giving her that infuriating smile again, all white teeth and patronage. If anything was calculated to annoy her, that smile was it.

"Precisely, lady. And that is why we shall be near Verdato. It is often better to hide things in plain sight where no-one will expect to find them. Gentile will assume that we are making for safety as quickly as possible and all his efforts will be bent on trying to cover his borders. He will not be looking near home for us, you may be sure of that. And then, when he begins to weary of the chase, we shall make our slow and careful journey to safety."

Marco was nodding as he spoke, but Marina was still doubtful. "Yet we are conspicuous, are we not? Two soldiers and a noblewoman, strangers travelling through territory where people are looking for strangers..." Her voice died away as he smiled again.

"True, lady—if that were how we shall seem. But that is *not* how we shall seem." He stood back, and looked her over. "A lady, hmm... So long as you keep that lovely mouth closed, and don't deluge all those about you with orders and questions, we may yet pass you off as something other than you are. Come." Without more ado, he took her hand and led her over to where the ashes of the fire were awaiting their covering blanket of branches, leaves and scrub.

"This is how we shall transform you. Kneel, my

lady Marina, kneel." Uncomprehendingly, wondering what was to come, Marina did as she was bid.

"Now, do as I do." He placed his hands where the fire had been and began to rub them hard among the cold ashes, before lifting them to his face to smear it so that he was covered in soot and grime. He repeated the action and smiled at her again, his teeth showing whiter than ever through the dirt which surrounded them.

"Thus we disguise ourselves. We shall appear to be a travelling pedlar, Gianni of the roads, a jack of all trades, his wife Angela, and his assistant, Beppo. Fortunately, Marco and I came this way on another errand some years ago, and none will think it odd that I return with a wife, as grimy as myself. For we must hide that splendid hair as well." He began to smear his hands over it, saying regretfully, "Only the direst need could compel me to commit such a sacrilege, I do assure you."

It was now the turn of Marina's grey eyes to blaze at him: a feat in itself it being difficult for grey eyes to blaze.

"On the contrary, Ser Niccolo," she gasped under his ministrations. "I have the feeling that you are enjoying yourself, rather than regretting your actions." The stroking motions of his hands were more in the nature of a caress than anything else.

Niccolo took his hands away and looked sadly at them before plunging them into the ash again, Marco joining him.

"Very well, then, lady. But now you must do to yourself as Marco and I do, and presently we shall dress ourselves to match you." His wicked eyes mocked the peasant's clothing which she was already wearing.

There was nothing for it. If she wished to escape Gentile, she must do as he bid her, but Marina murmured angrily as she smeared earth, grey ash and soot on herself, and her clothing. "But a pedlar travels in a cart, Ser Niccolo, not accoutred with broadsword and helm, and he has his farings with him. Where are your farings and cart?"

"Patience, patience," he told her, thinking that, as usual, she was showing herself willing to demean herself, provided the cause was good. Whilst she might argue with him at first, sweet reason from him usually had its way with her in the end. "We shall acquire them all before we are on the road out of Verdato, I assure you."

Oh, he had an answer for everything! And, whatever else, it was plain that the whole scheme to rescue her had been most carefully planned. So that when, presently, they rode down the mountain to come to a small farm in the foothills, she was not surprised to discover that the peasant who farmed it was an old soldier of his, and that hidden in his barn was the pedlar's cart and equipment of which he had spoken. There were rough peasant's clothes for him and Marco, too, and in the cart a strong sack where his and Marco's broadswords could be hidden away.

The other military accoutrements which they were wearing were to be left behind, but not before Azzo, the farmer, had fed them, and had given them, in return for more money from Niccolo, a supply of food to start them on their way. It was plain from the manner in which he spoke of Gentile that he had no intention of betraying them and helping him.

Niccolo improved the occasion by remarking sententiously to Marina, "You see how important it is, lady, not to be over-tyrannous in your rule. To be so means that you lose hearts, not win them. Remember that."

It was plain that he thought they were going to escape, for such advice could only be of advantage to her if she were to become the lady of Novera and Montefiore. Not, she thought resentfully, that she needed it. Ugo's rule had always been benevolent, and he had been her teacher.

When they had eaten they were on their way again. Marina and Niccolo bumped down the track towards the road which led from Verdato behind a spavined horse which bore no resemblance to the splendid steeds which they had left with Azzo. They were an extra payment to him for the risk he was taking in helping his one-time commander. Marco was riding a mule on which more of their possessions had been packed, including a lute—though which of them was going to be playing it, and why, remained a mystery for the time being.

Both Marco and Niccolo, like Marina, looked as though they had not washed for weeks, and Niccolo bore no resemblance at all to the dark Apollo whom Marina had first seen at Verdato. He was wearing a dirty scarf around his neck, and when he walked he sported a spectacular limp. They had eaten food heavily spiced with garlic at Azzo's and they all reeked of it, adding to the odour of sweat on the old clothes which Azzo had given them.

Marina had been given a soiled piece of white cloth to tie round her head, and she could not help but think of the fastidiousness which she had always practised when she had been the pampered lady of Novera. The daily bath in scented water. The oils which Lucia had rubbed into her skin to keep it sleek; the clean clothes, smelling of the herbs which had been placed between each layer of them in the painted chest at the bottom of her bed. She felt as though she had truly turned into the peasant which she now looked.

Except when she said so to Niccolo, his answer was a dry, "Best not let anyone see your hands, lady. Your nails are unbroken and your palms and fingers have none of the callouses which a true *contadina* would possess. But think nothing of that, a week's cooking of our meals, washing clothes occasionally, and helping me unload the wagon and sort the simples will soon change all that."

"Cooking your meals!" Marina could not prevent her voice from sounding hollow. "I cannot cook your meals. I have never cooked a meal, I should not know how to begin."

"Lady, you seem to me to have some intelligence, and that being so, you must learn to cook, and do all the other necessaries of our life. I cannot be seen to have a wife who does not know the duties of a wife. That would be to give us away, at once. Marco and I will tell you what to do, but yours must be the doing. There is no escape from that—unless, of

course, you would prefer to surrender yourself to
Gentile? If so, say the word—not that I should necessarily do as you bid me, but it would be useful to
know where I stand.''

Oh, he was hateful! Had he no idea how difficult
this masquerade was for her, coming as it did on top
of all that had happened to her since she had left
Novera? Apparently not, for he began to deluge her
with information about cooking, washing clothes,
making a fire, and all the other duties expected of a
pedlar's doxy—''for I doubt me anyone will think
that you are truly my wife, marriage and giving in
marriage not being the custom of those who travel
the roads.''

His doxy! Did he mean it?

And performing all the duties of being his wife!
Could that conceivably mean that he expected her to
share his bed? Having escaped Gentile's assault on
her person, was she now to endure his? She looked
sideways at him, at the strong profile, at the mocking
twist to his long mouth, and found no reassurance
there. That shapely mouth with its full lower lip had
doubtless kissed many women, and doubtless they
had taken pleasure in being kissed. But she, Marina
Bordoni, had no wish to be kissed by him, and would
certainly take no pleasure in it if he forced her to kiss
him…or worse.

Only to think of it had Marina going hot all over,
and a slight sweat, not wholly attributable to the
growing heat of the day broke out on her upper lip
and forehead.

It did not help matters that he suddenly looked at

her, and said in that annoying slight drawl of his, "You are well, lady? You look a little feverish."

What to say to that? I am feverish at the mere idea of being kissed by you, for that would give him entirely the wrong idea. She should be shuddering at the notion, surely, not running a temperature! So she answered him as coolly as possible. "No, I am not feverish, it is merely that I am not accustomed to travelling outside of a litter in the heat of the day."

He nodded gravely at that and said nothing more. Well, at least by her reply she had stopped him from continuing his long catalogue of all that she was expected to do whilst they were fleeing from Gentile. And once they were on the road from Verdato, Niccolo remained silent whilst he concentrated his whole attention on driving the cart.

Marina felt uncomfortably conspicuous, even when they shared the road with no-one but the odd boy driving geese. What did surprise her a little was the number of travellers whom they passed, both then, and later in their journey. When they approached a village through which the road ran, she thought that the whole world must be looking at her, and thinking, There is the missing lady of Novera. How much will the lord Gentile reward me with if I capture her and take her back to him?

But no such thing. The whole world or, rather, that part of it through which they were travelling, apparently saw what Niccolo da Stresa wished it to see. A pedlar who had visited them at sometime in the past and who had returned, to unpack his cart after he had lowered its rude leather canopy, and set out his wares in the village's little square, which had at one corner a chapel with a tiny bell tower.

Marina had often visited such small settlements when she had been moving about Novera, but she had never before stopped in one, other than to look out of her splendid litter and be handed a cup of the coarse local wine, which she drank to please the giver rather than because she needed it.

Niccolo first stopped the cart before the inn, which stood at the other corner of the square from the chapel, and bade Marco fetch them all a drink. Marco, who looked, if possible, even more villainous than Niccolo, for his clothing was so ragged and elderly that it barely fitted him, showing great expanses of sun-burned chest, arm and leg, grumbled loudly and surlily at them both before making his way into the inn. Even when he was inside it, Marina heard his curses still being hurled at them out of the door through which he had disappeared. It was plain that he and Niccolo had practised their deceits before, so that they had become second nature once they had exchanged their military clothing for a peasant's garb. Marco, from being gravely obedient, had turned into every surly under-servant whom Marina had come across in her previous life.

Niccolo's reply was to hurl curses of his own after Marco before driving across the square to take up a position before the church steps. He jumped down from the cart, threw the reins to Marina and in a brusque voice ordered her to "Look after the horse and cart for me, wife, until I have gathered us a crowd." He then unstrapped the lute from Marco's mule, which had ambled after them, and walked to the centre of the square where a small well with an ornamental wall around it stood.

Look after the horse and cart, indeed! Marina had never done such a thing before, and it was fortunate for her that the horse was a weak, tame creature, quite unlike the lively chargers who graced the court of Novera, and stood meekly before her as though Niccolo still held the reins.

Meantime Niccolo sat himself on the wall around the well, crossed his legs, tuned the lute and began to sing, ogling and winking at the first few curious housewives who had already made their way over to him. His song was one which Marina had never heard before, but which the women obviously had, because they all began shrieking with laughter, poking one another, and waving their hands at the singer. They made so much noise that men, too, crossed the square to listen to him, and to throw small coins into his small round hat which he had doffed and placed on the ground before him.

The song over, Niccolo graciously acknowledged their applause by bowing his head, and launching into another ditty, apparently even more scandalous than the first. He was singing in a lowish voice so that Marina could not distinguish the words, other than the occasional amore which floated over. Before he began the second song he called over to her. "Go and help Beppo—" Marco's new name "—carry out our bread and wine. Look to it, Angela, don't dawdle."

It was becoming less and less difficult to remember that Niccolo was Gianni, she was Angela, Marco was Beppo, the horse was Nello, and the mule was "Hey, You" or "Damn Your Eyes", apparently not being considered worthy of a name. It was also difficult to believe that Niccolo was drawing attention to them quite deliberately, and that everyone was taking the three of them at face value, three gypsy-like pedlars making a sparse living as they travelled the roads.

Muttering rebelliously to herself, Marina took from Marco the wine, bread and cheese which the innkeeper's wife had cut for them, and placed them on the steps of the chapel, behind the cart. Marco began to set out the bits and pieces of the pedlar's trade, which had the women ignoring Niccolo's songs, in favour of haggling over a new broom or a fine scarf. "All the way from Florence for your delight, ladies," half-sang Niccolo, who now put his lute away in favour of money making, rather than entertaining to gain a crowd to whom to sell his wares and make a few coppers.

Marina continued to help Marco by showing off the few pieces of women's finery they carried by holding it up, or draping it round her shoulders, remembering Niccolo's admonition that she was to speak as little as possible.

An old grey beard who had hobbled over to see the fun was so entranced by this silent woman—all the village women apparently being singularly noisy—that he congratulated Niccolo. "Hola, Messer pedlar, you have a treasure of a wife there. Dumb, is she?"

"Not exactly," riposted Niccolo with his most impudent grin, as he sold one of the village women a trumpery comb decorated with small glass beads. "She has a fine turn of speech when she thinks it necessary." He turned his grin on Marina. "Is not that so, wife?"

Marina could not help herself. She did something which no lady of Novera would ever have contemplated doing. She was holding a ladle in her hand, a copper one, to show to the group of housewives who were admiring Niccolo's wares. Without even thinking about her dignity as the lady of Novera, but only of her anger at his insolence, she cracked him smartly on the top of the head with it. That would teach him not to make fun of her in public!

All of the women, and the old greybeard, let out joyful screeches at the sight, and Niccolo, holding his head, jumped backwards with such a comical expression of alarm on his face that Marina, who had begun to advance on him, ladle upraised, dropped the ladle and started to laugh.

For the first time in her sheltered, dignified and ordered existence she was letting fly with a full-bellied roar, the sort of roar she had heard the older ladies of Ugo's court give when a crowd of mummers came to perform a masque for them, and did a suggestive comic dance. She had always turned her nose up at such a coarse and vulgar lack of reticence, but here, in the square of an unknown village, dressed like a fishwife, answering to a name which was not her own, and at the mercy of an impudent scoundrel who apparently did not give a ducat for her rank, she was laughing as she had never laughed before. Side-splitting laughter, which presently Marco joined in, and then Niccolo himself, still holding his insulted head, so that the little square rang with their mirth.

She was weeping tears of joy when Niccolo came up to her, and pulling a battered square of linen from his pocket began to wipe her eyes, and murmur gently, "Enough, wife, enough." He could hear that the unforced joy was beginning to turn into the hysteria of someone who had been sorely tried for a long time, and he wanted her to say and do nothing which might betray them.

Marina was in the circle of his arms, and oh, it was pleasant to lean against his strength, and be gently petted by him, for he was crooning something to her, and it was the naughty song which he had been singing. It was as though she were a child again, and she fell into a pleasant stupor and let him lead her to the church steps where he held the flagon of wine to her lips for her to drink, and oh, it was so delicious after the hardships of the day that it tasted better than the finest Falernian.

He was being kind to her—for the first time.

Later, they made their way to the stable at the inn's rear. They had eaten the remains of their own food, given to them by Azzo, and each drunk as much wine as they wished, the gift of the landlord, who had admired Niccolo's singing, and had rewarded them accordingly.

"You may sleep with the horses, Messer pedlar,"

he had roared at them. "And free, though many would charge you."

"Oh, the generous fellow that you are." Niccolo had bowed to mine host, staggering a little, for the wine had been strong, and they had drunk hard and deep. "Blessings upon you, and may the Lord God reward you as you deserve!"

Marina thought that this was perhaps a little fulsome, but did not say so. Her own balance was not all that it should be, and she needed Marco's steadying arm to steer her into the stable, and to help her to make a comfortable bed in the straw. She had tried to refuse to drink the freely offered wine, but Marco had whispered into her ear, "You must, Angela, if you are to play your part correctly. This is no time to court suspicion."

So now she was sitting in the straw, her head whirling, and Niccolo was throwing himself down beside her in the straw, staring at her, his blue eyes feral. Marina found herself shivering beneath the hypnotic blaze of them and, flown with wine, ready for sleep, tired as she had never been in her old life, she only thought that like her he wanted to rest. Instead, he leaned forward and tried to pull her down beside him. Even through the haziness caused by the unaccustomed amount of drink she had taken, some instinct for self-preservation had her trying to push him away, saying faintly, "No, Gianni, no. I wish to sleep."

Only to have him throw an arm about her, and say, his voice hoarse between drink, singing and laughter, "Come, wife, a good wife lies with her

husband, does she not? And you are my good wife."
Now she was fully underneath him and his mouth
was on hers. Marina tried again to push him away,
but Niccolo only lifted his mouth from her enough
to whisper, "Do as I say, wife. Do not fight me,"
before his lips were back on hers again, and he was
teasing them open with his tongue.

Gasping, she felt the full weight of the length of
him until he lifted himself above her a little—but he
kept his mouth on hers whilst his hands roved her
body. He had pulled down the bodice of her dress
and was beginning to caress her revealed breasts,
which had her gasping again, and lifting her body to
meet his, giving a little throaty cry as she did so. She
had ceased to resist him, and the pleasure he was
giving her.

Yes, he was about to make her his wife, there was
no doubt of that. Her senses reeling, giddy with drink
and the delightful feeling induced by his roving
hands, Marina found that her mouth had also taken
on a life of its own, and was responding avidly to
his kisses, as her body was responding to his ca-
resses.

And then, even as some warning bell began to ring
in her mind, she heard above them a coarse voice
bellowing, "Hola, Messer pedlar, I came but to see
you comfortable. Alas, I am too late. You are comfortable already, could not even wait to pleasure your
doxy, so I bid you goodnight—and may the nightingale sing for you until dawn!" Suddenly struck
stone cold sober, Marina heard his muffled laughter

which only ended when the stable door shut behind him.

Niccolo rolled off her at last when he was certain that the landlord had gone. He sat up, and Marina was left lying alone and bereft, as his mouth and his body retreated from her. Instead of relief, shamefully, she felt that she had been deserted. And then, sanity returned. What could she have been thinking of? She, the lady of Novera, had been willing to be tumbled in the straw like a very whore, by Messer Nobody, who had kidnapped her as cruelly as Gentile had done. Almost, at the end as he had left her, she had been ready to beg him to come back into her arms again and end what he had begun.

Something of what she was thinking and feeling shone on her face. Niccolo da Stresa cursed to himself a little, not only because he had roused her, but because he had roused himself. He had drunk just enough to inflame desire, not cool it. Pulling himself away from the sweet and soft body beneath him, which he knew by Marina's response had suddenly become a willing body as well, was one of the hardest things he had ever done.

He rose, bent down towards Marina, and taking her hand he pulled her into a sitting position, saying gently, "Forgive me, lady, for handling you so freely, but none must suspect that we are not husband and wife, or lover and doxy. None do now, and none will, if we behave as though we are what we appear to be. Remember that at all times, and now, sleep."

He moved over towards Hey, You, who had been put in his stall for the night, beside Nello their horse, and fetched a blanket for Marina to sleep on, so that she should not be prickled by the straw. Her eyes filled with tears. His kindnesses to her, because they were so rarely given, had the effect of moving her powerfully. And looking at him in the dim light of the stable, she acknowledged to herself that he was also beginning to affect her after a fashion which she could never have foreseen when she first met him.

His strength, the power of his shapely body, the brilliant looks which she knew were hidden beneath the grotesque disguise he had assumed, were working a strange magic on her. A magic which Marina did not fully understand, which frightened her, but which she was beginning to be powerless to resist if he turned it on her as he had done this night. She had never before wanted a man to as much as touch her hand, but Niccolo had touched much more than her hand, and her whole body throbbed pleasurably at the memory of it.

What she did not know, but which the vigilant Marco did, was that Niccolo was beginning to feel exactly the same about her—and that was no part of the plans he had for her!

Chapter Five

"Kidnapped! Again!"

The messengers who had unwillingly carried the unwelcome news to Ugo that Marina was no longer in Gentile's hands, but had been carried off by an unknown adventurer, whether to claim the reward which was being offered for her return, or to keep her for himself, no-one knew, cringed before his anger. What was known, they told Ugo fearfully, was that Gentile was running mad looking for her, and that she and her new captor had vanished into thin air.

Ugo, normally a kind and equable man, was nearly as choleric as Gentile himself on hearing this latest piece of bad news.

"No-one!" he roared. "No-one? Some nobody pulls off such a coup against a man of Gentile da Cortona's known capacity, and neither Gentile nor any of his lieutenant's recognised him?"

"He wore a helm with a nasal," said the leading messenger, "and all that could be seen was that he was young and dark. His lieutenant was recognised as Marco Despini, but who he has worked for lately is unknown.''

''Unknown, unknown,'' raved Ugo, sounding as fierce as Gentile for the first time in his life. ''And my poor niece is at his mercy! The Lord God has countenanced a bad month's work, first allowing Gentile to abduct poor Marina, and now in allowing some *nobody* to carry her off. At least whilst she was with Gentile, bad though that was, we knew *where* she was. Now we know nothing, nothing. Would to God that I had agreed to Gentile's demands at once, however monstrous they were—at least I would know her to be safe.''

Ugo had risen from the couch where he had been resting, and his face ashen, he began to shout for Rinaldo, the man who had replaced poor slaughtered Benedetto as the captain of his guard. Rinaldo came at the run, saying fearfully, ''Yes, lord. What want you with me, lord?''

''Make up a goodly troop of men and, without fear or favour, enter the territory of Gentile and any other lord where you think my niece may have been taken, and try to recover her for me. If you do, bring back this nobody who has made off with her, and he shall die slowly before me. I shall give you a paper authorising you to act in my name. Quickly, man, for who knows where she may now be, or what she may be doing. Oh, my poor niece, it was a bitter day when I agreed to marry her to Montefiore, and the devil take me if ever I let her out of Novera again, if the Lord God wills that she is restored to me.''

"Yes, lord, at once, lord." Rinaldo went running into the courtyard, calling for his lieutenants, his sergeants, to make the necessary arrangements to carry out his lord's orders. And if he thought that he and his men were going into danger to enter Gentile's lands at such a time, he did not say so.

Never before had he seen his kind and considerate master so desperate. And no wonder; like Ugo, he dared not think what might be happening to the most gracious and gentle lady Marina Bordoni.

The most gracious and gentle princess, Marina Bordoni, was seated between Marco and Niccolo on a bench in the inn at Ostuna, a small town ten miles down the road from the village where she had been baptised into the life of a travelling pedlar's wife. She had never found out its name, but as they left the villagers came out to wave them goodbye and bid them return—with more wares to sell them next time. They, at least, had no inkling that the lady of Novera had stayed among them for a brief space.

Seated beside Niccolo and behind the spavined horse, Marina watched the poor road unfold before them as they ambled north-east through wild and beautiful country. Alas, like Marco and Niccolo, she was suffering from a thundering head, a noisy witness to last night's drinking. She had woken in the small hours in a strange cold sweat, shuddering not only at the memory of the wine she had drunk, but at her own shameless wantonness in Niccolo's arms. How could she have virtually offered herself to the monster who was at present ruling her life?

It had taken some time for her to fall asleep again, and then she had woken up unrefreshed. Well, at least she had the satisfaction that Marco and Niccolo looked no better than she felt! Marco even grumbled at the bright sun, and when the time came to eat and take their siesta, they camped by a stream and drank the pure water from it. Niccolo made her eat the bread, cheese and slices of cold meat which they had bought from the innkeeper, telling her that she would feel better when she had done so, even though the mere idea of food had made her feel quite ill.

As usual he had been right—which Marina was beginning to find boringly predictable. It would be a pleasant change to prove him wrong for once. The road climbed into the foothills of the mountain above them and they could see in the distance a small town, clinging to its sides.

"Ostuna," announced Niccolo reminiscently, tickling their poor horse gently with his whip. "I remember Ostuna, they made us welcome. I wonder if they remember us, eh, Marco?"

Marco turned and looked at them from Damn Your Eyes's back. The mule was Damn Your Eyes today, because when they had left the village he had refused to move, however much Marco had kicked, cursed and sworn at him. And then, without warning, he had kicked his heels into the air, throwing Marco on to his back in the small square and had trotted away to bray evilly at him, before allowing Marco to mount him again, walking away as though he were the most docile beast in Italy.

Marina had found herself laughing heartlessly at

poor Marco on his back, his legs in the air, looking like an upside-down, stranded, black beetle. It had occurred to her as she gasped into silence at last that she had never before enjoyed herself so much as she was now doing, roving the roads of Italy, dirty and in danger.

Something of that remembered joy was on her face as Marco told Niccolo that, yes, he remembered Ostuna, and that there might not only be a welcome there, but that no-one would possibly identify them as Gentile's fugitives. "And, yes, lady," he finished, forgetting to call Marina "Angela" for once. "I heard you enjoy my downfall in the village square, but patience, patience, our journey may be long, and I may have the pleasure of the last laugh."

"Hardly likely that I shall be unshipped by Damn Your Eyes, though," returned Marina pertly, and heard Niccolo's laughter at her quick retort.

"You might suffer an even worse fate, wife," he told her. "Pride goeth before a fall."

"And tall trees may be cut down as easily as small ones," she reminded him, quoting a saying of Lucia's, designed to remind her that the great and the tall may suffer the same fate as the weak and small. "Remember *that*, husband."

And then he surprised her once more by leaning sideways and planting a kiss on her blushing cheek— the pallor caused by her sheltered life was rapidly disappearing. "And impudence is sometimes rewarded, wife." His bright blue eyes were shining at her again, and Marina registered that they were an indication of his feelings. He was pleased with her, and she wondered why.

No need to wonder had she been privy to Niccolo's thoughts. He had thought her a cold, haughty piece when he had first seen her in the church by Gentile's side. He had felt some fear that rescuing her might be difficult given his plan of campaign, which depended on its success for her willing cooperation in disguising herself as a peasant's wife.

What he had not bargained for was that she would enter so wholeheartedly into the spirit of the thing after her first misgivings. The change in her had come when she had struck him with the ladle. It was as though she had been liberated: that out of the stiff cocoon of haughty propriety in which she had been wrapped, a mischievous butterfly had emerged. He thought that the odds on them all escaping alive from this risky venture were much better than they would have been if she had been as stiff-necked as he had at first feared. What was still to be discovered was how she would react if they were ever in any real danger...

And so they rode into Ostuna, where, as at the unknown village they had just left they received what was almost a royal welcome. Ostuna was larger than the village and richer. The church in the main square was beautiful, showing signs of wealth, and the steps which led up to its noble doorway were high and wide. The church door itself was of bronze on which episodes from the lives of the saints had been hammered in low relief: it reminded Marina a little of

the door which adorned the Duomo, Florence's giant
cathedral.

She was not given much time to admire it. As she
stared interestedly in its direction Niccolo smacked
her smartly on the backside, bellowing good-
naturedly, "No day dreaming, wife! Work awaits
you. Help Marco to unpack the cart whilst I entertain
the good citizens of Ostuna."

For the first time Marina understood why the
maids who served her were given to flouncing and
tossing their heads if she were a little peremptory
with them. She found herself behaving in exactly the
same way as she obeyed Niccolo's orders and joined
Marco in laying out their stock of knick-knacks and
necessities. Her tormentor wasn't idle, either. He was
singing the same ballad with which he had begun
their huckstering at the village. This time his audience was larger and better dressed, and not quite so
free with their laughter—but they were more free
with their money, so that Niccolo rewarded them
with more songs than he had sung before.

The inn, again situated at the corner of the square,
was larger and better appointed than the one at the
village had been, and presently the landlord walked
over to where their cart stood. But he hadn't come
to buy anything: instead he listened intently to Niccolo playing and singing, and when he stopped, flung
a coin into his cap before saying, "Messer pedlar,
you came this way a year or so agone. I remember
your voice and your impudence. I would have you
entertain us tonight and then stay tomorrow to play
for us at our early summer festival. Our own musi-

cian has fallen ill and we need one to take his place. The Lord God knows that since Captain Gentile began to rule us, we get but small pleasure in our lives. Do as I ask and your reward shall be that I will not charge you for the bed and board of your woman and your servant whilst you stay here.''

He hesitated, looked dubiously at Marina, and then asked, ''Does the wench dance, too? Give her a good wash and a decent gown and she might be passable looking.''

The voice with which Niccolo answered him was full of laughter. ''Why, let me but command her, ser innkeeper—for I remember you, too—and she might perform a rondo for you, if she feels so inclined. Wife!'' He bellowed at her again as he had done a moment ago. ''How say you? Would you dance for the townsfolk—and help us to earn our supper?''

Oh, the insolence of him! To suggest that she, the lady of Novera, for whom other people danced, should be reduced to cavorting to entertain peasants! Marina began to open her mouth to tell him so—and then she caught his eye, remembered the danger she was in, that Gentile was doubtless at this very moment scouring Verdato to find her, kill Niccolo and Marco and take her back to his eyrie—and held her tongue.

''Wife?'' queried Niccolo gently, but there was steel in his eye and in his voice.

She faltered, ''If you so will, husband, but I have no fine clothes to perform in—as well you know.''

''Oh, there's no minding that,'' roared the innkeeper. ''She may borrow the dress that Primavera, the Lady of the Spring, wears when we celebrate Easter—after you have washed her, of course. The gown must be handed back in good condition for next year's procession.''

Oh, this was impossiblel She was to be washed and decked out for all the world to see—and what would that do to the anonymity which Niccolo had said that he wanted to retain? And she was to dance for them, who had never danced on her own before. Just let her corner Niccolo on his own for five minutes and she would tell him exactly what she thought of him! But not now.

The townsfolk were drifting away, and the innkeeper was urging them over to the inn. He was promising them wine and a hearty meal and room for the night. Marina's treacherous stomach was telling her that was exactly what she needed as the sun sank in the sky. Oh, and a wash. However much she might regret the danger being clean might place her in, the thought of being so was attractive.

This time the innkeeper was showing them to a room for the night—and not the stables; they were left for Nello and Damn Your Eyes, and their cart. Marco was pulling their bags from it and carrying them in. He had been given a straw palliasse on the corner of the landing, but she and Niccolo were led with some ceremony into a room with a big bed in it, and a chest on which stood a large earthenware pitcher and some coarse towelling.

A bed! One bed! For the pair of them! For were they not man and wife? Marina opened her mouth to protest, to say that this would not do, then closed it again as she caught Niccolo's eye. The worst of it was that the innkeeper chose to twit them about it, turning back the sheets and poking Niccolo jovially in the ribs. "The nightingale will sing all night, Messer pedlar, now that you are bedded in such comfort!" They could hear him roaring all the way down the stairs.

But the moment that he had left them, Marina hissed at Niccolo, "No, ser Niccolo, we cannot sleep here, nightingales or no."

Niccolo, engaged in untying the scarf which he wore around his neck on their travels on the road, swung round, his face innocent, to ask, "And why not, wife? Has the room not a bed, and a fine one, where three might sleep in comfort—and there are only two of us."

"Oh." Marina wrung her hands at his wilful misunderstanding of what she was saying. "I am not your wife, as well you know. Neither am I your doxy. *You* must sleep on the floor."

"Oh, no," murmured Niccolo softly, advancing on her. "It is I who am doing all the hard work necessary to keep us fed. It is I who am risking my life to rescue you from Gentile. If anyone is to sleep on the floor, then that anyone must be you. And there is no need for you to do so. The bed is big enough for us both. And now, cease to nag me. My mind is quite made up, and I cannot have you scolding me like a fishwife—" this as she began to open her mouth again "—that would never do. None in these parts respects a man who cannot keep his wife in order."

"But I am not your wife!" Marina, glaring at him, stamped her foot.

"No, but the world must think so—as you agreed with me when we began this masquerade."

"I never thought…"

"No," he told her, his face suddenly stern. "You never thought. You have never had to think, lady. Others have always done your thinking for you. Now you must do your own. We are in desperate straits, and fortunate it is that the landlord takes us at face value, but he will not go on doing so if you insist on playing the fine lady with me. Do not worry about being recognised. When you have been washed we shall paint you as the mummers in the masques you have seen are painted, and we shall braid your hair and deck you out in a fashion that no lady of Novera would ever adopt. Does that satisfy you—or must I treat you as a peasant would treat his disobedient wife—and beat you until you do as you are told? Choose, lady, choose."

He meant it, by St Michael and all the angels, he meant it! And she was alone with him and helpless. She bowed her head and muttered sullenly, "I have no choice, and well you know it. I will do as you wish."

"Good, and in the morning we may tell them that the nightingale sang sweetly for us." As Marina looked her incomprehension at him, he laughed gently, blue eyes alight again. "Oh, lady, I forget how innocent you are. The landlord but echoes what Messer Boccaccio hath hinted. The nightingale sings are but polite words for the act of love itself, and as man and wife, he expects us to take our ease in the comfortable bed he has provided for us, instead of making do with the hard earth.''

Marina's cheeks flamed, and she turned her head away from him. It was not the only part of her which flamed, and oh, how she hated him for affecting her so. Being close to him, sharing in the intimate acts of living, if not yet loving, feeling his strong hands on her as he helped her in and out of the cart, were all combining to let her know that she had a body and that body was demanding satisfaction whether she willed it or no.

He must be in league with Satan himself to make her forget so easily who and what she was, and oh, somehow, sometime, Marina raged to herself, she would pay him back for all that he was doing to her—and that included the attraction he was beginning to possess for her. But first there was the evening to be got through, and then the night, when she would be in the big bed with him...

Yes, the pedlar Gianni of the roads, his wife and his servant were good value for money, thought the innkeeper smugly. The inn was full of customers, the wine flowed freely. Niccolo sat on the bench provided him, singing whatever song his audience demanded of him. His voice hoarse from his exertions, he turned at last to Marina.

"Come, wife, I know that you can sing. Let me play whilst you entertain our friends." When she would have demurred, shaking her head a little, he turned to the waiting drinkers, winked slyly at them, murmuring confidentially, "Oh, but yestereve as we prepared for rest, I heard her sing *The Blackbird's Song* so sweetly, I would have sworn that it was the blackbird himself singing it." He began to play, gently and lyrically, the song which she had sung all unconscious that he had heard her.

There was no help for it, sing she must. And had he not said that it was he, and he alone who was earning the money for them to live? His own store had soon been spent, and she would like to show him that he was not their only provider.

She stood up, as she had stood up to sing for her uncle and his little court, her sweet, true voice ringing out to the sound of the lute. Never mind that she was in a smoky inn, full of the fumes of drink and sweaty bodies, for a moment as she sang she was back in what now seemed a lost paradise, an improbable place which she must have imagined, not truly experienced, so far away did it seem.

As the last notes of the song hung in the air, the lute following them faithfully, until it, too, was silent, there was silence from the roystering drinkers. It was as though, for a space, they had been in a forest glade, and the blackbird had truly sung for them... Marina bowed to her audience, as though to Ugo, and life began again. A rough voice shouted to Niccolo, "Oh, aye, pedlar, bravely done, and what betting but that the nightingale sings for thee tonight." The coarse allusion which would have passed Marina by earlier that day, set her cheeks flaming once more.

Coins were thrown to them, and several called for her to sing again, at which Niccolo whispered in her ear, "If it be too much for thee, Angela, then rest," because he knew what strain she must be under and wished to spare her. Marina, however, rejected his offer. She would show him, that she would, that even a great lady used to ease and comfort could play her part, if needs be, as well as any man. She shook her head vigorously, and asked him if he knew *Lucia's Prayer*. He immediately began to play it, and she sang again; this time the song was short and sad, telling of love lost and never regained.

For the first time Marina sang it with deep feeling. Why, she knew not, but since her abduction the calm passivity with which she had always met life had disappeared. It had depended, she was beginning to understand, on the knowledge that she was sheltered from everything that the ordinary people whom she was meeting on her travels experienced. It had begun to crack when Gentile had abducted her, and her safe world had disintegrated around her. Her snatching away by Niccolo, and the plan he had devised to rescue her, had carried the process on further.

These new emotions which she was beginning to experience wrote their message in her voice, which broke in the last verse telling of Lucia's despair and death after she had lost her love. The song had never moved her before, but as she ended the tears were falling, unbidden, down her cheeks.

They did not go unnoticed by Niccolo. This time, after she had finished and the drinkers had roared their approval, he pulled her gently down beside him, and muttered, "Rest, wife, rest. Your labours are done for this night."

The landlord brought her a goblet of wine, and bade her drink it. "You must sing tomorrow, Angela, as well as dance," he told her. "Such a voice must not be wasted."

The drink tired her. She was content to sit back and watch the passing show. Niccolo, his voice recovered a little, sang again, but even as he launched into his last song, Marina's eyes were closing. The strain of the escape, the new experience of living most of the day in the open air, the novelty of the evening which she had just spent among carousing farmers and peasants had all taken their toll of her.

The man who had jested to Niccolo of the nightingale singing looked down at her as she slept against his shoulder. "You have a treasure there, pedlar, and not ill-looking beneath the dirt, I'll be bound." He threw Niccolo another coin, and joined his rustic fellows who were falling out of the door, singing a bawdy song, the one which Niccolo had ended with. He could hear the echoes of it floating behind them as they straggled down the narrow road to their beds. The landlord was collecting pewter pots, Marco was helping him, and Niccolo, an odd smile on his face, was bending over Marina.

She was so deeply asleep that she made nothing of his lifting her and carrying her upstairs. A sweet smile curved her mouth as she dreamed that she was a child again, playing in the palace garden at Novera. Her second song had brought back old memories, and she was roving among them. Even when he carried her into the bedroom to lay her down on the big bed which had so affrighted her, she did not wake.

He pulled back the covers, took off the peasant's sandals which Azzo had given her, before stripping off his own clothes to leave himself only in the long shirt which he wore whose points fastened into his hose which he also removed.

Then, with a wry and rueful expression painted on his face, Niccolo climbed into the bed beside her, pulled the covers over them both—and tried to sleep. But sleep was long in coming, not the least cause of its absence being the temptation which Marina presented to him, lying unconscious beside him in the bed. Finally he too, bone weary, slept...and the nightingale never sang for them once.

''Sit still, wife!'' Niccolo's voice was exasperated, and no wonder. He had spent the last hour helping Anna, the innkeeper's wife, to dress Marina for the festival. Between them they had laced her into a heavy blue dress, stiff with tarnished gold embroidery and dressed her hair for her in the most outlandish fashion which Marina had ever seen. To her astonishment the wash which she had been promised turned out to be nothing but a rub with a damp towel which removed most, but not all, of the grime from her face. Her hair had not been touched. Washing in the town of Ostuna, it seemed, was very different from what it was at the court of Novera.

So was hairdressing. After a perfunctory combing, Anna began to plait coloured ribbons through her hair so that presently it did not matter whether it was its usual brilliant gold or the duller ochre shading towards brown into which her travels had transformed it; the ribbons hid it completely. The plaiting completed, Anna placed a chaplet of fresh flowers on Marina's head before standing back to appraise her work. Marina could only marvel at what she might look like, but Anna had no doubts about her own artistry or the improvement in Marina's appearance.

"What a pretty child you are, Angela," she exclaimed, "and will be prettier still when we have painted you. You will rival the ladies of the Signoria in Florence, no doubt about it! Is not that so, Gianni? Does not your wife look even more lovely than the ladies of any court you may care to name?"

"Oh, indeed, Signora Anna, she looks as beautiful as the Virgin on the wall of Ostuna's church," was Niccolo's enthusiastic response—but he took good care not to catch Marina's eye whilst he was making it. Lacking any sort of mirror she could not judge exactly how she looked, although she thought that no-one at Novera would have agreed with them—but she kept her opinions to herself, safer so.

The promised painting she endured. Anna smeared various strange substances on to her face—they were coarse and vivid, nothing like the delicate cosmetics used by the ladies of her own court. A brilliant scarlet for her cheeks and lips, a bright blue smeared on to her eyelids, and a piece of charcoal to emphasise her eyebrows were all deployed by Anna with more enthusiasm than skill.

"And now," she announced proudly, when her work was done, "all may see and admire the lady of the fiesta, however far away from her they are." She turned her charge about and about for all the spectators who had gathered around them to wonder at, just as Marina's own waiting woman did after she had made her mistress ready for some great occasion such as the arrival of an envoy from the Florentine Republic. For the first time in her sheltered life, Marina became aware that in matters of dress and display, all women, whether high or low, tended to share the same interests and mannerisms.

No time to think of that now, for Anna was poking Niccolo in the ribs and shrieking joyfully at him, "Kiss your wife, Gianni. So lovely as she is, she deserves a reward from you."

Marina had no time to protest for Niccolo, taking Anna at her word, leaned forward to kiss her on the lips, his eyes closing as he did so. Not that Marina saw that, for her own eyes closed as his lips touched hers, and they stood for a moment, twined together, all in all to one another, before Niccolo stood back lest he become aroused before all the world.

Stars in her eyes, her mouth a little open, Marina stared at him. The scarlet from her lips was now smeared on his, and without thinking, she put forward two long and shapely fingers to brush the betraying colour away. So intimate in nature was this lightest of touches that Niccolo drew in his breath with a hissing noise and Marina, stunned by her own daring, defied him with her eyes and put the traitor fingers to her own lips.

But this served only to compound what she had done. Not only was the taste of him on her lips and in her mouth, but it was as though she had kissed him by proxy as it were, as children blow kisses at one another to tell their love. She had not willed this thing, but she had done it all the same, and a profound shock ran through her whole body.

For the first time she had initiated a form of love play with a man, and like all the new things which she had experienced since Gentile had snatched her away and Niccolo had come into her life, it was telling her things about herself which she had not known—and which she was not sure that she wanted to know.

What she *did* know was that, for once, she had surprised the man who now owned her, for she was also coming to understand as she flowered and matured under the strain of living this dangerous life, that she had always been owned by some man or another. First she had been owned by her uncle, and then he had proposed that she should be given to another man, the heir of Montefiore. But instead fate had stepped in and handed her over to yet another man, Gentile da Cortona and, if that were not enough, she had next acquired a new master, the one who stood before her, who might be her saviour or her betrayer.

At the moment she had nonplussed him a little, which pleased her, and also told her that, though he might have one kind of power over her, she had another power over him. She had the power to make him tremble, to desire her, but this power was two-edged, for if she exercised it, she was in danger of giving him yet another power over her. Not simply to dispose of her freedom, will she, nil she, but the power to make her desire him…

So she gave him a dazzling smile and swept him a great curtsey which had Anna shrieking at her. "Oh, you have gained a lady's manner with a lady's face! Look to her, Gianni, lest she seek a lord for herself instead of a pedlar." Anna collapsed into bawdy laughter.

Once Marina would have moved away from, or reprimanded anyone who spoke so before her, but today, freed of all constraints, she laughed herself, and flung back at him and Anna, "Oh, tempt me not, *signora*, lest I take you at your word!"

It was as though, shedding her identity, assuming this new one, she had truly become someone else, a someone who could express her own feelings, not carefully stifle them in case they destroyed the mask of propriety which she had worn since she was a small girl.

Spontaneity had not been her friend.

It might be now.

As though he was aware of what she was thinking and feeling, Niccolo took her hand and gently led her away from the giggling Anna into the square, where he and the landlord began to explain to her what they wanted of her. That she was to walk behind the leading men of the town, who would be carrying wreaths of flowers to adorn the shrine to the Holy Virgin which stood at the entrance to Ostuna. An entrance which was also an exit; the gate by which she and Niccolo and Marco and Damn Your Eyes would leave in the morning, their tasks here completed.

Today Niccolo would walk at the head of the procession singing and playing. But before they left the square, she would dance before them all, a grave dance to honour Christ's mother.

"I have never yet danced alone," she wanted to say to them, but Niccolo had told her earlier, that he would have none of this. "You have danced often and often in the court at Novera," he had said in his most persuasive voice. "All that you are required to do is to dance on your own as you would have danced in company."

"But so many will be watching me..." she began, falteringly.

"And how many do you think watched you when you were the lady of Novera? Many and many, I have no doubt. Think only that once this is done, we may leave, and we shall have behaved in such a manner that none will doubt that we are what we say we are. Courage, wife," he had finished. "The devil is dead, as they say, and the devil which is Gentile cannot harm us if we remember that!"

Yes, she was remembering what he had said as the crowds began to gather in the square. The small crowd which was to walk in procession to honour the Holy Virgin, the larger one watching and cheering it, before they all returned to start the feasting and drinking which was designed to celebrate the longest day of the year.

"It is a small enough thing to ask of you," Niccolo had finally said, his eyes grave, before she had nodded her agreement. And now, suddenly, the excitement of the town was infecting her, and her feet began to itch, ready to launch themselves into the dance which was to start the celebrations.

Men—and women, too—propose, but God disposes. Marina was never to dance for the townsfolk of Ostuna, for even as Niccolo began his song, and she moved forward into the centre of the square, there was a great noise and a thunder of hooves. A party of horsemen, followed by men-at-arms, came charging through the crowd, driving them in all directions and striking at them, so that men, women and children were thrown to the ground, injured and dying.

Like Moses parting the waters of the Red Sea, they thundered into the square, to come to a halt directly before the steps of the church where the procession was still standing. One of the leading citizens, a goldsmith whose name was known throughout Verdato, moved forward to remonstrate with the leader of the horsemen. Even before he spoke, even before the leader raised his whip and slashed him across the face with such force that he fell to the ground, writhing, Marina, her heart sinking, recognised him.

It was Braccio degli Uberti, one of Cecco's lieutenants, a man as brutal as Cecco himself, and his master, Gentile da Cortona. Marina was in no doubt as to why he was here, and what he was about. He was in charge of one of the parties of Gentile's men who were searching for Gentile's lost prize—and here she was, standing in the square for all to see, immediately before him...

Chapter Six

Braccio degli Uberti's hard stare swept the crowd of townsfolk who were stunned by the sight of the dead and wounded, stunned by the ferocity with which their leading citizen had been struck down, denied even the right to speak. The stare passed over Marina, passed over Marco, passed over Niccolo, saw them as merely part of the herd of cattle who called themselves the citizens of Ostuna.

Satisfied that he had cowed them, as cattle should be cowed, he relaxed in his saddle, smiled a grim smile, and spoke to his herald who rode beside him.

"Do your duty, man. Tell this scum why we are here, and tell them that if I find that they have lied to me, why, I shall hang every man and boy in the town in the square, and hand the women over to my troops."

He needed no herald. His bellow had reached the ears of all. Nevertheless the herald dismounted, and standing in front of his master unrolled a scroll from which he read aloud.

"Know ye, that I speak for your lord, the most merciful and righteous Gentile da Cortona, and demand that all who may have knowledge of the whereabouts of the most noble lady Marina Bordoni, and the piece of filth who stole her from me at the very moment of our nuptials, shall at once inform those who stand before you of it. Your reward shall be my thanks. Your punishment, should you withhold that information from me, is death."

He fell silent and Braccio swung his fell head in an arc which took in all who still stood in the square.

"Well, you have all heard the herald. What have you to tell me? For sure, it must be that the lady and her abductor passed this way with their troop."

Silence fell on the square. In the distance a bird began to sing, its pure sound rebuking the dirty intrigues of man. Standing quite still, as though by doing so she might somehow vanish from Braccio's sight, Marina scarcely dared to breathe. His stare darkening, Braccio pointed his whip at an elderly man who had been standing at the front of the procession, and demanded imperiously, "You there! Answer me!"

"Most noble lord," stammered the man. "I have seen all who passed through Ostuna within the last week. None such as you describe have been seen here. Of what kind was this troop?—not that we have seen one, you understand, but should we do so, then we shall inform the noble lord your master, at once."

Braccio leaned forward, his grim face grimmer still. "Come nearer, yes, nearer." Paralysed with fear the man hesitated. "The troop comprised some twenty men-at-arms, as well as ten crossbowmen and their captain. The lady they have made off with is most delicate, blonde and as beautiful as an angel. The devil is with them for they have all disappeared. But at some time they must surely have passed through Ostuna. Remember, if you lie…'' He bent down and flicked his whip so that it curled round the man's neck. ''Your life is not worth a ducat—trades-man!''

Clutching at the whip which was strangling him, Braccio's victim gasped. ''They may have passed through in the night, lord…'' and screamed a little as Braccio tightened the whip.

''Passed through in the night, eh? And yet you heard nothing?'' Braccio's laugh at that was a snarl.

''I said *may* have passed through in the night, lord,'' panted the man. ''All here will bear witness that I speak true.'' He fought for words, for something to say which would placate the monster before him. ''The pedlar, Gianni of the roads, will confirm what I have said,'' he finished.

''Pedlar?'' Braccio's head moved as though he were a falcon about to stoop, to kill. ''Where's he? Let him come forward.''

Niccolo, his lute in his hand, limped forward until he stood before Braccio.

''Here I am, lord. I have been travelling the road these many weeks, and have seen none such as you have spoken of.''

Marina's inward trembling grew so strong once Niccolo had been called for that she was fearful that it might begin to show. Surely if Braccio looked hard at her he would recognise Gentile's wretched captive, the woman whom he had so nearly made his wife— the delicate woman as beautiful as an angel... True, she did not now appear to be either delicate, or angelic, but if Braccio looked hard at her he would surely see that...No, she must not even think it, the very thought might betray her.

But Braccio's gaze swept over her, unseeing, and now all his attention was on Niccolo. "Pedlar?" he mused. "So, why the lute?"

Niccolo bowed his head deferentially, avoiding a direct look at Braccio and replied as meekly as a very priest, so that even in the grip of terror Marina could only admire the cunning impudence of him. He seemed as fearful of Braccio as his previous victim had been, who was now nursing his neck, the red weal around it a mute witness of Braccio's cruelty.

"Why, lord, I do but play and sing at the towns and villages I visit to add to the little I make from my trade. It is a hard life on the road." He bowed his head submissively.

"No doubt." Braccio's lip curled. "And you say that you have seen nothing untoward on the road?"

"Nothing, lord. For sure if I had I would not hesitate to tell you."

"No doubt." Braccio's lip curled again. "Look me in the eye, man. I hate a coward."

"Yes, lord." Niccolo raised his head to stare Braccio full in the face.

Braccio's smile was ugly. Here was another chance to cow the cattle who made up Ostuna's citizens even further.

"Why, man, you have the seeming of one doomed to hang. I'll improve your looks for you, so I will." He brought his whip down across Niccolo's face with such force that he staggered and fell.

Marina could not help herself. She screamed and fell on her knees beside him, to turn her heavily painted face towards Braccio, who was laughing at her distress, to cry at him, despite her fear, "Coward, to strike an unarmed man, not ready for a blow."

There was no doubt that this time Braccio's laugh was a genuine one. "The doxy is braver than her owner, I see. Were you a trifle cleaner I'd have you sent to the castle, but, faugh, my palate is a trifle dainty to need such as you. But should you wish to earn a few ducats, why, you may come up to the castle to entertain my men this night. I'll see you well paid. Hey, pedlar." He leaned forward to speak to Niccolo who, still dazed, was rising to his feet, helped by Marina. "Your woman may add to your exchequer for you, if you are so willing. I will not force her. Her courage deserves more than that."

Marina was not to know that this kind of twisted chivalry was common to such as Braccio. Niccolo was not so damaged by Braccio's blow, which had left a scarlet and bleeding weal diagonally across his face, that he was unable to understand that Marina's reckless intervention had, surprisingly, saved them both from worse mishandling. All the more reason, then, not to provoke Braccio or to attract further attention from him which might cause either of them to betray who they were.

"It is for Angela to choose what she shall do,

lord." The wound on his lips made speaking painful, but none listening would have guessed it.

"Say you so, pedlar? Well then, *signora*. Choose." His tone was imperious and he had gone from ferocious brutality to ferocious goodwill almost in the course of a sentence. Inspiration struck Marina. She bent down to recover Niccolo's lute which had fallen from his hand, and which was, miraculously, undamaged, before putting a tender hand on his arm.

"Why, most merciful lord," she faltered, bending her head submissively, as much to hide her face from him as for any other reason. "Of your mercy you will excuse me, for my husband will need me this night to nurse him, to tend his wound."

"Enough." He was pleased by her flattery. He was not to know that Marina was inwardly seething at his brutality and was regretting that she was not still the lady of Novera so that he could be punished for his cruelty as he deserved. Ignorant of her true thoughts, Braccio was prepared to be merciful.

"So," he waved a dismissive hand, "you may continue with your revels, but mark me, I shall visit the lord of Ostuna in his castle, and should either of us learn that you are keeping anything regarding the kidnapping of the lady of Novera from us, be very sure that I shall not be so merciful again, as I am now."

Marina bowed her head as he finished speaking, although inside she was screaming, "Merciful! You call yourself merciful surrounded as you are by those you have killed and injured for no reason at all. May the Lord God visit you with such mercy—and soon."

Niccolo had taken her hand. He could feel her trembling. He thought that it was fear which was moving her, but for once he read her wrongly. It was not fear, but red rage, an emotion which had never troubled Marina before, an emotion which had no place in her previously placid life.

And the cause of it, surprisingly so far as Marina was concerned, was not only the carnage about her which Braccio had created, but the vicious blow which he had struck at Niccolo. It was as though he had struck her, and had wounded her to the quick. Later, much later, she was to think that if there was one moment in her odyssey across Italy when she turned into Angela, and Niccolo and Marco into Gianni and Beppo, it was when Braccio struck Niccolo. The lady of Novera had disappeared, to be subsumed into the pedlar's wife. Marina Bordoni was no more.

No time to think of that then. Nothing to do but watch Braccio order his men to follow him up the slight hill which led to the lord's castle, high above the town. The lord was old and ailing, rarely seen, and was wont to leave the townsfolk to themselves. His nephew and heir lived in Florence, a rich merchant whose interest in Ostuna was small, seeing that it was but a fief of Gentile's, over-taxed and exploited by him.

Whatever Braccio said it was plain that the festivities were over. Once the last of his men had entered Ostuna's castle, the townsfolk began to gather up and tend their dead and wounded. Fortunately, the dead were fewer than had at first been feared, although several had been grievously wounded. But all thoughts of a day's pleasure had disappeared in the need to mourn the dead and to tend those still living. The festivities were abandoned.

Niccolo, or Gianni, as Angela now thought of him, took his lute from her and to test it ran his fingers over the strings, creating a melancholy sound. Beppo emerged from the crowd in which he had been hidden and began to examine Gianni's face.

He shook his head ruefully, then said, "Not a bad wound, but a nasty one. You were fortunate that the eye was not damaged. It may even leave you with a scar." The wound was open and bleeding across the cheekbone and temple where the lash had struck Gianni with most force. "Angela, best you take him back to the cart and dress it for him." When she opened her mouth to tell him that she had no notion of how to do so, he smiled kindly at her, and said, "Never fear, I will show you."

Trembling a little, still from anger, and not from fear, Angela did as she was bid. Gianni's expression was unreadable as she slipped her arm through his. He handed the lute to Beppo and was content to sit by the cart and have Beppo and Angela clean his wound and dress it. The landlord and landlady of the inn watched them: both had been fortunate not to have been among those cut down.

"Alas, Angela," murmured the landlady, throwing her arms around Angela, her high spirits dampened by the day's events. "Your dance will not now take place. The procession to the Virgin has been abandoned, so this year Ostuna will not be blessed by her. Oh, the devil is in it, for not only has Braccio killed our townsfolk, but he has taken our luck away!''

Angela freed herself from Anna's embrace. She was still wearing the chaplet of flowers which Anna had placed on her head in the early morning. Now she removed it, looked earnestly at them all and said, ''But if, Signora, you and your husband were to escort Beppo, Gianni and me to the Holy Virgin's shrine at the edge of the town, we could place my chaplet at her feet and we could all pray to her to take pity on us. We could explain to her that it was not the wishes of the folk of Ostuna that she remained unhonoured today, and ask her to accept this offering instead.''

Anna's response was to throw her arms around Angela again and impulsively kiss her on the cheek. Angela thought that she had received more open affection from this new met peasant woman than she had received from anyone in all the years in which she had been the lady of Novera!

''Oh!'' Anna exclaimed. ''You are a good girl, indeed you are. I'll never have a word said against those who travel the roads again. You have the right of it, Angela. Come, husband, and Gianni, too, if you are able, and Beppo, and let us go honour the Virgin as she says. Our holy Mother will surely not ignore our prayers, reverently offered.''

And so it came to pass. Their small procession, Angela leading and holding her chaplet before her, began its walk to the shrine. On the way they told those fellow citizens whom they met of their mission.

Many joined them. Some, who had been carrying flowers to take to the shrine before Braccio arrived, returned to their homes to collect them and follow Angela.

Under the bright sun, her face smeared with paint and perspiration, wearing her tawdry finery, holding a crudely made crown of flowers, the missing lady of Novera, hot and tired, but full of a fierce determination that the townspeople of Ostuna who had been kind to a humble pedlar and his wife should not have their day completely ruined by lordly cruelty, led them to the shrine which stood just outside the far gate of the town. Always before when she had taken part in such ceremonies, she had stood cool and aloof whilst others did the work and organised matters, leaving her only to smile graciously, to be above the throng, accepting the plaudits of the crowd, having done nothing herself. Never before had the lady of Novera initiated such matters or taken part in any ceremony in such a way that she felt and bled with those around her.

She was unaware as she walked along, her eyes fixed on a distant goal, that Gianni was watching her in some astonishment. Her expression of grave but enthusiastic determination was so different from her usual calm indifference that it might almost have been another woman who finally knelt to lay her chaplet at the feet of the Holy Mother. Others followed her with their offering. Some, who had no flowers to bring brought fruit. Finally, Father Francesco, who had been one of those leading the original procession, arrived, having been informed of what was toward. He had been looking after the spiritual affairs of the dead and wounded, but came at once when told what the pedlar's woman was about.

"My daughter!" he said to Angela, who knelt before him for his blessing, after he had blessed the decorated shrine. "I salute you for your determination to see that our shrine was honoured. May the love of the Lord God be with you always."

"Well, lady," Gianni said, when at last they were back in the square again, forgetting for once to keep up the fiction of their false names. "I think that the Lord God is also responsible for your transformation, for I cannot think who else is."

"Angela," reproved Angela gently. "My name is Angela. And as for my transformation, I cannot think of what you are speaking." Her surprise was genuine, not assumed.

My transformation? she queried to herself, as she helped Gianni and Beppo to pack the cart, preparatory to their leaving Ostuna before night began to fall. Although in pain from his damaged face, Gianni thought that they ought to be on their way. Whatever can he mean? For the one person least conscious of how much she was changing under the impact of her new life was Angela herself, late the lady of Novera.

They slept that night under the stars. Anna and her husband had begged them to stay the night at Ostuna, but had reluctantly agreed that under the circumstances they had best be on their way, even though Anna argued that Niccolo needed a night's rest in a good bed, rather than sleep by the side of the road.

His wound, whilst not severe, was painful and, as he had argued earlier, to do what one was expected to do disarmed suspicion rather than created it. They would be expected to fly from Braccio's persecution, so fly they did.

Gianni caught Angela's pitying eye on his injured face as she sat by him whilst he drove them along the road from Ostuna. He smiled painfully at her, and said, "Do not feel sorry for me, Angela. Remember that it is likely to make it even more difficult for anyone who might recognise me to do so! Looked at in that light, one might almost consider it a boon."

"Nothing so painful could possibly be considered a boon," was her spirited retort. Once, when she had first met him, she might have felt pleased that he had been so cruelly attacked. But in the short time which she had spent with him on the road, Angela had come to know a different man from the one who had mocked her in their earliest encounters. He was both brave and resourceful, and the affection displayed for him by those who had known him in the past, such as Anna and her husband, showed a different side of him from the one which she had first encountered.

Angela did not ask herself whether her own changed manner might have altered his to her, because she was not yet aware how much she had changed and was changing. Beppo's manner to her had remained constant. It was impersonally kind and helpful. He spoke little, either to her or to Gianni, but what he said was always down to earth and full of common sense.

It was he who persuaded Gianni to stop earlier

than he had wished to and persuaded him to rest. "Sleep now, and make an early start tomorrow."

So exhausted was she by all that had happened to her that Angela thought she would fall asleep immediately, despite the fact that her bed was a blanket laid on the hard earth. But sleep was long in coming. All that had happened during the long day ran through her head. Again and again she heard the screams of the townspeople as Braccio's men carried out their murderous work. Again and again she felt Braccio's fell gaze on her. Again and again she saw him strike Gianni. Again and again she saw Gianni fall to the ground... The litany of all that had passed was long and oft repeated.

And then when she did fall into a restless slumber she was awoken by Gianni calling out. He was lying not far from her, and she had heard him tossing in the night. He was probably finding sleep as difficult to achieve as she did. His cry was so piteous that she sat up, and when it was repeated she rose and walked over to where he lay.

Somehow he had become tangled in the blanket which Beppo had wrapped around him, and was struggling to release himself from it. He was not properly awake for when she knelt down beside him and whispered his name he stared blindly at her. Nevertheless she persevered.

"What is it, Gianni, may I help you?" She put out a hand to him, to have him seize it and pull her to him.

He was hot, his hair was wet, and his voice when he spoke was hoarse. It was plain that he did not know her, for he muttered brokenly, "Oh, yes, mistress. Only lie with me, and after that mayhap, I shall sleep without dreaming."

Still holding her in an iron grip, he pulled her down beside him. Angela struggled, but it was hopeless. She could not free herself and, once she was by him on the ground, he put his arms around her, saying, "What angel comes to give me rest?" and made as though to kiss her.

But the effort pained him, and he rolled away, putting his hand to his injured face. As swiftly as she could, Angela moved away, to sit from him at some distance, saying more loudly than before, "Wake up, Gianni, you are dreaming. Shall I fetch Beppo?"

This time he sat up, shook his head, threw aside the blanket and murmured petulantly, "I am as hot as though I were in hell. How far gone is the night?" Then, staring at her, he said, "What brings you here, lady? Are you one of the moon's servants, come to haunt a poor devil in his fever?"

"Angela," she said firmly. "I am Angela, remember. You rescued me from Gentile's clutches and now we are fleeing from him. Shall I fetch you water? There is a stream nearby if our skin is empty."

He was fully awake now, and he yawned and stretched. "I remember. Your pardon, Angela, I believe I nearly gave you an unwanted baptism into life! Yes, I should like a drink. Braccio's vile blow has made me feverish. But do not wake Beppo. He at least is sleeping. What made you come to nurse me?"

Angela rose in one supple movement. "I heard

you call in your sleep. I could not sleep, and it seems that your dreams were all evil, so you cried for help. A moment, and I shall bring you water.''

It was pleasant to lie there even though the fever gripped him, Gianni thought, and to watch her walk to the cart to find that the skin still contained water. She poured it into one of the metal goblets they carried with them. All her movements were as elegant and controlled as though she were still a great lady in the court at Novera, instead of walking barefoot, clad in a peasant's rude gown, her hair streaming down her back.

Pray God he managed to keep her out of Gentile's vile clutches even though she might have landed in his! He remembered how a moment ago he had thought to have her in his bed, not knowing who, or what, she was. More and more on their journey she was coming to tempt him, who at first had seemed so cold and distant that she could not be a temptation to any man.

He drank the water which she handed him and patted the ground beside him. ''Sit with me for a time, Angela. Neither of us can sleep this night, and perhaps if we talk a little you may forget what happened today, and I may be able to ignore my fever and the pain in my face.''

''Now, how did you know that I could not sleep because of Braccio, and what he did to Ostuna?''

Propped on one arm, Gianni was able to admire the planes of the perfect face so near to him. The moonlight softened her severe expression, and made her more of a temptation than ever. He swallowed, and then said, "Why, that is not difficult. I think that you have led a sheltered life, and have never seen cruelty inflicted before. Ugo Bordoni is reputed to be a kind ruler, and I suspect that he has never allowed you to see the inevitably harsher side of his rule."

Angela nodded thoughtfully. "That may be true, but I cannot think that my uncle would ever behave as Gentile and Braccio do."

"Alas," and Gianni's voice was heavy for once. "Those who rule men, and those who lead men may occasionally be constrained to order many things which would soil the ears of an innocent like yourself. Harsh decisions have to be made—and be carried out harshly—as you would discover if you were ever to rule Novera on your own. Even a princess, if she were not to lose her throne, would be compelled to behave like a prince—remember that."

Strangely, Angela did not wish to be reminded that she was in truth the lady of Novera, who might need to rule it alone if she never married. She could not imagine ordering men to carry out massacres for her, but she had read enough of Messer Plutarch to know that a great princess could be as cruel as a great prince. Sitting in the open in the balmy warmth of a night in late June, talking to a nobody of a *condottiero*, was making her face facts about the reality of the life she lived—a strange thought. For the first time she was not grateful to Ugo for keeping her so innocent of the world.

Another thought struck her. "I would like to ask you a question, Gianni. I hope that you will answer it truthfully." She paused to watch him nod his head.

He was already looking less feverish, so she pressed on. "How can it be that these peasants, aye, and even the townsfolk of such as Ostuna, the people I have met in our flight, be so happy and kind when they have so little? Anna and her husband would have let us stay for nothing at their inn tonight. I have not always found that those about me at Novera, rich though they were, were as kind."

"It would be untrue to believe that all the lesser folk are happy all the time," Gianni told her, "but, having little, they are grateful for the small blessings which life brings them. And not all are as kind as Anna and many of those we met at Ostuna and the first village, but again, having little, they know how hard it is to have less—hence their kindness."

This made her think, and thinking made Angela sleepy. Unselfconsciously, and forgetful in her tiredness that Gianni was a man—and therefore not to be trusted—she lay down beside him on the hard earth which was not nearly so hard as it had seemed earlier and, blanket-less, let sleep claim her. Before she did so she murmured drowsily, "What makes you so wise, Gianni?" But she did not stay awake for his answer, nor did she see his rueful expression as he picked up his blanket and covered her with it to sleep unprotected on Mother Earth himself.

Astonishingly and surprisingly, sleep claimed him, too, and the moon shone on them both as she sailed down the sky towards dawn.

Chapter Seven

"Two rabbits!" exclaimed Beppo gleefully. "And mushrooms—large ones. We shall eat well tonight."

He and Gianni had been foraging for food. They had told Angela that it would be many days before they came to another town or village, and at first, in her ignorance of what life on the road meant, she had not fully understood that once their small stock of food ran out, they would have to hunt and forage for it. For drink they had water from the many streams in the woodland and scrub through which the road ran.

While Angela helped Beppo to skin, draw and cut up the rabbits and prepare the mushrooms—he had begun instructing her in the art of cookery from the day on which she had been renamed Angela—Gianni was looking with distaste at the stained linen shirt which he was wearing.

"Even to keep up our disguise I am not prepared to wear this filthy shirt much longer," he complained. "It will shortly be walking away from me!

Tomorrow, Angela, I shall show you how to wash clothes. This afternoon, whilst I looked for mushrooms, and Beppo hunted our noble prey, the rabbit, I discovered that we are near to a small river, with a shelving beach. We can all wash our shirts at the very least.''

''And our feet as well.'' Angela was looking with equal distaste at her small feet, which were beginning to show the signs of their long journey...

She remembered the day, nigh on a week ago when Gianni's fever had returned, and Beppo had driven the cart instead, leaving Angela to ride Damn Your Eyes. The mule's name was well deserved, for when Angela tried to ride it, it would have none of her, either throwing her off or refusing to move at all. In the end she had walked along, leading it, slowing them down, which was just as well for any rapid motion of the cart disturbed Gianni. Fortunately his relapse was not lengthy. He was well again the next day, but Angela steadfastly refused to return to the cart, saying, ''Ride in my place until you are fully recovered. It will not hurt me to walk.''

''By the Holy Virgin, no, Angela,'' he told her forcefully. ''I will not sit while Beppo drives and you walk, and that's final.''

Angela did not relish another day's plodding along the rough track into which the road had degenerated, but she was determined to make him rest—at least for a day—in case the fever returned again.

''No, it isn't,'' she announced, in her most daunting lady of Novera manner, and sat down in the road before the cart. "There. I refuse to move until you agree to ride in the cart and allow me to walk."

Both men stared at her. Beppo began to laugh, his stern face amused for once, but Gianni was furious—*his* usually cheerful face was stormy.

"Get up at once," he roared, "before I lift you into the cart myself. Dear God, why have you blessed me with such an obstinate shrew?"

"It was you who kidnapped me, not I or God, so there is no use in blaming me or God," returned Angela incontrovertibly. "You have made your bed and must lie on it, as my nurse so often told me."

"Damn you and damn your nurse. You are the most obstinate..." Gianni paused for breath, red faced. He had jumped from the cart to advance on Angela where she sat in the dirt, the mule beside her idly cropping the grass at the road's edge.

It did not help matters that she smiled sweetly up at him, murmuring, "Wench? Is that the word that you were looking for, Ser Gianni? Or were you thinking of a worse one? If you try to lift me into the cart I shall resist you. I know that you will win in the end because you are stronger than I am, but it won't do your health any good, even so."

Gianni knew only too well that he had no wish to struggle with her, that was for sure. For one thing, ever since he had woken up to find her by him in the night, she had begun to present a very real temptation to him. And now, looking down at her as she sat in the road, her smiling face was provoking him in more ways than one. To pick her up, to hold her in his arms—and do nothing with her, except throw her into the cart like a bale of goods—was more than a mere frail and mortal man could bear...

"You tempt me, *wench*," he muttered morosely. "When I first met you, you seemed to be as orderly and dignified as a woman could be. And now look at you, sitting in the road, exchanging words with me like a fishwife."

The devil was in her, no doubt about it, and where he had been all her life, and why now, on this long and tiring journey he should choose to whisper in her ear, Angela did not know.

She smiled prettily up at her captor, saying, "Oh, Ser Gianni, and there was I, congratulating myself that I was acting the part of the pedlar's wife so well that I thought to earn praise from you, not blame. A fishwife is what I appear to be, and you," she put her head on one side, "look exactly like the fishwife's husband," for he stood before her, scarlet in the face and angry, his hands on his hips, head flung back and as dirty as...as...the...devil.

Yes, he was the devil who was provoking her.

He glowered at her.

She smiled sweetly at him.

Beppo was hard put to contain his sniggers. The irresistible force had met the immovable object. He had seldom seen his lord and captain so nonplussed.

"I will bargain with you," uttered Gianni at last and reluctantly, his distaste for the whole business plain.

"You will? Oh, bravo. And what is it, this bargain? Go away, at once!" This last was to the mule which had advanced on her and was licking her hand appreciatively, as though in admiration of her outrageous behaviour—for it was outrageous, Angela knew, no doubt about that. But it was all *his* fault for being so domineering and disagreable.

"If you will agree to spend the morning riding, whilst I drive, then this afternoon I will agree to rest while Beppo drives and you walk."

"A very judgement of Solomon," replied Angela approvingly. "The lord of Novera himself could do no better. Yes, I agree."

"Sense at last," remarked Gianni sourly, rolling his eyes to heaven as though imploring the Lord God to pity him, saddled as he was with a contrary woman.

Angela's response to *that* as she took her place beside him in the cart, and Beppo mounted Damn Your Eyes, who had turned into Hey, You again, was to inform him cheerfully, "My old nurse used to say that there was no pleasing men. I cannot say that I had occasion to agree with her until I met you, Ser Gianni."

Gianni muttered an oath beneath his breath, then said aloud, "I can spare your old nurse's sayings, Angela. Let her disappear into the limbo from which you have chosen to summon her!"

"But she said so much that was wise." Angela's pious face as she uttered this monstrous fable was no reflection of her thoughts, for she had found her old nurse both sententious and boring. She was proving, however, a useful whip to attack Gianni with, he being so unattackable otherwise. "For example—"

She got no further. "By all the devils in Gehenna,

and those roaming the world, enough! No more. I feel a fever coming on,'' and Gianni clutched at his head.

''You do?'' He had delivered himself unto her, as Father Anselmo was given to saying when he played Benedetto at chess, and Benedetto had made a false move. He had given her a delicious opportunity to bait him again. ''In that case, Ser Gianni, I suggest that you surrender the reins to Beppo at once, and allow me to walk. We cannot be put to the trouble of nursing you again.''

She looked as soulfully concerned as she could for Gianni's health, and the success or otherwise of this whole expedition, which was taking her—where? Only Gianni and the Lord God knew, and neither of them was choosing to enlighten her.

Gianni stopped the cart. ''What Pandora's box did I open, lady, when I rescued you from Gentile? Report said that you were quiet, modest, would not say boo to a goose, and had hardly a word for anyone, man or woman. An ideal wife for a man who wanted an ideal wife. At first I thought that, for once, report said true. But look at you now... And do not call me Ser Gianni. Gianni will do, no pedlar is Ser.''

''Certainly, if you will refrain from calling me lady. I am Angela. As for reproaching me for my behaviour, you would do well to reproach yourself. For safety's sake, *you* said, I was to be Angela in word and deed. No one was to suspect that I was the missing lady of Novera. If you wish her back again, then I will gladly oblige you. You have only to ask.''

Even Angela was stunned by her eloquence. For,

of course, all he had said of her behaviour before he had arrived in Gentile's church was true. She was, at last, beginning to realise how much she had changed—as Gianni had already tried to tell her. And now he was glowering at her again, before suddenly laughing as though he were demented,

"Great God," he choked, throwing an arm around her, regardless of Beppo, or poor drooping Nello and Hey, You. "That should teach me not to argue with a woman, and a pretty one. Angela and wife you shall be. I think, after all, she is preferable to pious perfection—which is what you were." He gave her a kiss, which rated somewhere between the loving and the brotherly, and started Nello on his way again.

Pious perfection. Was that what he had thought of her? But, of course, he was speaking no less than the truth. Her cheek burned with his kiss, for every time he touched her, however lightly, Angela found herself quivering and shaking. Did it happen because she was turning into Angela, or would Marina, the lady of Novera, respond in the same way?

Now that was definitely not the kind of problem which she could discuss with Father Anselmo. Nor could she ask Beppo, who was looking at both her and Gianni in the most speculative manner, as though he were trying to decide whether to buy peaches or apricots in the market. And why was that? What were they doing which was both intriguing and amusing him?

But, of course, here was another thing which she knew. She was behaving like the ladies of her court when they flirted with the men who surrounded them! They teased and tormented, eyes shining, sometimes from behind their fans, sometimes more openly. She had always despised them. She would never do such a thing. Not she! She would never talk in their double fashion, taunting to gain attention.

But that is exactly what you have been doing, said a sly little voice inside her, and as though you have been doing it all your life. No wonder he is surprised at you—after all, are you not surprised at yourself?

And if I behave in this wanton manner with a...nobody, chance met, who means nothing to me, shall I do so with Leonardo di Montefiore? If I ever chance to meet him, that is. If Ser Nobody from Nowhere ever lets me out of his clutches. Suppose I only wish to behave like the lady of Novera with Messer Leonardo...? Suppose...suppose that I do not jump and quiver at his touch...what then...?

A sardonic voice broke in on her troubled thoughts. "Silent so long, Angela, and so thoughtful. What are you musing on to make you look so soulful? Trying to recover pious perfection?"

Oh, how wrong he was! At this moment, pious perfection was a long way from her thoughts. So far away that she actually jumped when he spoke—and he hadn't even touched her!

Angela turned her head to look closely at Gianni. At his strong and beautiful profile, at his arrogantly held head with its crown of curling black hair, at his long athletic body, his powerful hands, meant for the broadsword, but now controlling the reins of an elderly and ambling horse.

He should be wearing the clothes of a Leonardo

di Montefiore with a face and body like that, not the threadbare canvas of a poor pedlar, or a mercenary soldier's battle-worn armour. Never, in all her years at Novera had she ever met anyone like him. So young and so sure of himself. He was like the Greek heroes of whom Father Anselmo and Girolamo Borgioli, Ugo's secretary, had told her of. He resembled Apollo himself…except that Apollo was fair like the sun…

And now he was staring at her, his expression quizzical. "Yes, Angela, you have something to say?"

Did she? Have something to say? What she wanted was something to do. To put out a hand to touch the apricot of his warm cheek, gilded by living in the sun. To stroke the one black curl which had fallen across his brow. To touch his sun-warmed lips, and gently soothe away the pain of the wound which Braccio had given him, healing now, but which must still be troubling him. To… She must be going mad! But she was not. Angela knew at last what was wrong with her, what had been wrong with her from the moment he had lifted the helmet from his head. No, from the moment she had heard his beautiful voice taunting Gentile in the church at Verdato.

She loved him and was in love with him! She, the lady of Novera, untouched by a man either physically or emotionally, who had only enjoyed the intellectual companionship of men, was in love with a nobody, a mercenary soldier on the make, who was certain sooner or later either to ravish her, or even to sell her to the highest bidder.

"No," she almost stammered in her very real distress and confusion. "I was...thinking."

His beautifully arched brows rose higher still. "Thinking, Angela? Of what?"

"Of nothing, Gianni, nothing." All the charming self control with which she had defied him a few moments ago was gone. Her eyes wide, she was staring at him as though she had never seen him before. Which, in a way, she hadn't. To discover that she loved him had new-minted him for her. And even if it was proximity to him over the last few days which had undone her, delivered her to him, there was no going back.

"Nothing?" In the contest between them, which had begun from the moment they had first met, Gianni was now the winner, whom a little earlier had been the loser. "A strange nothing which has you frowning so hard."

"I was thinking—of something which Father Anselmo told me once," she lied desperately.

"Father Anselmo? You are sure you don't mean your old nurse?" Oh, he was enjoying himself, damn him, and somehow she must wipe the smile from his face.

"Yes, Father Anselmo." Angela searched her memory feverishly for something to say, then came out at last with, "We were debating whether it was ever permissable in the Lord God's eyes to commit a wrong that right might follow," she ended triumphantly.

"Oh, I would hardly call that nothing, Angela," was his deceptively soft reply. "On the contrary, it is a problem which has troubled mankind since the time of the ancients. No wonder your brow was so furrowed. I am surprised that it is not permanently so if you ponder often on such deep matters!"

"You are pleased to jest, Gianni." Angela's voice was stiff.

"Not so. I can only commend you for inwardly debating on such profundities when we are fleeing from your would-be ravisher, and are in danger at any moment of being discovered."

"It helps me to forget." Angela was startled to discover that there was truth in what she said. She remembered her discussion with the good father vividly. With a sly glance at her companion, she remarked coolly, "I don't suppose that you have anything to contribute to the debate, Gianni?"

"Again, on the contrary, Angela. For it seems to me that, whereas in the convent or in the study one may spend hours considering whether to do a wrong that a right may be the result, in the real life of the state or the battlefield, poor wretches like myself may have to make a decision on the spur of the moment. It is only afterwards that the magnitude of what we have done may strike us.

"What seems to be the right and sensible thing in the heat of battle, or in a busy council chamber, may look quite otherwise afterwards. And sometimes, of course, we have no choice. We must do what is to be done, and to the devil with the consequences— and sometimes, it may in truth be the devil."

He was being quite serious for once; all mockery had fled from his voice. His whole manner had changed. There was a bitterness, no, a sad resignation in what he was saying, which struck Angela so hard that she could make no light comment back.

On the contrary, as he had said. So now she spoke slowly and sincerely to him, her head bent. "You speak from experience, Gianni?"

It was a moment before he answered her. "Yes. Would that I did not."

Silence seemed the best answer to that. So silence Angela offered him, and for the next few miles they travelled slowly along the road until, as the sun grew higher and hotter in the heavens, they stopped for their afternoon siesta after a light meal.

And when the siesta was over he was mocking Gianni again, teasing her, but for a space he had shown her quite another man. A man to respect. Which made it harder than ever for Angela to tell herself that she must not, should not, love him. But all the same, she could not help but wonder at what busy council chamber or battlefield he had been present, so that he could remember that the decisions which had been taken there were bitter ones...

She was back in the present again, the smell of cooking rabbit strong and sweet in her nostrils. Beppo, whose turn it was to cook, had gathered herbs on his journey back to the cart and had smeared the rabbit joints with a little oil from the phial they carried with them and rubbed the herbs into their skin. He was holding each joint above the flames of the fire at the end of a small pitchfork and, as each was finished, he wrenched it free and handed it to Gianni or Angela. They were sitting, as always, at a little distance from the road, with a view before and behind them of a forest wilderness, the road they were travelling on now barely a track.

"How far to Burani, do you think?" Gianni was asking Beppo after he had demolished a second joint.

"A day, a day and a half," Beppo shrugged. "If we are lucky. Remember, there was a bandit king near here when last we passed this way. We should make speed to reach Burani before he finds us."

"We dodged him last time." Gianni was lying back, his hands behind his head, his eyes closed, the scar on his face still livid, but beginning to fade. "We have nothing to offer him in the way of plunder, so we should be safe."

"Such creatures are capricious, as well you know. No-one, high or low, is safe from them."

Beppo held out another piece of rabbit to Gianni who waved it away, saying, "Give it to Angela, she must keep up her spirits, and besides, we cannot have her growing thin."

Oh, dear God, after that taunt she would like to refuse the rabbit, but even after eating two of its small joints she was still hungry, and was already salivating when she took the third from the end of Beppo's pitchfork. She ate it with a relish she had never felt for the fine and delicate food which she had been served at Novera. How strange it was that rabbit, eaten in the open as she sat, bare legs crossed on the hard earth, tasted like the food of the Gods. Ambrosia, Messer Ugo had called it, and she had always wondered what that food might be. She had never thought that it could be rabbit.

"This bandit king," she asked Gianni. "Who is he?"

"He calls himself Guido Orsini, but you may be sure that no Orsini would claim him as either their legitimate, or illegitimate, get. He is young, dissolute and violent."

"Worse than Gentile or Braccio?" This with a shiver.

"Much like Braccio, but worse." Angela pulled a face. "With luck we shall escape him."

But luck was not with them.

They were still some miles from Burani when fate struck again. They had spent the night in the forest, well away from the road. Somewhere in the small hours, the waning moon already falling down the sky, they had been awoken by the sound of a troop of men and horses moving along the road. Their fire had long been out, and they were hidden from sight by the trees amongst which they had camped.

Gianni, apart from the one night when he had been troubled and Angela had reassured him, was a light sleeper, and on waking, all his senses were at once alert. He sat up, pulling a long dagger from under his improvised pillow, and rose in one lithe and silent movement to look in the direction from which the hoofbeats were coming. Beppo woke, too, and finally, Angela. She was learning to be wary, and in any case, found sleeping in the open more difficult than in her comfortable bed. The untoward noise had roused her.

She rose to stand beside Gianni and whisper at him, "What is it?"

"Soldiers," he told her, "and from what I can make out of their pennons and badges, Gentile's. They are still searching for the lady of Novera." He spoke of her as though she were someone none of them knew.

"But why at night?" Angela tried to keep her voice down.

"To surprise those whom they might meet, particularly if they think that they have found the lady. She and her captors have disappeared so completely that Gentile must suspect magic." He gave a low chuckle at the thought. "He needs to recapture her soon, for it is likely that both Novera and Montefiore have troops looking for her by now."

This was a new thought for Angela. Of course, both her uncle and the Duke of Montefiore—to say nothing of Leonardo—would be looking for her, trying to find her before Gentile did.

"Should we not look for them, and surrender to them?" she asked, as artlessly as she could.

Angela only knew that Gianni was laughing, soundlessly, because she could see his shoulders shake in the dim light. "By no means, Angela. I have no wish to share you with anyone. Once we are away from them all, then, and only then, shall I make up my mind what to do with you."

"You forget that I am promised to Leonardo di Montefiore and by now but for Gentile, and then you,

I would have been his bride and safe in a comfortable bed," was her tart reply. The noise of the soldiers had died down, and they were out of danger again, so she was not worried when her voice rose in honest indignation.

"On the contrary—" Gianni's favourite and most mocking answer "—it is something I rarely forget. But I am intrigued that you mention the lord Leonardo so fervently and wish to be 'safe in his bed'. I understood that you were not in favour of marriage to him."

"And that is true. I wish to marry no man. But at least if I were with Messer Leonardo I should not be standing in a forest wearing the garb of a peasant woman, with a man who rarely shows me any respect and has not yet made up his mind whether to wed, ravish, or sell me!" She shot this at him with all the venom she could muster.

His answer was to put one hard arm about her shoulders. "Oh, Angela, do but confess to me, as to your confessor, honestly before the Lord God, how much you have been enjoying yourself these last few days! How much you enjoyed yourself at Ostuna before Braccio arrived. Your cheeks have now the most charming colour which were formerly wan. Your manner is enthusiastic and brisk, which was cool, measured and indifferent. Your walk is lively, not stately. And you ate your rabbit with such gusto that I cannot believe that you wished it other than it was. Of your clothing—yes, that is a pity, I grant you. I have a mind to see you dressed as you should be. But if you were, then..." and by the light of the waning moon she could see that his eyes were aglint with mockery "…then I should never have seen your shapely legs and ankles. For sure, fine clothes may conceal an ill-made body, but your clothes conceal little—to my pleasure."

"Oh…!" She tried to wrench away. "How dare you? I am sure that Messer Leonardo would not speak to me so shamelessly."

"Then the more fool he not to treasure what he sees, and let his lady know of it."

"Think you," came a weary voice from behind them, "that you could cease this verbal jousting and return to your beds? I, at least, wish to get some sleep this night. Between Gentile's men and a pair of flapping tongues, I am like to be awake until dawn."

"I do but seek to quiet a fractious woman," Gianni tossed over his shoulder.

"Ser Beppo, pray tell your comrade to cease from distressing me with his ill-considered remarks and I shall be only too happy to end my share of our conversation," was Angela's response to his plea.

"There is nothing to choose between you," grumbled Beppo, lying down and pulling a blanket over his head. "Cry truce and let a poor devil sleep."

"Truce," both parties cried together, looking a little guilty at their lack of consideration for Beppo, who ran their commissariat so well and so unselfishly.

Beppo lifted his head for the last time to proclaim sardonically, "Let us run up a flag to celebrate your rare accord—and sleep on it."

Sleep they did, later than usual and, after a drink

of water and a hard crust of bread—the last which remained to them of their supplies from Ostuna— they set off down the road again. Burani, Beppo assured them, was now but a day's travel away, at the very most. There they would find food and perhaps a bed to sleep in, for one night at least.

"For today, cold rabbit," Beppo exclaimed.

They made good time. Nello was friskier than usual. Gianni was less frisky than usual, Beppo was even more silent, and Angela was even more talkative. She was on the point of asking Gianni where he had been campaigning before he had turned up to kidnap her from Verdato, when they heard in the distance the thunder of hooves again.

She hardly had time to pray that it was not Gentile's men returned, and that neither Gentile nor Braccio was with them, when the troop came round the bend of the road and were upon them.

By their pennants, the badges on their surcoats, and by their general condition, it was plain that, whoever they were, they were not Gentile's men. For all his faults, Gentile's troops were well turned out and well disciplined. This small troop was as slovenly a crew as any of the three of them had ever seen before.

They were led by a young man as ill-turned out as his band. On seeing their little procession, he held up his hand and commanded his troop to stop. Which was just as well, thought Angela, who had for one dreadful moment been under the impression that he intended to ride over them.

He leaned forward on his horse's neck, as Braccio

had done, to demand of them, "Who the devil are you, and where are you making for?"

Gianni did everything but actually pull a forelock. "Of your mercy, lord, I am Gianni of the roads and this is my wife and my partner, Beppo. We are on our way to Burani to sell our wares there."

"Hmm..." The ill-favoured man on the seedy warhorse allowed his feral eyes to rove over Angela; Beppo was not worth a stare. "And what have you seen on the road, of which you might care to tell me, pedlar?"

"Seen on the road, lord? Why, what should I have seen? Only the birds, and the rabbits which infest these parts. And last night, a troop of soldiers broke our sleep—and that is all, most gracious lord."

If Angela thought that this was overdoing the humility somewhat, the man on the horse did not think so. He put his chin on his mailed fist and after a moment ground out with an evil smile, "Now, why do I not believe you, pedlar? I have never seen you before. You are a stranger in these parts?"

"Gracious lord, not exactly. Beppo and I came this way nigh three years agone, before I married Angela here. We but thought to come this way again, business was good last time."

The man worried his lower lip with his teeth, then asked, "Do you know who I am, pedlar."

"Not for sure, lord, but I would hazard a guess that you are Messer Guido Orsini of the great house of Orsini, and if so, I salute you, lord."

"You may do more than salute me, pedlar. You may follow my men and me to my castle, for I would have more words with you. My men's women would be glad to inspect your wares and,'' with a sideways glance at Gianni's lute, "I crave entertainment, so you may play and sing for me, and your wife may dance for us. After she has been washed, that is. You understand me?"

"Yes, lord, I understand, lord." Gianni twisted and turned as though he were in truth a cowed peasant confronted by one of the great ones of his world and not knowing quite what to do to please him.

"Good. Then follow my troop. To make sure that you do, one of my men will ride beside your cart. If you should try to escape from us, why, he shall have orders to cut you down on the instant. You understand me, pedlar?" His grin was evil.

"Yes, lord, assuredly, lord," Gianni gabbled. Not all his fear was assumed, for he could see the capricious nature of the monster before him. Even if he were only Braccio writ small, he was none the less deadly for that. More so, perhaps, for he was not as clever as Braccio.

Nothing for it but to follow Guido and his little band. They left the road which led to the north, and ultimately to safety, and were soon struggling along a lesser track up the hillside, for Guido's eyrie was perched on high so that he might easily see all who made their way towards him.

It had once been owned by another bandit lord, long dead, who had gone on to greater things than preying on passers by. He had ended up with a little state of his own—which Guido might do one day. Angela had heard of such rogues, but had never thought to be a prisoner of such a one as Guido. She remembered what Beppo had said of him the night before, and shivered inwardly. She would not show fear, for she was sure that Guido and his men thrived on the fear of others.

After an arduous climb they had reached his stronghold, or rather, they had reached the outworks and the small village which lay on one side of it, behind a strong, easily defended wall. It was less of a true castle, and more an elaborate version of the towers which the nobility of Tuscany had built in towns like San Gimignano, which lay in the hinterland between Florence and the North. In these more peaceful times the nobility had deserted them, but here, lost in the woods of the Appenines, Guido still lived as men had lived for the last few hundred years, before the order and civilisation which had been lost after the fall of the Roman Empire had returned to Italy.

There was a wall around one side of the tower, the other side stood above the sheer rock which fell away beneath it. Guido's soldiers and servants lived in the little village. His small garrison was quartered inside the tower with a guard house at its entrance, through which all visitors had to pass before being admitted to Guido's presence. His living quarters were at the top of the tower, so arranged that an invading force would be compelled to fight its way up the stairway and landings which led to it—a difficult proposition.

Few of the rulers of Italy's city states cared to try to rid the countryside of such minor bandits; it was easier and cheaper to allow them to live, unless they became too much of a nuisance—like the flies and wasps which plagued people in the summer.

"Drive your cart into the main courtyard, pedlar," commanded the soldier who rode with them, "where the lord may see it. There is a hut in the living quarters where you, your wife and comrade may sleep and eat. The lord will provide you with food in return for your entertainment while you stay with us. But before I take you there, he wishes to question the three of you further."

No help for it, again, but to do as they were bid. Guido had not yet treated them as foully as Braccio had treated the citizens of Ostuna, but he was even more frightening, Angela thought, than Braccio had been. There was a barely reined in savagery inside him, something which she had never seen before she had left the safe haven of her uncle's palace. She had never known that such human wolves roved the earth, but her education in the realities of the world in which she lived was growing apace.

They were not taken to Guido's apartments but to a great hall on the ground floor opening out of the guard house, where there was a huge fireplace, empty now that summer was with them, and a noble oak table which ran the length of the hall, benches on each side of it. Beyond it was a large open space before a dais on which stood an elaborate if battered carved chair, on which Guido had seated himself in morose state. He had pulled off his helm and his mailed gloves, and was now biting his fingers as he stared at them.

"Come closer!" he snarled irritably at them. "Now, pedlar, I would question you further. You say that you have seen nothing out of the way on your travels, but I know that such creatures as you do not betray at once all that you know. Listen carefully: has the news reached you of the spiriting away of the lady of Novera?"

Gianni, who had been nodding his head earnestly in time with every word which Guido uttered, and whose dragging limp had been at its most pronounced on his walk to the hall, said eagerly, "Oh, yes, lord. We learned of it at Ostuna. One of the lord Gentile's captains, Braccio degli Uberti, came to the town to question the citizens and my humble self as to whether the lady and those who had captured her had passed that way..." He paused, almost, thought the shivering Angela, as though he were tantalising the monster before him. Had he learned nothing from Braccio's treatment of him at Ostuna? Was he not putting all their lives at risk?

Apparently not, for the caprice which Guido so frequently displayed was of a different order from Braccio's. He laughed a little, bit his fingers again, and commented drily, "You are a teller of tales, I see, pedlar, and tell your tale after such a fashion as to keep the attention of those who listen. That is good, I await your entertainment this night with interest—but do not toy with me overmuch. This is a serious matter of which I speak. I have a mind to try to find the lady myself—to enrich myself, you understand. The ransom for her will be a goodly one, since both Novera and Montefiore will have to join together to pay it. Did Braccio give any hint of where his master thought that she might be? For the word is that she has vanished, and the troop with her. What magician, think you, has spirited her away?''

For one ghastly moment Angela, and Gianni and Beppo, too, thought that Guido was toying with them, had guessed who and what they were. But Gianni, whose cunning brain was whirling, continued as though all were well. ''Why, lord Guido, the thing is beyond the understanding of a poor pedlar—as it was beyond Braccio's and his greater master. Certes, no party resembling the one which took her had passed through Ostuna. Nor have we seen, or heard, aught on the road but the troop which passed by us yesternight—and that was one of the lord Gentile's.''

''Um...'' Guido bit his fingers again, leaned back. Thanks be to the Lord God, thought Angela, whose legs were almost failing her, he was not suspicious of them. But, as Gianni explained to her later, he plainly thought that they might be withholding what they knew to gain a greater reward.

''No matter,'' Guido came out with at last. And then, as a thought struck him, ''And the troop which passed. Did they question you?''

''No, lord Guido, for it is our habit always to lie well off the road, safe from any marauders except four legged ones, you understand. They did not see us.''

''Better the bears than the men? Eh, pedlar?''

''Exactly, lord, you have the right of it, lord.'' Bowing, Gianni's head nearly reached the floor.

This greasy humility from an inferior, which

would have revolted Ugo, appeared to be exactly to Guido's taste.

"Now, pedlar, had you information which I could use, I would have rewarded you, but seeing that you have none, then your only reward will be for the entertainment which you will provide for us this night."

Gianni smote his brow and appeared to think. Both Angela and Beppo gave him apprehensive looks. Oh, Holy Mother, what was the rascal up to now?

The unholy rascal on the dais leaned forward eagerly. "What is it, pedlar? Has the sound of gold refreshed your memory? What have you to tell me?"

"Nothing much to the point, lord, but a packman we met on the road outside Ostuna, after we left— he was making for Ostuna, you understand, lord— told us of something strange which he had seen."

He had? What packman was this? Neither Angela nor Beppo remembered meeting a packman. Beppo gave a silent inward groan which was, had he but known it, echoed by the one Angela was internally emitting.

Gianni put his hand to his head, and closed his eyes as though trying to recover a memory almost lost. It was a gesture which Angela had seen deceitful servants make time without number. Had their condition not been so dangerous she could almost have laughed at it.

Finally he muttered so that Guido had to strain to hear him. "He said, lord, he said that he had passed a strange party of men by the roadside, who were arguing with one another, and a lady who was on horseback. When they saw him, the man who was their leader swore at him, and told him to be off. I remember, yes, that I do, that he said that the lady had given him a most piteous look, and that one of the rogues with her had turned her horse away, and shouted at him again, so that he travelled on, for fear of his life.''

"And that is all? In which direction was this party travelling?''

"Oh, lord, of your mercy, that I cannot tell you. Indeed, the matter had almost slipped my mind, until you jogged it.''

"Until the promise of a ducat jogged it. You've told me something, but little enough, and little is what you will get for it, you naughty rogue.'' Guido slipped his hand into the purse which swung at his side and drawing a coin from it, threw it on the floor at Gianni's feet.

With a delighted crow of joy, Gianni grovelled before him to recover it as the coin spun and rolled away from him. Guido laughed at the sight. "Be off with you. And Matteo,'' to the soldier who still stood guard over them, "bid your wife wash the wench and give her something fit to wear. She may help her rogue of a husband to entertain us this night. If his singing and playing are as good as his impudence, we shall have a splendid night of it.''

He flapped a regal hand at them and turned his head away to indicate that the audience was over, before bellowing at one of his sergeants to make up a troop to search along the road for such a party as the imaginary packman had seen. Angela could only

marvel at Gianni's cunning. He had satisfied the
monster, but he had not invented a story which would
put the good citizens of Ostuna in danger. So she
told him, when once they were alone together in the
hut assigned to them, after she had been the recipient
of another so-called wash, and yet another tawdry
piece of finery calling itself a dress.

"How did he know that I could dance?" she asked
Gianni, after she and Beppo had reproached him for
his fertile imagination which had had both of them
in a stew of fear that Guido might guess what he was
doing. His answer to that was a shrug.

"I had to tell him something, you understand, to
divert any suspicion that he might have had of us,
and that was all that I could think of. It seemed to
do the trick—for the moment, at least."

He went on to answer her question. "All those
who travel the roads for a living have a myriad of
such talents. Tonight we will play and sing for him,
and pray God he will let us go in the morning—but
with such a dangerous beast who knows what he
might think to do with us? I did not like the way he
looked at you, but at least he did not guess the
truth."

The truth? What was the truth? Did Gianni know
what telling the truth meant? He already had two
names, Niccolo and Gianni. But, come to that, so had
she—and Beppo. But it was at his behest that they
had them. What was his real name? All that she truly
knew of him was that he was a soldier, that when he
was not disguised as a pedlar he was a most handsome man, that he was brave, foolhardy even, and

had an inventive tongue. So inventive that truth and lies were inextricably mixed in what it said, so she could not fault Guido for not guessing that he was being lied to repeatedly.

The question was, and it was one which had plagued her since she had met him, could all of his talents get her safely out of Verdato—and then... what? She drew in her breath as she looked at him where he sat opposite to her, tuning the lute and singing beneath his breath, his face rapt, his whole shapely body at rest—and pray God that he did not forget to limp, for she thought that though he might have deceived Guido this afternoon, Guido might not necessarily stay deceived if he thought that there was something false about the pedlar and his household.

They were trapped in the eagle's eyrie, and had yet to escape from it.

Chapter Eight

Flambeaux painted shadows in Guido Orsini's great hall; there were no windows in it, only slits so that even on the long evenings of summer their light was needed to work and eat by.

The long table was heaped with food. Angela's mouth watered at the very sight of it as she, Gianni and Beppo were led in, to sit at the far end of it. Guido was seated on his dais: a table had been laid before him, and his lieutenants sat on either side of him, their women in between them.

Seated on Guido's right was a big-bosomed beauty, black-haired and black-eyed, magnificently dressed and bejewelled. Her headdress was a chaplet of gems which held down a filmy veil lifted away from her face, simply there to emphasise the glossy lustre of her hair, shining through it.

Even as Gianni and his company began to sit down, Guido spoke to his obsequious major domo and crooked a hand in their direction. It was thus no surprise that the major domo arrived busily before them to bid them attend on the lord Guido's pleasure.

"All of us?" demanded Gianni, a little insolently.
"As the lord wills it, yes."

Gianni took Angela's hand, and stood at a little distance from her, holding her hand high in parody of a great lord leading his lady into court, and processed down the room, a little slowly because of his limp, to stand before Guido. Beppo followed them, his hand on his heart, the parody of a perfect second-in-command.

Nothing escaped Guido it seemed. "You are pleased to mock, pedlar," was his grim comment. "Take care lest you become too insolent: a whipping might improve your manners, induce a due humility. For the present, I am content to allow you licence, but not for ever."

He turned to the woman by his side. "What think you of the rustic beauty, my lady Isabella?" Now it was he who was doing the mocking. His question was meant to provoke one woman, and perhaps humiliate the other.

Lady Isabella duly supplied the humiliation. Her eyes roved dismissively over the seething Angela. "Were she a little cleaner, my dear lord, she might be passable," she finally announced. "It is to be supposed that the Lord God has given her other attributes to make up for her lack of beauty."

"Do you say so?" Guido, it appeared, was bent on mischief making. "But I suppose it is too much to expect that one woman might be able to judge another's looks fairly. I see promise there, perhaps to be fulfilled when the pedlar's wife dances for us."

"Wife?" The lady Isabella's eyebrows rose dismissively. "You honour her overmuch, surely? Such creatures do not marry, I understand. I see that the pedlar carries a lute. Do you play and sing as well as huckster, fellow?"

Gianni was suddenly greasily humble again. "To please so fair a lady as yourself, I am willing to essay anything."

This flattery patently delighted her. She turned to Guido. "Now, my dear lord, had you asked me about the pedlar's claim to be well-favoured, rather than his wife's, I might have given you a different answer. Had he not such a bad limp, he would be as well set-up as any peasant might expect to be." She rewarded first Gianni and then her husband with a smile, toothy in its dazzling intensity.

Gianni could almost feel Angela's rage. The hand he still held was quivering in his. So, the lady of Novera had progressed from being a woman so detached from ordinary humanity that she could hardly be considered to be a woman at all, to one who could feel wounded pride and jealous rage! Wounded pride because of the lady Isabella's dismissal of her looks, jealousy because she was making eyes at Gianni! It was not conceit which told him this, but his knowledge of men and women. He also knew that the lady Isabella's dismissal of Angela's looks had angered him as much as Guido's lecherous eyeing of her.

Guido's answer to his wife was a stare of such malignity that Angela shuddered at it. "Who do I reward for such a statement, lady?" he finally snarled. "The pedlar, or you? Or the pedlar's wife?" And now the stare he turned on Angela and Gianni was baleful in a different way from the one which he had directed at his wife.

She seemed little troubled by it. Perhaps, thought Angela, she was used to walking the tightrope which had her husband's affection at one end, and his feral temper at the other. But her principal fear was not for the lady Isabella, but for Gianni and herself, who had suddenly become two bones of contention between husband and wife.

Something else frightened her, a something which she hoped Gianni was considering. How long would it be before the two monsters before them began to grasp that Gianni of the roads and his wife were rather more than ordinary pedlars? The very fact that each of them had felt attracted to a pair of peasants might cause them to question why this should be so.

A short and silent prayer to the Lord God appeared to be in order. Angela hastily composed one and inwardly offered it up to heaven. Surely the Lord God was failing in His duty to mankind to allow such creatures as these to hold power over helpless men and women? This dreadful piece of heresy nearly overset Angela, for never before had she had occasion to question the will of God—mainly because the will of God towards Marina, the lady of Novera, had been so unfailingly benevolent.

So overset was she that she missed Guido dismissing them, with a warning to Gianni not to let the favour which the lady Isabella had chosen to show him encourage him to commit more insolence. "Be very careful," he grimly ended, "that you do not provide entertainment for me and my men of a kind which you may not like. The whipping post and the rack make men sing a different song from those sung to the lute.''

"I hear you but to obey," grovelled Gianni. "Come, wife." As Angela, her mind for the first time fixed on the capriciousness of the Lord God, hesitated and stared blankly at him, he informed the closely watching Guido, "Oh, great lord, my wife is so overwhelmed by your magnificent presence that she has been transported out of this world into contemplation of the next." A remark which was truer than he knew.

It was also true, and fortunate as well, that the lord Guido Orsini was sufficiently full of himself and his importance to take such grotesque flattery at face value, and he forgave Gianni his recent impudence, and lordly waved the pedlar, his wife, and his man back to the far end of the table where he bade them eat and drink their fill.

Even her fear of the man who was providing it could not prevent Angela from enjoying the good food set before them. Gianni, watching her frank pleasure as she looked around her, remembered the cold woman who had shown enthusiasm for little when she had first travelled with him. Now she was eating with even more enjoyment than she had shown when demolishing the rabbit which Beppo had cooked for them.

"Bravo," he whispered in her ear while consuming the boar's meat which rested on the manchet of bread before them. "Alway's eat well when good food is provided in plenty is an excellent motto for a soldier and a soldier's wife. One never knows where the next meal is coming from. Drink the good wine, too, Angela.'' He poured it from the big earthenware pitcher which stood in the centre of the table into her pewter goblet.

Angela needed no further encouragement. When she had finished eating she looked around her at the motley crew which made up the senior members of Guido's household. She did not have long to look for they had barely finished their meal when the major domo was with them again. They were to go to the lord Guido's end of the room and play, sing and dance for him.

''What shall I dance, Gianni?'' asked Angela fearfully.

''Dance the dance with which you would have favoured the good folk of Ostuna. Remember that you are not at the elegant and civilised courts of either Novera or Montefiore, but in an outlaw's stronghold. They will not expect what would be expected there. Have courage, and all will be well.''

It was all very well for him to talk. He had obviously done this sort of thing before. While she had been prepared to dance for the good folk of Ostuna, she was not happy about capering before the greedy eyes of the lord Guido. But there was nothing for it but to do as Gianni told her, for she was as much his prisoner as she was Guido's, with the difference that he did not seem to be as cruel as Guido. She could only hope that she would perform well enough and not give the three of them away by her clumsiness.

Cross-legged on the corner of the dais, Gianni

tuned his lute and began to sing. The song he sang, and the manner of his singing of it, was quite different from the earthy songs he had begun with at Ostuna. His voice was as beautiful as the rest of him, when he was not disguised as a travelling huckster, and the love song he had chosen rang melodiously through the hall. After he had finished, even Guido's rough soldiers were quiet for an instant before demanding more.

He bowed his head in acknowledgement of the applause, and said, "Now my wife will sing *The Blackbird's Song* for you." He played the first bars of the introduction, looking encouragingly over at her where she stood, hands modestly crossed before her, her head bent.

As always, Angela found that while singing she forgot for a moment where she was, and who she was pretending to be. She could look away from them all, towards the flambeaux flaming in their glory and pretend that it was to her uncle that she was pouring out her song. She was transformed.

For a moment, watching her, Gianni was gripped by two strong and powerful emotions. The first was one of fear that those around them would see the transcendent beauty hidden by her poor clothing and uncared for face and hands. The second was the sudden untoward knowledge that she was beginning to wind her way into his heart. That he not only lusted after her, but was beginning to fall in love with the simple bravery which she was consistently showing.

Sheltered, spoiled, cosseted, thrown into a world so unlike her own that she must be in a state of constant bewilderment, she refused to show fear, or petulance, or any of the petty selfishnesses which he would have expected from her.

Her stoicism almost shamed him, if only because he had dismissed her before he met her as the worst sort of indifferent pampered beauty, who thought that the whole world only existed to revolve around her. But she had shown compassion for, and understanding of, the sufferings of the townsfolk at Ostuna, and once the first few days of fright and shock after his kidnapping of her were over, she had done her best to live her new and difficult life cheerfully.

And now he must be careful not to betray what he felt for her before Guido's band of rogues, lest he betray the pair of them.

The song drew to its end, and again, there was silence after its ending. Guido shook himself, leaned forward and said, "Enough of this maundering, pedlar. Let us have a song fit for soldiers first, and then your wife shall dance for us."

Gianni grinned up at him, and launched into a soldier's marching song of such surpassing indecency that the whole hall erupted with joy as the first words rang out into it. Titled *The Englishman and the Venetian Tart*, it ran through innumerable verses, each more filthy than the last. The lady Isabella put her fan before her face, and several of the women hid their faces in their hands—but took care to peep through their fingers at Gianni whilst they did so. The men hammered on the tables and stamped their feet at the refrain which followed each verse. Angela, standing before them all, was one vast blush, particularly when Gianni winked in her direction—and shouted, "Dance, wife, dance."

So she began to dance and realised that he was being kind to her, for concentrating on her steps she heard only the music. The women began clapping in time with it to drown the words, and the men shouted them out more than ever, so that the oak beams of the hall echoed with the sound. The lady Isabella dropped her fan in order to gain a better look at Gianni. Like his wife he would benefit from a wash but, Lord God, what shoulders he had, what thighs!

At long last it was over. Breathless, Angela sank down in a great curtsey, and Gianni, scarlet in the face, passed his hands gently over the strings, calling to Guido as he did so. "A rest, lord, I crave a rest. Let my comrade Beppo tumble and juggle for you before Angela and I sing and dance for you again."

Half drunk, as most of his men were, Guido nodded, and Beppo, who had been standing silently by, opened the canvas bag he had brought in with him, fetched out the clubs which he had been carrying in it, and began to juggle to the sound of Gianni's lute. Angela sank down on the dais by Gianni, who winked at her again, before rewarding her for her dance with an idle kiss. A kiss jealously noted by the lady Isabella, who was suddenly determined that if her husband had his way with the pedlar's dirty doxy this night, then she would sample the delights which the pedlar might have to offer.

Fortunately not privy to either the lord or the lady's thoughts, Angela was beginning to think longingly of her bed. Would this day never end? Her feet ached and her head was spinning as a consequence of the first rich meal which she had eaten since she had left Novera. The wine which she had drunk and the unaccustomed exercise she had been taking had also exhausted her. For the moment she was content to watch Beppo, who, having laid down his clubs, was beginning to tumble, bringing off a series of backward, forward, and twisting somersaults before he called on Gianni to help him with his final pièce de résistance.

Remembering to limp, Gianni laid down his lute, and legs apart, braced himself whilst he held out his hands to Beppo who, taking them, leaped lightly on to his shoulders. Beppo balanced there for a moment before throwing himself upwards into a double somersault which brought him to the ground some yards in front of Gianni, who maintained his own balance, just.

Both men bowed and, before she could check herself, Angela began to clap, shouting bravo and leading the hall's applause. Fortunately those around them only thought that she was acting as the tumblers' assistant and touting for approval, instead of admiring the trick for the first time. "Again!" shouted Guido and his lady, so they performed the trick once more, with a slight difference this time; Beppo facing in the opposite direction, landed behind Gianni—which allowed the lady Isabella to admire the pedlar's body all over again.

Beppo bowed to the lord Guido and, his part of the entertainment over, picked up his bag and his clubs and melted into the background. Unknown to

Angela—or to anyone else for that matter, other than Gianni—he slipped from the hall and slunk silently into the courtyard where he harnessed Nello and made certain that the uncertain mule—who was not sure whether its name today was Hey, You or Damn Your Eyes—was also ready for immediate departure. He liked the looks of neither Guido nor his lady, and thought that they ought to be ready for anything.

His activities went unnoticed, helped by the fact that Guido's men, secure in their eyrie, had become careless and, apart from the sentries on the walls, were nearly as drunk as their master.

And then he sat down to wait on events—and Gianni.

In the hall, Gianni was playing and singing again. But his audience was no longer attentive. Some had slipped to the floor, dead drunk, others lay with their face on the table, snoring. Still others had pulled serving wenches from their places at the back of the hall and disappeared into the shadows with them.

Gianni seemed tireless: helped no doubt, thought Angela sourly, by the nods and winks he was receiving from the lady Isabella as her husband descended towards drunken oblivion. He had earlier told Gianni that he expected him and his wife to wait on his pleasure at the feast's end, but it was becoming plain that by the feast's end he would take his pleasure with no-one.

Isabella prodded her husband, who had slipped sideways in his great chair and had begun to snore. Only one of his lieutenants looked even remotely so-

ber, and several of the ladies had forgotten themselves enough to join their lords in abandoning so-
briety and restraint altogether. The whole dissolute
scene was so different from anything which Angela
had experienced at Novera that she might be living
in a different world. She saw the lady Isabella looking mockingly at her and Gianni, and wondered what
new torments she was planning for them.

Nothing, apparently, for she leaned forward to say
to Gianni, who had stopped singing, and was idly
strumming his lute, the only sober man in a room
full of drunkards, "Enough, pedlar, take your dirty
doxy with you and leave. The lord, as you see, is too
far gone to entertain her, and I would not have her
stay here another day to be a temptation for him.
So—be on your way."

"And nothing tempts you, lady? And should I not
fear your lord's anger, if we disappear, incontinent?"

Oh, how dare he make eyes at such a…a…painted
maypol! Why, she was old enough to be his mother,
which was an exaggeration, Angela knew. But had
he no shame? For, after all, she was supposed to be
his wife, or his woman, or his doxy, and he was
looking at the lady Isabella as though he could eat
her—and she was doing the same to him. For no
reason at all, Angela wanted to weep.

She was not yet sufficiently aware of how the
wicked world wagged to know that one way of rescuing them all from the trap in which they were
caught in Guido's tower was if Gianni used the lady
Isabella's lusting after him to their advantage.

She heard Isabella laugh softly, then say, "Leave

now, pedlar, have no fear. One woman is very like another for Guido, and he dare not anger me too much for I have brought him wealth, and an alliance with my family. I was Isabella Attendolo—and,'' with a significant glance at him from her fine eyes, ''I do as I please.''

Attendolo! That explained much. For she was a member of one of Italy's most powerful dynasties which had provided great *condottieros*, dukes, marcheses, counts and lords to rule states without number. Why, the great Sforza himself, the Duke of Milan, was a member of this same family, and Guido would not gainsay a wife who had such power at her back.

But what would happen to a pedlar who gainsaid her?

No time to think of that, for she had arisen, stepped down from her chair of state so that she stood face to face with him, to throw insolently over her shoulder at Angela, ''Stand back wench, and look the other way. I would speak with your owner.''

For one shocking moment Angela was on the point of turning back into the lady of Novera, who would tell the Lady Isabella exactly what she thought of insolent bitches who annexed other people's husbands without a thought. No matter that Gianni was not her husband and never would be, praise the Lord God, the fires of jealousy raged within her. But prudence warned, Say and do nothing which might give away the game which you and he and Beppo are playing. And he is nothing to you. She says that he owns you and she speaks better than she knows.

What was the lady whispering to Gianni, her imperious voice low, the fan which she held in one begemmed hand tapping gently against his chest? Did she wish him to retire to her room with her? Even Angela knew that this would be a risky ploy. So, what was she plotting?

Isabella was laughing up into his face, was stroking it, and he had taken the gemmed hand which had caressed his cheek and was kissing it before she strutted away, the knowing eyes of the few who were sober, following her. She walked and behaved as though she had dismissed him, but Angela was not so sure.

"What do we do now?" she asked him anxiously.

He seemed at first not to hear her, then said at last, distrait, "She has dismissed us. We are to leave the tower at once. She wishes to thwart Guido by refusing him you."

Angela shuddered. "She does me a kindness, then."

"True, but that was not her aim. We will leave quietly, without undue haste. There may be some officious follower of Guido who might think to gain favour by detaining you for him."

"And that is all? We are to leave? Why should she agree to this? She seemed to want more from you than a public farewell."

Gianni waved an airy hand. "Who knows, dear wife. Such great ladies are capricious beings. Perhaps she felt sorry for us." He was urging her gently to the door with each word he uttered.

Why was it that she did not believe he was telling

her the entire truth? She was sure that he was not, for during their journey together she had learned to read him, and the tone of his voice told her that he was engaging in one of his deceits. But she could not question him further; they must use the respite which the lady Isabella had offered them to try to escape before Guido revived and called them back.

They strolled down the hall, Gianni whistling as though what he was doing was of no import, swinging his lute gently, his arm through Angela's as though he were intent on bed after a hard day's work. They passed the sprawled bodies of Guido's men lying below the sprawled body of Guido himself, only held upright by his elaborate chair. It was hard to tell how lost to the world he was.

Unbelievably, no-one stopped or challenged them as they walked through the guard house, where Guido's men, their superiors lying unconscious in the hall, were sleeping as careless as they. Hand in hand, they walked through the open door into the courtyard, where they could see the cart, Nello harnessed to it, and Hey, You standing by, Beppo's hand on his collar.

Angela's head was in a whirl. Was their escape to be as easy as this? After all her worrying about how they were to extricate themselves from between the lion's paws, had the lioness ordered the gates to be opened for them, and why? Not from the simple goodness of her heart, surely?

"Up with you into the cart, wife. You are ready, Beppo?"

"Aye, and you may tell me later how you performed this conjuring trick. Let us make all speed lest something untoward delay us.''

Gianni handed Angela his lute, but made no effort to climb into the cart himself. He seemed to be waiting for something.

Beppo called irritably from Hey, You's back. ''Get on with it, Gianni. This is no time to be standing about.''

True enough, and then the mystery was solved. Through the lighted doorway to the guardhouse and the tower a woman came, moving swiftly towards them. It was the lady Isabella! Her lustrous hair was down, she was wearing a plain black dress which fell just below her knees, all her jewels were gone, and her hair was tied back with a black ribbon so that she might be taken for one of the serving wenches roving the castle looking for satisfaction after an evening's entertainment.

In a voice as sweet as treacle, she addressed Gianni. ''Stay but a moment, pedlar. You owe me for allowing you to go free, and I would take my payment before you leave.''

So! This was what he had not told her. Angela set her teeth and stared at the lady as haughtily as she dare. To no avail. Her eyes were only for Gianni.

He turned to face her, his back to Angela. A flambeau set in a sconce in the tower's wall threw a flickering light over them. She saw that his fists were lightly clenched and that his whole body was at the ready, as though danger threatened. But when he looked full into the lady Isabella's smiling expectant face, Angela saw him relax, and when he spoke, his beautiful voice was as light and easy as a man's could be.

"Payment you shall have, lady. But surely you do not wish it here?"

Her laughter was honest and amused. "Why, pedlar. You surely do not expect me to receive you in my room. I want what you have for me now—and here. My husband is dead to the world—and I would not burn longer."

"But here—we are not private?" There was disbelief and a certain desperation in his voice.

"Why not, pedlar? Never tell me that you have not used a wall before to pleasure yourself. I have a mind to behave like the serving girl I appear to be."

Laughter still threaded through her voice, but Gianni knew that were he to deny her, her laughter would cease and condign punishment would follow. The lives of all three of them hung in the balance of the lady Isabella's pleasure. There was no help for it. In sight and sound of a woman whom he was coming to love and to respect, he would have to make love to another. He had counted on Isabella sending for him to go to her room—but she was maliciously intent on making him betray his wife in that wife's presence.

Now Angela was not his wife, but he could almost feel her distress as she listened to this exchange, could only imagine what she would feel when he began to pleasure the lady... Forget that.

He moved forward, said roughly, "As you will, lady," and seized her equally roughly. "You have chosen to have your pleasure this way, not I."

"Better and better," she told him blithely. "Your anger will fuel desire."

And there was truth in that, Gianni thought grimly, but not for him this time.

He dragged her to a niche in the wall, away from the light, out of Angela's view but not her hearing, and threw up Isabella's skirts. If the lady wished to play at being a peasant, then he would treat her as her kind treated peasants, roughly and without consideration. But, alas, that was what she wanted. And though, in the end, it might appear that he was raping her, she was raping him, for he had not the slightest feeling for her, and would never have touched her had not necessity demanded it.

His only prayer was that he would be able to satisfy her, for he knew as well as any man that it was not enough to will his body to arousal, for it had a will of its own.

And if he failed her, he had no doubt of the outcome. She would cast him off for not satisfying her and cry rape, and Guido's men would come a-running. The mere thought of that and what they would do to him before despatching him, and to Angela and Beppo afterwards, set him shuddering—and left his desire drooping still further.

Even her moans and sighs as his unwilling hands caressed her could not work the trick for him. The knowledge that Angela was watching him was like cold water thrown over him. Angela…! And there was his way out of this impasse. He could imagine that it was Angela pinned between him and the wall, that black-avised was fair, that black eyes were a clear and lucid grey, that lustrous black curls were blonde. To pretend that he held Angela in his arms revived his flagging self...

His last thought as he set about fulfilling the lady's wish was that either way, fail or succeed, he was dishonoured. But for once the Lord God was kind, even as he had at the last managed to coerce his unwilling body into submission. The sound of running feet, and a female voice trying to shout without shouting as it were, interrupted his desperate labours with the lady Isabella.

He heard her curse beneath her breath as her name floated towards them.

"My lady, my lady, come at once, the lord Guido is asking for you."

"Oh, Satan take the man and pitchfork him into hell where he belongs. I thought him dead to the world until morning, at least," exclaimed the lady Isabella, the milk of human kindness sadly lacking in every word she uttered. "Don't stop, pedlar."

"Oh, no, lady." Gianni stood back, trying to lace up his much darned hose again, and restore himself to respectability. "I have no mind to be cut off in my prime, and you may yet try him beyond reason."

By now Isabella's waiting woman was upon them. "Oh, lady, come at once. The lord Guido has asked for you, and will not be gainsaid. The drink hath made him wild." She turned her agitated face towards her mistress. "Delay not, lady, or worse will befall. He is raving." She was wringing her hands, and the tears were beginning to fall. What she dare not tell her mistress was that Guido had threatened her. "He thinks that you are with the pedlar, lady. Return, and prove him wrong."

Torn between wanting the pedlar to finish what he had started, and her fear of a man who was so capricious that he might forget his fear of her relatives, and punish her as he thought that she might deserve for her repeated faithlessness, the lady Isabella hesitated and was lost.

"Another time," she flung at Gianni, beginning to repair her own disarray, and then, with a flash of her old impudence as he walked away from her, "You have forgotten your limp, pedlar!"

He heard Angela's indrawn gasp at this taunt, and grinning, flung over his shoulder his final word for the lady Isabella, "Another night, lady, another time, and you might cure more than my limp for me."

She laughed at his impudence, showing white teeth, and called to the watching guard at the courtyard's gate, "Let them pass, man. They have entertained us enough for one visit."

Angela watched Gianni walk towards her, watched the lady Isabella run noiselessly back into the tower, her waiting woman behind her, still wringing her hands and wailing. No time to waste, though, for Gianni was in the cart, had taken up Nello's reins and was urging him on. Beppo was aboard Hey, You who was behaving well for once.

The yawning guard at the gate, who might have argued with them at their going, was too determined that once they were gone and the gate closed he would be able to sleep peacefully to stay them in their passing. Besides, the lady had given them permission to leave, and the Lord God knew, as did all the garrison, that in the end, the lord Guido always gave way to her—although one day he might not.

The pedlar's cart was being driven back down the road by which it had come, and Gianni's thwarted body was one vast ache for he had just reached the state required to pleasure the lady Isabella when her woman had arrived. Angela was quiet by his side, radiating fury. Between denied lust and his sense of shame at what he had been required to do to save them, he could not keep silent.

Once out of sight of the tower and when they were well on their way to the road he turned his head towards her, and ground out through gritted teeth, "Say it, then, Angela, say it! Do not sit there thinking it. The Lord God knows that I had no desire after such a hard day to please a female imp from hell such as Guido's lady!"

"Say you so! From the noise that you were both making I thought that pleasure was the one thing which both you and the lady were enjoying!"

"Body of God, Angela, I but tried to pleasure her to save us to get us out of Guido's clutches. It was my duty, woman!"

"Your duty, Gianni! God send us all such a pleasant duty! Sad it was that you were interrupted before pleasure became even more pleasurable."

Angela's voice was as acid as she could make it. Sitting in the cart, waiting for him to finish with the lady Isabella, consumed with jealousy, Angela had at last come to terms with the feelings which Gianni had aroused in her. The worst feeling of all was that she had but one wish: that it was she who was pinned against the wall, moaning beneath his ministrations, not Isabella. How dare he pretend that what he had been doing was his duty!

"Silent again," he snarled at her. "Admit that what I was prepared to do, much against my will, achieved what we wanted. Are we not on our way towards freedom, woman? It was a small price to pay, and you did not have to pay it."

"Freedom, Gianni?" Angela wanted to hurt him, yes, she did. Yes, she would. "Freedom? *I* am not free. You are free. Beppo is free, Nello is free, Hey, You is free, but I..." She was in full flow now, her voice soaring.

"Damnation and hell's torments, woman." Gianni's patience finally snapped. "Cease to nag me. There is no need to take the pretence of being my wife so far that everything which I do earns me non-stop reproach. Did you acquire that clacking tongue in Novera, only to save it to hit me over the head with it every time that I transgress your noble concepts of honour?"

"No, husband dear. I acquired it after I met you! When else? Know that I am your prisoner, that I have no notion of where we are, or where we are making for, or what you will do to me when we get to whatever destination you have in mind for me. And you prate to me of being free. By the Lord God..."

"By the Lord God, woman," began the incensed Gianni, to have Beppo, his patience exhausted, shout leather-lunged at both of them.

"By the Lord God, what has got into the pair of

you to make such a noise that Guido Orsini could
hear you in his tower? Have you both taken leave of
your senses? The lady has become a shrew, and you,
Gianni, a fool. Save your breath, both of you. Let us
get as far away from Guido's tower as we can, and
then, why even then, you must cease your quarrel-
ling. Survival is all.''

Chapter Nine

All that night Gianni's temper was no better than it had been on the day when he had quarrelled with Angela. They had stopped around dawn in order to sleep after they had travelled further at one time than ever before.

"Imperative that we get as far away from Guido as possible," Gianni had snarled at them earlier, after Beppo had taken one look at Angela's white face and suggested that they draw off the road and rest. "I am surprised at you, Beppo. We don't want Guido Orsini on our trail before we have put a good distance between him and us. We will sleep when we can see Burani, and not before."

Beppo held him to that, even though they were in sight of Burani's towers and its cathedral earlier than they had expected. They travelled further off the road than they normally did, and at last Angela could lie down. But not to sleep.

All that had passed during the last twenty-four hours ran through her head. She had thought herself hardened to her tribulations, but Gianni's cavorting with the lady Isabella, as she thought of it, had hurt her more than she could have believed possible. Which was stupid, because he was nothing to her as she was nothing to him, so how could she conceivably see his behaviour as treachery?

In the middle of her tossing and turning, for Angela found that it was difficult to sleep in broad daylight, she became aware that someone was sitting beside her and had taken her hot hand in his. It was Gianni. She brushed her hair out of her eyes, looked up at him and snapped, "Yes, what is it, Gianni? Has Guido found us—or his lady?"

The moment that the words flew out she regretted them, for he looked even more tired than she felt. As she finished speaking, he closed his brilliant blue eyes. If she had had a hard day yesterday, then he had a harder, and needed his rest.

He opened his eyes again, looked down at her, and amazingly, smiled. "Not long ago," he told her, "you comforted me at night when I was restless. I heard you cry out just now, and I thought that it was my turn to supply comfort. Send me away if I am wrong."

His voice was so kind that Angela wanted to cry. She turned her head away as the tears forced themselves out of the corner of her eyes, however much she willed them to stop.

He put out one of the shapely hands which Isabella Orsini had admired, turned her face towards him and began to speak earnestly to her. "Look at me, Angela. I know why you are unhappy and cannot sleep, and I know that it is my fault, doubly so, I admit. Imprimis, because in your presence I had to do something which should only be performed with love and in private, and I was compelled to perform in hate and publicly, before you. Secundus, afterwards in my distress, I was vilely rude to you, brutally ignoring *your* distress.

"For Secundus, I beg forgiveness. But for Imprimis, I do not. I only ask you to remember what we so recently discussed. That one might have to make decisions on the spur of the moment as to whether one should commit a wrong in order to achieve a right, and I told you how difficult it was to make such a decision. Rightly or wrongly, last night I agreed to what Isabella Orsini demanded of me in order to gain our freedom and to preserve you from rape by Guido—for that is what he intended. I am not proud of what I did, or so nearly did, but neither did I commit an act for which you, or any other, ought to reproach me. You see how difficult it is to make these important decisions in the heat of daily living, however easy it may seem when one is sitting comfortably in a garden or a study.

"Like you, I am finding sleep difficult, but if you can bring yourself to forgive what ought to be forgiven, and to understand why I acted as I did with Isabella, why then, perhaps we may both be able to sleep," and he kissed the hand which he was holding.

Angela did not pull it away. She let the tears fall freely now. He put out his other hand, wiped her cheek, then put his hand to his mouth and licked the tears away.

"Do not cry, sweeting. None of this is your fault."

"Oh, yes," she choked, "it is. I was cruel. I did not think of your feelings. Only of my own."

"Then we are quits, dear child, for when we quarrelled afterwards, I did not consider how outraged you must have felt, delicately reared as you have been. I thought only of my own shame, and I wanted to strike all the world in the face—instead, the face which I struck was yours."

He was being so magnanimous that the least she could do was not cry over him. "I forgive you both Imprimis and Secundus," she whispered, and now she was kissing *his* hand. "Quits, Ser Gianni, and let us sleep."

He nodded his head. "With this proviso, that I stay with you until sleep claims you, so that I may earn my own." When she opened her mouth to deny him, he shook his tired head at her, and said simply, "Do not argue with me. I am bone weary."

So Angela lay down and, as he had promised, sleep claimed her. When she awoke towards noon she found him lying beside her on the hard earth, still asleep, his hand held out towards her. Rising, she was careful not to disturb him, and when Beppo, who had been preparing a light meal for them came towards them to wake him, she put her fingers on her lips and shook her head at him.

"He is so tired, let him sleep." Beppo did not argue with her.

But when he awoke he was demanding, domineering Gianni again, and their early morning talk might never have taken place. He broke his fast impatiently, as though the food irked him, and said, before Angela and Beppo had time to finish their repast, "It is urgent that we talk. I have decided that we must change our plans and change them drastically. For one reason and another, we have drawn more attention than I had hoped." He paused, and Angela's glance at him was a worried one. What he said next added to her worries.

"Beppo knows that I had alternate plans prepared in case things went ill. It would be wise, I think, to implement them now." He walked over to the cart and began to haul out of it some of the packs which were stowed towards the back of it, and pull them open.

"From being three, we must become two, plus any servants whom we shall hire in Burani, in order to deceive any who might suddenly ask themselves who Gianni of the roads, his blonde doxy and his partner, truly are." He began to extract from the first pack a set of rich clothing which included a man's beautiful gold and emerald hose, and an emerald tunic to go with them, together with a fine linen shirt, lace edged around the collar. An emerald and gold houppelande with ampler skirts than was common completed the ensemble. Gianni followed this by fishing out of a second pack another set of men's clothing, darker and more sombre in nature, black with silver trimmings. Conical black hats and leather boots followed.

Gianni shook the beautiful clothing briskly, so that the creases began to fall out of it. He tossed the black suit at Beppo, bade him go to a pool nearby, wash himself, find shelter and then change into the suit. He plainly intended the glorious emerald suit for himself. With some amusement he watched Angela look down at her shabby brown dress, her bare legs and her crude peasant's sandals; an unlikely outfit, she thought ruefully, for a woman to wear who was travelling with such a pair of peacocks.

She was about to say so when Gianni forestalled her. "Never fear!" he told her gravely. "A good general is known by his attention to detail. Look!" With a conjuror's flourish he drew from the second parcel a dress, which whilst not so magnificent as the one which Isabella Orsini had worn, was still sufficiently handsome as to show that its wearer was richer than the common run. It was made of a deep blue velvet, with silver trimmings, sturdy enough for its owner to wear while travelling. A pair of elegant black leather shoes followed and a fine linen chemise to wear under it.

Angela gave a little gasp at the sight. She had almost forgotten that such beautiful things existed.

"I had no idea of what you really looked like, my lady," he told her suavely, "but I knew that such a lovely thing would not only suit you, but please any woman with a claim to beauty. When Beppo returns you must do as he has done, and transform yourself into someone, who, if she is not quite the lady of Novera, is sufficiently wealthy as to wear this dress with pride. And after that I shall turn myself into your husband, a rich merchant. And after *that*, our little party will split up. Beppo will return alone to...his home, and you and I will travel on together, looking quite unlike Gianni of the roads and his doxy.''

''But how shall we pretend to be rich, and be able to hire servants to accompany us, seeing that all the money we have is that which we have gained from your peddling and our singing and dancing on the way?''

Gianni's smile was a naughty and a knowing one. He placed his finger by his nose in a vulgar gesture which again reminded Angela of sinful servants at Novera. ''Now there, Angela, I have to confess that I have not told you the entire truth about our financial standing. The less you knew, the less you could give away. I had no knowledge of how discreet you could be, so I thought it best to err on the side of caution. But here,'' he took from its hiding place in the cart a leather pouch with a drawstring, opened it, and began to pour gold ducats from it into his hand, ''here, as you may plainly see, we have more than enough to enable us to pass as wealthy merchants.''

Angela turned crimson and then pale. Was there no end to his deceits? ''We have been scrimping and saving and eating poor food this last ten days, and all the time we were carrying a fortune with us...'' she exclaimed. She thought of how she had sung until she was tired, in the belief that all they had was what they earned. ''Oh...! You have done nothing but lie to me since we first met.''

''Dear girl,'' said Gianni gently. ''Had you known the truth, you would not have been as convincing a poor peasant as you appeared to be. We could not be both pedlars and rich as well. And this store was a reserve, to be called on only if needed. Now it is needed, and we shall still have to be careful, until we reach Burani, though not as careful as we have been. Ah, Beppo, you look uncommonly respectable, so respectable that I hardly know you.''

And that was true enough. Angela stared at the burly bourgeois who had just emerged from a thicket and who had replaced the scruffy and disreputable looking peasant who had been riding Hey, You. She could not believe that he was the same man and so she told him. "And you cannot ride Hey, You looking like that! It would not be proper."

"No, indeed," agreed Gianni. "We also need to dress the cart up, and say that we are riding in it because recently you have been too frail to go on horseback. Beppo can hide in the back until we are safely inside Burani. There he will leave us, buy himself a horse, hire a servant and return home by another route from the one which we shall be taking.

"Who will think that the merchant Ottone Rinieri and his wife Emilia are Gianni of the roads and his doxy, Angela? Now be off with you, my child, assume your new clothes and be quick about it for I am eager to wash myself and wear some clean linen for a change."

Oh, he was intolerable, calling her child and sweeting, and ordering her about as though she were truly some wench he had picked from the hedge rows, instead of the lady of Novera whom he was manipulating for his own ends. What had happened to the kind man who had comforted her earlier in the day? Then commonsense told her as she washed herself in the little pool, dried herself on the towel which Gianni had given her, and put on her new dress, that he was doing the thinking and planning for them all. More than that, he had rescued her, and was still rescuing her from Gentile's dreadful clutches—to say nothing of those of Guido Orsini.

Angela had forgotten how handsome he really was until she saw him clean again and in his beautiful clothing. Like Beppo—who was now Messer Ettore Manfredi—and herself, he was quite transformed. All in all, they formed a handsome trio, very different from the ragged pedlar and his company.

"I shall forget who I am supposed to be," she announced as she paraded round the cart which Gianni and Beppo were beautifying, trying to get used to being a lady in exquisite clothing again. "After all, this is the third name I shall have answered to in less than a month, and not one of them is Montefiore, which I had expected to be addressed as by now!"

And then she said, a little anxiously, "What are we going to do with Hey, You? We are not going to abandon the poor creature, I hope."

"Oh, we shall sell him and put the money towards buying us a pack horse. I am afraid that we shall have to sell Nello as well, faithful though he has been, and buy a good horse to pull the cart, for I fear that you must be a delicate ailing creature, Emilia. Do you think that you can assume a die-away manner and be petulantly demanding of your put-upon husband?"

Angela thought poorly of this as a proposition, and grumbled at him. "I suppose it would be all the same if I said that I preferred to be a haughty creature like the lady Isabella, I should still have to do your bidding. Are you sure that this pantomime is really necessary?" And then she brightened a little. "Although I must say that I prefer wearing handsome and clean clothes after the dirty rags I have been crossing Verdato in. I thought that we should have been safely out of it by now."

"Burani is the last large town in Verdato, and we shall soon be across the border, but even then we shall not be quite safe. Gentile makes little of borders. Now get into the cart, Signora Emilia, and prepare to be demanding—that should surely please you."

But his voice was kind again and he was only teasing her, not cruelly mocking her. In his manner to her he had almost reverted to the man he had been in the night. So it was in amity and in some state, despite the poorness of their horse, and the ambling mule, happily free of his burden, that they drove towards Burani, Beppo hidden in the back of the cart.

What Marina, Angela and now Emilia did not know was what Beppo had said privately to Gianni before he had been hidden in the cart. "You will be kind to her, will you not? She is a brave lass, not at all what we had expected."

"Now what do you take me for, Marco? Of course I shall be kind to her. I have always been kind to her, have I not? But I have also to get her safely away, and to do that I need to have her obey me unquestioningly."

Beppo knew that his lord was being wilful, he also knew that he could speak to him freely without restraint. "I know that you have expectations of others which they do not always live up to, and that she is desperate to prove that she is not overcome by what has happened to her. I think that it might be a good idea to tell her the truth, and that you might regret it if you do not."

Gianni took refuge in ambiguity, a favourite trick of his when challenged. "The truth, Marco, Beppo, Ettore? Do you know what the truth is?"

Beppo's answer was sturdy. "Yes, I do, but I sometimes fear that you do not. There is such a thing as being too clever. You would do well to remember that. Be kind as well as clever, and the Lord God will reward you."

Gianni's answer was a shrug. "I bid you farewell and good luck on your journey home. God grant that it may not be long before we meet again." He embraced his friend and suddenly grave, held him at arms length, looking deep into his eyes. "Trust me, Marco, my faithful friend. I have never let you, or any man or woman down yet, and I do not intend to start now."

"But you have never been in these circumstances before, nor with such a lady as that of Novera. She has proved to be true gold, never forget that. *Addio*, and God be with you, too."

It was all the farewell which they could have. For once the merchant Ottone Rinieri and his wife Emilia had passed the guards at Burani's gates and had brought their cart to a halt before Burani's best inn, Beppo, now Ettore Manfredi, slipped silently and unobtrusively away, leaving them to their fate.

Burani was bigger than either Verdato or Ostuna, and richer. Had Emilia the ordering of it she would have chosen it for her headquarters, and not Verdato as Gentile had done, and so she told Ottone.

"My thoughts, too. But he conquered Verdato first, and Burani later, and by then he had made Verdato his capital. But it cannot hold a candle to Burani. Its cathedral is a gem, and its merchants are richer than those of Verdato—but then, they do not have Gentile perpetually on their back."

That was true enough, and once again Ottone had demonstrated his knowledge and grasp of the ways of the great world where fortunes and decisions were made. He must, Emilia thought, have been a successful *condottiero* if his military skill had matched his political and economic understanding. She wondered why she had not heard of him before, for she was sure that the name of Niccolo da Stresa had never been mentioned by her uncle.

Oh, but, she reproached herself, why did she assume that that was his real name? He seemed to shed identities and change names more often than he changed his clothes, and now he had her doing it, too. They drove down Burani's main street to a great square. Just off the square was the street where the goldsmiths and bankers had their headquarters, and it was thither that they were bound. To replenish their exchequer, Ottone said.

He stopped the cart to ask to be directed to the offices of the goldsmith, Giuseppe Farfalla, which were, they found, housed in a noble building. Once inside they were conducted to an airy room, where Ottone produced a note of hand from the Medici bank in Florence which had the goldsmith who was, as was common in smaller towns, also a banker, bowing and smirking at him. And where had Ottone got the note of hand from? Not honestly, Emilia was sure.

When told that they had planned to stay at an inn, the goldsmith flung an arm around Ottone's gilded shoulders and insisted that they lodge with him.

"But for one night only," Ottone insisted. "We must be on our way. My wife is delicate—you understand?" He placed his finger by his nose again, and winked.

Oh, the devil! He means that I am with child! Whatever next! But all that the bursting Emilia could do was what Marina and Angela had done, obey him by lowering her eyes, simpering, and waving the fan which Ottone had taken from one of the pedlar's packs in the cart and given to her.

"I understand." Giuseppe winked back, adding, "Lady, it will be my pleasure and my wife's to see that the food which we give you will not distress a delicate stomach."

Slops! They were going to feed her on slops, and here she had been congratulating herself that she might be about to eat a decent meal again. No hope of that with Ottone's fertile brain spreading lies in all directions.

"Now why did you tell him that?" she exclaimed crossly when they were in the elegantly appointed bedroom which Giuseppe had given to them. "Now I shall have nothing to eat but thin gruel, milk, and…slops. Why could I not have had a damaged ankle and a limp—like the one which you have lost—then they would have forced food on me to assist my recovery!"

"Dearest wife," said Ottone smoothly, bending down to kiss her. "Think how useful and disarming a breeding woman is. Besides, you were plainly not breeding at Guido's tower, or Ostuna or the village, and a rich merchant with a sickly wife, and several servants bears little resemblance to Gianni of the roads and his tattered train."

"Why does everything you say sound so right and proper and—clever—whilst everything I say sounds the contrary." Then, brightening a little, Emilia added, "I suppose it is because I am not so lost in deceit and trickery as you are, Messer Ottone. Tell me, what are you truly like? Is there someone real hidden beneath your many disguises? Or do you change as the wind changes, so that no-one ever knows who exactly you are?"

She had nonplussed him at last. He turned his back on her to stride to the window to stand staring out of it at the goldsmith's garden, as tidy and orderly as he was.

He swung round again to face her, and if she had distressed him, there was no sign of it on his face.

On the contrary, it was as smooth as a calm sea and about as readable. But she thought that somehow she had touched a nerve in him, though he would never confess to it.

"Alas," he told her, his voice as sweetly reasonable as he could make it. "My knowledge of the world is so much greater than yours that you must respect it. Later, when we know each other a little better and are not living in constant danger of death, or worse, then we may debate matters more fully, but for the present I must ask you to do as I bid without question. Safer so."

"As Master Ottone wishes." Emilia swept him a great curtsey, bowing her head to lift it to find him gazing at her with smiling approval.

"Trickery and deceit," he said softly. "Why, I must commend you as an apt pupil. You are already Ottone's consort to the very life, and Marina and Angela are long gone and forgotten. Shall I reproach you for the ease with which you change yourself— or admire you?"

Yes, he had an answer for everything. And, as usual, he was right. In the short time since she had met him, and had begun to live a life of danger on the roads, she had begun to change, and now she did not know who she was—other than that in a little while she must be in the goldsmith's parlour pretending to be two months pregnant, the merchant's ailing wife!

She looked around the bedroom, dominated as it was by a great carved and gilded bed. Its dimensions were noble but, alas, she would have to share it with him. There was a day bed before the window, but she suspected dismally that she would not be able to persuade him to sleep on it—and she was right.

"Oh, no," he told her. "We are a loving husband and wife. But be reasonable, sweeting, the bed is large and we may put the bolster between us."

"But I am not your wife," Emilia wailed, "nor your sweeting either, and if you will not sleep on the day bed, then I shall."

To no avail. He took her by the arm, and pulled her to him to hold her tight against him, blue eyes bright and glittering. "And would you not wish to pretend that we are truly husband and wife—for one night only? No-one need ever know."

Oh, he was the most cunning and tempting devil from Messer Dante's deepest hell, the vile Inferno itself! To lie in the cradle of his arms, to feel the strength of his shapely body, to be tempted by the very scent of him—clean Ottone, as handsome as the devil himself—was torture for a poor girl who wished to remain virtuous. How easy it would be to turn in his arms to offer him her lips—and everything that was hers. Oh, Mary Mother help me, for I not only love him, but I desire him, and I never knew before that love and lust are so intermingled. My knees are so weak so that he may yet take me, even without my willing it.

But that was a lie. She must not, could not yield to him. For was she not the virtuous lady of Novera who was promised to the lord Leonardo di Montefiore in marriage? It was her duty to marry that lord, and she could not go to him from the bed of a handsome fly-by-night mercenary soldier—who was offering her nothing but that bed.

Before propinquity and opportunity could do their dreadful work on her so that she would lie beneath him without willing it, but only because her will was as weak as her body, Emilia tore herself away from him, and retreated to the far wall of the bedchamber, trembling violently.

She put up a hand before her as though to conjure him away. "No! No!" she exclaimed. "I will not be your doxy, clean or dirty. I am the lady of Novera and I must do my duty and marry the lord Leonardo. Tempt me not."

Ottone never moved. He stood impassive before her, except for those speaking eyes. At last he said, "But you feel nothing for him, Emilia. Confess, you do feel for me what you ought to feel for him, for I could tell as you lay trembling in my arms just now that what I wanted, you wanted, too."

"And if I did?" she spat at him. "Honour forbids. Duty forbids. By all the Bordonis, living or dead, who kept their honour intact then I, too, must keep mine intact. *Amor vincit omnia*, the poets say: love conquers all, but that is not true: for it cannot conquer my honour or my duty." And shuddering from the very strength needed to refuse him, she turned away from him.

She did not see the strange look which crossed Ottone's face as she uttered her proud declaration. Nor did she see him close his eyes and clench his fists.

"Enough," he said at last, to her back. "I will sleep on the day bed if that is what you wish."

"I do not wish it." Her voice was as melancholy as a dying wind. "I would wish quite otherwise, but my wishes do not count against what I owe not only to Leonardo di Montefiore, but to what the Lord God demands of me."

She heard him leave the room and then, once his footsteps had died away, Emilia threw herself on the bed and began to cry for what could never be.

In the end they stayed in Burani for two nights. To rest and recover, and to allay any suspicions which their eagerness to be gone immediately might create. Ailing she might be, but under the pretence of wishing for the Lord God's blessing, Messer Ottone's wife Emilia visited the cathedral which, like Burani itself, was smaller than Florence's Duomo, though larger than Gentile's church in Verdato which pretended to be a cathedral.

Alas, she could not go to confession, for she dare not tell the priest the truth of her situation. But she could stand anonymously among the other men and women and pray to Almighty God to get her safe home again—only she was becoming a little confused as to where home was.

Novera and Montefiore both seemed so far away. The place which she knew, and the place which she did not know, both lacked the same thing. And, monstrously, that would be the presence of the man who had come to loom so large in her life that it seemed as though she had always known him. Could it be that home was where he was, and nowhere else? Could she bear to be alone with him, now that he knew she loved him?

And how and why had she come to fall in love with a man of deceits, who was carrying her to God knows where, and of whom she knew nothing, except that she loved him?

Emilia would have liked to stay longer in Burani and, perhaps one day when her flight was safely over, it was possible that she might visit it again, and admire its elegancies with a lighter heart. A river ran through it and villas and summerhouses had been built on its banks: it seemed like a miniature of Florence itself, possessing all of that city's civilised grace.

Their host was a man of parts with a small library of beautiful books: it was a pleasure for Emilia to renew her acquaintance with Messer Dante on the afternoon when the goldsmith took Ottone to the stables where he sold Nello and Hey, You and bought a more powerful horse to pull their cart.

He also hired two large men, Pasquale and Roberto Albini, the sons of a saddler who was a neighbour of the goldsmith. They did a good business by hiring themselves as guards and escorts to travellers out of Burani and into the neighbouring duchy of Montefiore. Occasionally they travelled as far as Milan, to the north of Montefiore's capital, and then hired themselves out again to escort another train back to Burani.

"Little chance that they will betray us, as wandering ex-soldiers offering themselves for hire might do,'' confided Ottone to Emilia before they made their farewells to the goldsmith and set off on the road which led into Montefiore, and to relative safety. They would not be completely safe until they were near to the city from which the duchy took its name. Whether he intended to visit the city, or where they were ultimately bound for, Emilia did not know. They were moving into lands of which she knew little, far from the familiar names of the territory around Novera.

Travelling as the merchant Rinieri and his small company was very unlike travelling as Gianni and his wife. Astonishingly, although she enjoyed the good food and the relative comfort of the inns and farmhouses where they stayed, Emilia found herself missing the friendly and easy life of the road. She would have thought when Ottone had first captured her that she would have been only too glad to live in relative comfort again, and without ever-present danger dogging their footsteps, but no. She missed Nello and Hey, You and even the silent Beppo, and the rabbit he cooked for them. Their escorts were friendly enough, but in a distant way. Inn landlords bowed and scraped to them, offered them their best fare, but the fun of country living, as well as its hardships had disappeared.

She said as much to Ottone, who had given her a slightly twisted smile: he had been a little distant with her ever since the scene in the bedchamber, and she was sorry for it, for she also missed his affectionate teasing.

"You would not have liked it in winter," he told

her, "but for a time, especially in the summer, it has its attractions. And I believe that you enjoyed shedding the responsibilities you carried in your old life." He was always circumspect in what he said to her in case their escorts overheard anything incriminating, and he taught Emilia to be the same.

No doubt he was right about their old life, and why she had enjoyed travelling the roads as poor Angela so much.

"And do not think that we are safe yet," he told her. "I hope that we are, but there are other dangers on our journey besides those which Gentile might create for us. I doubt that anyone will make the connection between us and a poor pedlar, but we must be careful still."

The habit of years ingrained in Ottone made caution a second nature with him, and he was right to be careful. They were three days out of Burani and travelling steadily away from Verdato when Gentile and Braccio degli Uberti paid Guido Orsini a visit.

Guido was someone of whom Gentile made use, and the reverse was true. Furious that Marina Bordoni and her mysterious captor had vanished into thin air, Gentile was still quartering Verdato and its borders when he decided that Guido might have something to tell him.

They sat at table together after a private feast where little had been drunk. Both men wanted their wits about them when dealing with the other. Gentile had Braccio with him. He had demoted Cecco after his failure to trace Marina, and had turned him away. Cecco's fall was Braccio's opportunity and he was determined to make the most of it. His leading sergeant sat at table, too, but so far had had little to say. That was not in his duties. He was there to listen and to learn.

Guido had no adviser with him but the lady Isabella. Woman she might be, but she was as shrewd and as wild as a mountain cat and saw possibilities hidden from Guido's duller sight. If Gentile was surprised by her presence he did not say so, which was fortunate. They had been talking for some little time, or rather Gentile had, of the steps which he had taken to find Marina.

"And all to no avail," he finally grumbled. "It is as though they all vanished into thin air when once they were out of Verdato."

Isabella had been staring at the sergeant, a comely man, who reminded her a little of Gianni of the roads, although he was cleaner.

"This wench of yours, this lady of Novera. What was her seeming?"

Bad enough that the woman should sit in their councils, but even worse that she should question him. Nevertheless to keep Guido quiet, he answered her.

"A blonde woman, tall. Haughty in manner: a very pillar of virtue. Thinks too much of herself. Once seen, hard to forget."

"A beauty?"

"Aye, very much so."

"And the man who captured her. Of what like was he?"

"Were you not heeding us, lady?" Gentile was

pleased to have the opportunity to rebuke her. "You heard us say that we never saw his face. That he wore an old fashioned helm with a nasal."

Isabella's smile was as poisonously sweet as she was. "Aye, I heard you, lord of Verdato. But what else of him? Tall, short, broad shouldered, good long legs, bandy legs, a pot belly? Lithe in his actions, or clumsy? Or were you all so stricken that you saw naught of him?"

For a moment there was silence. Gentile had seen little of Marina's captor, being held by him in such a way that all he saw was the roof of the church until he was thrown headlong before the church's altar. Braccio had been away with a troop putting down a village which was slow in paying its taxes. Only the sergeant, who had previously been Cecco's, had enjoyed a good view of the man, and into the silence he said so.

"Tall, lady, well shaped, good shoulders, long, powerful legs and thighs, and lithe, like a wild cat. No belly, and malignant."

His reward was a dazzling smile from the lady which had him uncomfortable for reasons which he would not have liked to confess to his superiors. "So, your sergeant is observant, Gentile. Now, has it not occurred to you that the reason why you could not discover the lady's abductor and his troop was because there was no troop, once Verdato had been left behind?"

"No troop!" exclaimed the three from Verdato. "But his troop was seen, a goodly one with seasoned soldiery."

"Aye, but your man is cunning. Witness how he brought off his coup. Suppose he disposed of his troop, and disguised himself and the lady, what then? He has you running around Italy's roads and forests looking for quite the wrong thing."

Guido began to laugh. "I should make you my battle tactician, wife. You are as cunning as the devil himself. Why not, eh? You had not considered that, Gentile?"

Gentile began to look downcast. Braccio said nothing. His moment of embarrassment was yet to come.

"This is all very fine, lady, but where does it lead us?"

"This." Isabella joined her husband in his laughter. "A tall blonde woman, and a large and well built man with the cheek and conceit of the devil, as lithe as a wildcat. Where met we with such lately, husband?"

"Why, where, lady?" Guido was staring at her. Cleverness was all very well, but Isabella was too often reckless with her suppositions—on the other hand, she was also frequently right in them.

"Where but here? The pedlar you brought in. Tall and well built, and lithe as a wild cat. Remember the tumbling act he and his man performed? He sang for us, too."

"But he had a limp. Had your man a limp?" And Guido addressed the sergeant who shook his head.

"No limp, on my life."

"Neither had the pedlar, as I have reason to know," stated Isabella triumphantly. "It was a pretence, a deceit. And the blonde woman with him, for whom my husband had a fancy. He thought her a beauty beneath the dirt.'' She thought a moment. ''Wait, he had the remains of scar on his face. Someone had struck him with a whip recently. Had your man such?''

There was a dreadful silence.

Braccio's sergeant said faintly, ''By the Lord God, the pedlar at Ostuna, three days out of Verdato. Remember, Lord Braccio, the one you struck in the face after he had said that he had seen naught on the roads. If he were the man who took the lady and she travelled with him in his cart, they would reach Ostuna at about that time if they had started from Verdato and tarried at the village of Perrone... The lady is right—and that is why they disappeared. They didn't...''

''They turned into the pedlar, his doxy and attendant,'' almost sang Isabella. ''Body of God, he was a man to remember, not much like a pedlar if you looked closely at him. And he sang a good song.''

Gentile was incandescent with rage. ''If I catch him he'll sing such a song as would fetch the devils out of hell! And you had him in your hands, and the woman too, and you let them go!'' He was rounding on Braccio whose face was as white as the cloth on the table before them. ''God's teeth, have I but exchanged one fool for another?''

''Lord, how was I to know? And are we sure that this was the same man who took the lady...?''

''You have but one chance to save your skin, dolt, and that is to go after them, and bring them here. I'll

warrant the lord Guido and I will make such mince-
meat of him that no part of him will be left to defile
the ground between earth and sky if he is the fellow
who took my bride from me.''

Now he rounded on Guido. "And why did *you* let
them go? Seeing that you had a fancy for the wench
yourself. But if your lady is right, she was no
wench—only in seeming—although I find it hard to
believe that such a haughty piece could pretend to
be a peasant's trull!''

Isabella, delighted to prove once more what fools
men were, put her oar in again. "Oh, she did a merry
dance before us all, your virtuous and haughty lady,
and she and the pedlar were lovers if all the looks
they cast on one another could be believed.''

Guido, ignoring her spite, snarled back at Gentile.
"No need to reproach me. The lady Isabella sent him
away to keep the wench from me, though I have half
a mind that she had the pedlar to herself before he
left.'' He began to laugh helplessly, for the true joke
was on Gentile, not on him.

"We were all fools together, were we not? The
richest heiress loose in Italy, and my dear Isabella
told her that she was a dirty doxy and she never
turned a hair!'' He began to weep with laughter.
"Why, I could almost congratulate her for her impudence, and the man, too, if I didn't wish to rack
him until the trickery oozed out of him with his life.''

But Gentile wanted to hear no more. He was bellowing for Braccio and the sergeant to saddle up, and
take the road into Montefiore to catch the bastard
who had made such a laughing stock of them all.

Chapter Ten

At much the same time that Guido and Gentile were conferring, Ugo Bordoni and his entourage arrived in the city of Montefiore. Even age and infirmity could not prevent Ugo from journeying there to discover what might be done to recover his missing niece. She had disappeared so completely that it was almost as though some magician had taken her, and was hiding her somewhere far from the haunts of men. All Italy was slowly learning that Marina Bordoni had been snatched away at the very moment when her forced marriage to Gentile da Cortona was about to take place, and gossip and speculation were rife.

Ugo had travelled at great speed from Novera, haste post haste, as the phrase had it, and had brought with him a large troop of his most trusted men-at-arms. It was his belief that together he and the Duke should be able to track down whoever it was who had stolen the heiress of Novera away.

Duke Theodore di Montefiore met him at the very

doorway of his palace in order to demonstrate to the utmost his consideration and respect for his visitor, once his companion in arms. He was in his late fifties, had been handsome in youth, and was still a man at whom people looked twice. His dark hair was now silver, but the power and nobility of his countenance made his age seem of little consequence.

"My poor old friend," he murmured, embracing Ugo. "I understand why you have come, but at your age, was it wise? I have this very morning sent another large troop on its way to Verdato to scour the countryside for your niece. They have my most express orders to stop and question all travellers, even those who show no resemblance to your niece and her captor."

"My duty, it is my duty," returned Ugo heavily. "I was wrong to palter when Gentile first took her, and I have paid for it. I should have sent an army after her to compel him to return her, but I could not believe that he would force her into marriage. And then, when he did, that another should snatch her away..."

"True, I had thought such adventures at an end." Duke Theodore was leading him into his palace, a superb building in the new classical style, filled with treasures gathered from all over Italy. Montefiore was on a par with Florence and Milan so far as power and wealth were concerned, and in marrying Marina to the Duke's son, Ugo knew that he was assuring not only her future, but that of Novera's. Like many rulers of Italy's smaller states he was coming to understand that power, in future, was going to lie with the larger ones. If a larger state was going to annex Novera, then better that it should be a benevolent one such as the Montefiores ruled, rather than a greedy one like Florence or Milan.

Later, after he had been taken to his apartments and had rested for a little time, Ugo and Duke Theodore sat down to dinner in a room distinguished by its civilised nature. It was as far removed from the crudities of Verdato and Guido Orsini's eyrie as the mind could conceive. The food was as splendid as the dishes on which it was served. There were no manchets of bread on which to put the food at the Duke's table, but plates of gold and silver, and forks were there for all. Fingers were for barbarians.

To Ugo's surprise, neither the Duke's son, Leonardo, nor his own wife, Caterina, were present at their meal. The Duke explained that his wife was an invalid who kept to her room. Her one wish in life, he said, was to see her son happily married. As for Leonardo, whom Ugo had hoped to meet, the Duke apologised for his absence, too, and his answer pleased Ugo. "Yes, I am sorry that my son is not here to greet you," he explained, "but on hearing the news of her abduction he took a troop with him into Verdato to try to find and rescue his bride."

"Good! It is what I should have expected of him from all you had said in his favour in Florence." Ugo drank his wine with a little more heart. "With your two troops as well as my own men quartering the countryside and questioning all travellers, we should have no difficulty in tracking down the monster who has snatched my poor niece away. Between us all, finding her should not be over difficult.''

For the first time since the dreadful news of Marina's capture by Gentile had been brought to him, Ugo began to feel hope.

The Duke, however, was not so sanguine. "True," he said gently, "but we must not forget that Gentile will be seeking her, as well as any other rogue *condottiero* who might see an advantage in capturing her. We must hope that Fortune smiles on us for a change, and not on them. Drink to it, my old friend. The red wine will put heart into you.''

Quite unaware that they were now being sought by no less than five small armies, all intent on capturing them, Ottone and Emilia were making their way across country. They were travelling at a faster pace than when they had been pedlars, and in far greater state and comfort.

But not in greater happiness.

Ever since their encounter in the bedroom of the goldsmith Giuseppe Farfalla, they had been constrained with one another. For the first time Emilia, the lesser experienced of the two, knew what Messer Giovanni Boccaccio had meant in his *Decameron* when he had spoken of lovers burning for one another. Oh, yes, she burned for Ottone, no doubt of that at all. She hardly dared to touch him, and yet touch they must, for they must not make their two bodyguards suspicious.

But torture it was for both of them to bill and coo at one another, to touch, to embrace discreetly, to pretend that they were ailing wife and loving husband. Because she was ailing, their guards were not suspicious when Messer Ottone and his wife lay apart—it was no more than was to be expected of a husband whose wife might lose their first child if they were not careful.

So, at night they burned separately. They slept apart from one another on blankets on the hard earth on those nights when they had not been fortunate enough to find an inn or a farmhouse with spare beds on their route towards safety.

"A farmhouse is better than an inn," Ottone explained to Emilia, "for few inns are as clean and comfortable as the two we lodged in earlier, and farmer's wives are houseproud."

Once Emilia would have stared haughtily at him and, remembering that in the first inn they had lodged at they had slept in the stables, she would have replied tartly that he had a peculiar notion of cleanliness and comfort. But her experiences had changed her, and she had become aware of the straitened conditions in which most of the children of the Lord God lived.

For the very poor whom she saw in the fields and the villages, in their ragged clothes, lived in huts and hovels of wattle and daub, and ate the hard crust of poverty. Even in her life as a pedlar's wife she had never descended into such depths as those lived in whom she daily passed.

They were sitting at dusk before a fire, and, as always, not far from water when he told her this. The life of the forest was all around them. In her wanderings Emilia had discovered that the birdsong of the night was different from that of the day.

"Where are you taking me?" she asked him abruptly. "And how far away are we from your destination?" She purposely did not say *our* destination.

Ottone lay back lazily, his hands behind his head. "You will find out soon enough, sweeting," he told her.

Sweeting again! He had not called her that since the fatal night in Burani. And if she were not mistaken the look on his face resembled the one he had worn that night, not the cold one of the few days since they had left Burani. Here, in the half-dark, almost alone, for their two watchdogs were seated at some little distance and could not overhear what they were saying, the old intimacy of the days when they had been pedlar and supposed wife, had returned.

The dim light softened his face, made him seem younger. She could imagine what he had looked like when he was a boy. Where had he been? What had he been doing when she had been a young maiden learning to be the lady of Novera? Ah, sweet Jesus, how handsome he was, and how much she now understood what Messer Boccaccio had been writing of in that book which Lucia had not wanted her to read, but of which her uncle had said roughly, earlier that year, "Let be, it is time that she grew up. Let Messer Boccaccio educate her a little."

But it was not Boccaccio who had educated her but Niccolo da Stresa, also Gianni and Ottone, who was looking at her with such sweet desire in his beautiful eyes, and with such a softening of his usually hard mouth that the lady Marina, also Angela and Emilia, felt her very joints loosen at the sight.

To distract her wandering and sinful mind, she asked him, as impersonally as she could, "You know everything about my life, Messer Ottone, for it was an open book, but I know nothing of yours. Of your goodness, tell me a little of it, for I have a desire to know something of the man who has carried me off."

"Now what, dear wife, would you like to know? That I was a wild boy, naughty as boys usually are? That my father despaired a little of me at one time, since I was so unlike my elder brother, who was a very paladin of all the virtues—which I never was, though I suppose that I do not need to tell you that."

"No, that is true," agreed Emilia. "And this brother of yours. What name had he? And where does he now reside?" For she thought to be a little cunning and have him betray himself and his origins a little as he talked so carelessly to her.

Ottone fell silent for a moment, and his face darkened. "He resides, I hope, in Messer Dante's Paradise, having passed through Purgatory. He is dead, wife, he died in a pointless skirmish. Being good, he lacked the knowledge to understand the brute cunning of those who are evil and so died of his virtues, which some might say—although not I—was better than living because of his vices."

He fell silent again, looking into the fire which was now burning brightly.

"And you, what do you say?" ventured Emilia at last.

"That good or bad I miss my brother, and wish that I had seen more of him, but we went our different ways. He to University at Pavia, and I to Paris."

"Paris!" Emilia was entranced. "You went to Paris!" She spoke with all the delighted enthusiasm of someone who, until her fateful journey to Montefiore, had never left Novera. "Of what like is Paris?"

He laughed, one of his mocking laughs, showing his splendid white teeth. "Paris? Large—and dirty."

"Oh," exclaimed Emilia. "You mock me. You know perfectly well what I meant, and it did not deserve that answer."

"No, but what I said is true. For the rest, it was the perfect place for a footloose boy who wanted not only to study at the feet of great teachers, but also to learn what life was about."

"And what is life about?" Emilia's smile as she said this was a little sly.

"Love and war, lady. Birth and death, what else?"

He was telling her nothing about himself, and yet in another sense he was telling her everything.

"And you speak French?"

He shifted a little so that he could see her the better. See the firelight on her face as the night grew darker. "Of course, and German a little."

"As well as Latin and a little Greek?"

"And a little Greek," he agreed smiling, "for who has more than a little, except the great pedants? And I am not a pedant."

"Indeed you are not. And speaking so, you serve both Venus and Mars?"

This delighted him. "Yes. The goddess of love and the god of war. Well said."

"And you have been a soldier? Marco called you captain once."

Questioning him was like being a dentist, the one who had visited Novera and had slowly, so slowly, pulled teeth. Except that he did not shout and scream like the dentist's victims.

"Yes, I have been a soldier." He was silent again. Oh, he knew what she was doing, and was evading her every question! He had all the arts, and was devious, too.

Emilia listened entranced. "Tell me a little of your life as a soldier, and how you came to be one, for your education was more like that of a scholar than a warrior."

He was silent for a moment, and then said, "Oh, my brother died in an ambush set by a man whom he thought his friend, and my father told me that the life of a scholar or of a clerk, or even a merchant was not now for me. I had been educated as a page in the house of a nobleman before I went to Paris, and I was skilled in all the knightly accomplishments. I sometimes think that Paolo, my brother, should have been the younger son, for he was more fit than I for a life indoors among books and papers— although I never fought against my father's orders that that should be my life.

"So when Paolo died my life changed completely. I became a soldier, not a clerk." He fell silent again, and Emilia realised that although he had told her everything, yet he had also told her nothing. He had given her no hint of his true name or family—for she was sure that it was not da Stresa, nor of where he had lived, or of the noble house in which he had been a page.

She knew that it was a commonplace for boys of good birth to spend some of their adolescence in the household of another nobleman, rather than with their own family, for only so, it was thought, would they be properly disciplined. There had been at least two in Ugo's household at Novera, and she had played with them when she was younger, but when she had reached the age of fourteen she had been forbidden their company.

And so she told Ottone. He laughed softly. "Your uncle did not want to expose you to temptation." He sat up suddenly, and asked her, "What would he say if he knew that you had been daily exposed to temptation and had so far resisted it? Would he believe you—or me?"

Emilia was honest. "I don't know. Sometimes…" she began and stopped, fell silent.

"Sometimes?" he echoed. "What were you about to say, Emilia? Why did you stop?"

She could not answer him, for a true answer would be that she was not sure that she ought to resist the call of passion—which might never come again. Instead she asked him again about his past as a soldier, and seeing that she would not reply to his question, he told her a little of it. No, not the horrors, but some of the commonplaces of comradeship and the problems of knowing what decisions to make when the lives of your men hung upon your every word.

She nodded gravely at this, but again, although he had revealed to her much of the man that he was, she was still in the dark about the essentials of his past. Perhaps, she thought sadly, she might never know them. Perhaps he would disappear from her life as swiftly and suddenly as he had arrived in it. She shuddered at the thought and to hide the shudder she turned the conversation again.

"You said that you studied at Paris. Was it at Paris that you learned how to deceive and to answer so that you gave nothing away?"

"No, I learned that from life. I was determined not to be deprived of it, like my poor brother, because I thought that men and women were naturally good."

Emilia shuddered. "But does not that make you unable to enjoy life as the Lord God intended it should be enjoyed? To be so suspicious? To be without trust?"

"No, not entirely without trust, for one has to trust someone. It is up to us to choose carefully those whom we trust, not assume blindly that all are trustworthy."

"And do you trust me?"

This came out heartrendingly. So heartrendingly that Ottone levered himself up and moved to where Emilia sat, hugging her knees, her eyes on him wide and questioning. He had forgotten that although she was innocent, she was also clever and intuitive.

"Implicitly," he murmured and took her in his

arms. He loved her for her intellect as well as her calm beauty and the courage which she had consistently shown in adversity. And also for the shrewdness with which she had questioned him, which had almost caused him to drop his guard.

She turned in his arms as lightly and easily as though she had done it a thousand times before, to offer him her lips. He trusted her, so she would trust him, and at that very moment, as they truly tasted one another for the first time on their travels, a nightingale began to sing.

They were lost. The liquid music which poured into the heavens, the touch and feel of another soul, the twin to their own, held them captive. If it was Emilia's first taste of true passion, then it was Ottone's first taste of true love. He had known many women, and made love to some of them, but he had never before felt what he was now feeling for the woman to whom he was beginning to initiate into the delights of love.

He was a boy again. The boy of whom he had spoken, who had lost the admired elder brother and was in a great city, alone but free, experiencing everything for the first time. Love and hate and learning. Her lips were sweet because he was the first man to whom she had freely offered them, and as blind passion began to hold him in its thrall, the cold something which had ruled him since his brother's death, cried warningly, "No, you are not to betray her by making her your doxy in truth as well as in pretence. She is innocent, and innocence is too easily betrayed."

He had spoken of trust, and he must not betray hers.

So he pulled away from her.

In Burani it was she who had ended their love-making, but here, in the dusk in the forest, it was he who called a halt, and she, her face lit with passion, who stared reproachfully at him.

"Duty," he said slowly, the word hurting him even as he spoke it. "You spoke of your duty, and because of it, you drew away from me in Burani. I would not have you go against your duty, nor would I betray you, after you spoke so touchingly of trust."

"It was not I who spoke of trust," she told him, "but you."

"Well, then, lady," and there was nothing mocking about him now, "if the word I used was trust, and the word you used was duty, then those are the words which must rule us, if we are to be true to ourselves."

"And love, Messer Ottone? What of that word?"

"Oh, lady, you denied it at Burani, as I deny it now. It is the splendour of the night and the bird which is singing to us so sweetly, which have together led us astray—as Messer Boccaccio once wrote."

But Emilia had not read that story. It was not in the manuscript of the *Decameron* which she had read, being one which the scribe who had copied it out had considered to be too improper to be repeated. But she remembered what Ottone, when he had been Gianni, had told her of the other meaning of the nightingale's song, and her face flamed at the memory.

Had she been so wanton as to forget what the end of their loving would have been? Had she forgotten that she was the lady of Novera, seduced by his answers to her questions which had revealed the boy he had been, a boy whom she wished to love—and be loved by?

"I forgot everything in your arms," she muttered miserably and turned away from him. "It was I who should have said no, not you. How weak I am, not to remember that I am promised to the lord Leonardo. I so nearly gave you what should be his alone."

He made no answer to that, for one of their bodyguard was coming over to them, to discuss the night's arrangements for sleep and for safety. So far they had met few on the road by day, and none at night, but as they neared Montefiore that might change.

Ottone felt Emilia shudder and mistook its meaning. He was all solicitude. "You are cold, wife? Shall I order the men to build us a larger fire—or shall I fetch you a shawl from the cart?"

He used the word wife so often that Emilia thought that he must like the sound—or the thought of it—which had her smiling sadly.

She shook her head. "No, I am not cold, but I am rather tired. Even so, before I retire I should like to walk a little."

"Not on your own," he replied, and rose swiftly.

"If you will permit I will walk with you for I, too, feel cramped after a day spent driving the cart."

She could believe that, so she allowed him to take her arm, and they walked a little way into the forest. It was not yet dark. They were in the half-light between night and day when objects were strangely clear, before they disappeared from sight altogether. They had only walked a little distance when the trees ended and they were on the edge of a cliff which looked down a great valley.

In the far distance, blue against the growing grey of night was a settlement, with its few evening lights already shining and twinkling. Ottone said, "If I were to take you to Montefiore, Emilia, it is there, beyond the town which you see before you, which is Morcote, the name of the lordship which Leonardo di Montefiore owns."

Montefiore, which if he so willed would be her journey's end. Did she wish her journey to end? Once, at the beginning, she would have welcomed it but now, all had changed. Could she marry Leonardo di Montefiore when her heart was given to another? For now she not only desired Ottone, but she had come to be his friend, someone to whom she could talk, as she was someone with whom he could talk. So strange it was that after all their amorous encounters they could be so impersonal, that he could speak to her of music and books, pick up his lute and sing to her as though they had never been in one another's arms…

It came to Emilia that in one thing they were alike. They were both strong-willed. Was Leonardo strong-willed? Would he speak to her of books and music, laugh over Messer Boccaccio's stories?

When he came to her in their marriage bed, would the nightingale sing?

The thought that it might not was unbearable. Especially since she knew that in the arms of the man beside her the nightingale *would* sing, and sing sweetly... Duty was only a word, and here beside her was life and love, and duty and Leonardo seemed far away.

It was not Leonardo who had saved her from Gentile, it was Ottone. Why should she not reward him? Was it not her duty to reward him? Passion rose in her, and as the night grew darker and the stars began to appear as they wandered back to their small camp, Emilia was wondering whether she was not being a fool to hold him off. If she but said the word...what then?

Because if she did not give him that word soon she never would, for were they not almost at journey's end? If nothing went wrong, that was. To tame her errant thoughts she said as much to Ottone. "Think you that we are safe?"

In between wishing Emilia in his arms and in his bed, Ottone had been thinking the same thing.

"I hope so. But experience teaches me to be wary. Until we reach our destination we cannot account ourselves safe. All our enemies are cunning, else they would not be alive and successful. I will only say that we are but a few days from deliverance."

She had expected that he would say as much, so said nothing herself. As on every night, they parted to lie down at no great distance from one another, but for their own different reasons, neither of them slept easily.

In the morning Emilia wondered how she would be able to look Ottone in the eye again after she had betrayed her feelings towards him so plainly but, strangely, she found that far from being embarrassed, some barrier between them which had existed since Burani had fallen. From that evening on they were easy with one another again, and the days passed happily and uneventfully by. So uneventfully that even Ottone began to believe that they might reach their journey's end without further trouble.

Such thoughts always tempt the Gods who watch over the affairs of men, for they mean that men consider themselves the masters of their own destiny. So, as fate, or the Gods, would have it, even as they neared Montefiore, Emilia's beauty brought them trouble again.

It was late afternoon. They were ambling along, Pasquale ahead of them, Roberto covering their rear, when a small party of young men on horseback, falcons on their wrists, galloped along the rough road towards them. Their leader put up a hand and bade them stop. His eyes roved keenly over their little party, and came to rest on Emilia as she sat silent by Ottone.

He was young, only a little older than Emilia, but carried himself with the arrogance of someone who has given orders all his life, and who expects them to be obeyed immediately.

"Why, who are you?" he asked. "And whither are you bound? It is Naldo da Bisticci who asks you, the lord of this valley." He waved a careless arm around him, so that his hooded falcon fluttered angrily at the movement.

"Lord, I am Ottone Rinieri, a merchant of Florence bound for Montefiore, where I have business." Ottone's tone was not as servile as it had been when he had been Gianni, but he was careful to speak after such a fashion that he did not offend the haughty boy before him.

"Oh, indeed! And the woman beside you? Your lady, is she? And why do you travel in a cart more suited to a peasant than a merchant of note?"

"My wife ails a little, lord, and this is an easier mode of travel for her." Ottone's tone was still decently humble.

"Indeed! She does not look as though she ails, merchant. Quite the opposite, in fact. But that being so, where do you intend to rest this night? For you are in territory where neither farmhouse nor inn is available."

"Why, on the earth, lord. It is summer, and the weather is kind."

"But not tonight, merchant," riposted Naldo, who was now frankly appraising Emilia so that she shivered before him. "My castle is nearby, and you may lodge there in comfort—as long as it may please you."

"That is most gracious of you, lord," replied Ottone, keeping his voice and his temper as level as he could. He had only one desire, and that was to strike the boy before him for the insolence with which he was stripping Emilia with his eyes. "But I may not stay for more than one night, if it please you. I am already late for my appointment in Montefiore, and would wish to hasten on my way."

"Oh, I would not have you reject my hospitality, merchant, and I would require you to remain for at least two nights. We lack entertainment and knowledge of the great world outside our valley, and would have you supply that lack. Is not that so?" And he turned in his saddle to address his men who loudly chorused a willing answer.

"You see, merchant, we are all agreed. Two nights, and you shall drink my best wine, and sleep in a bed more comfortable than that the earth supplies—or even an inn or a farmhouse. Come, follow me, you, your beautiful wife, and your twin guardians."

There was no help for it. Emilia whispered to Ottone, once they were on their way to Naldo's castle, travelling behind him, out of his earshot, "I do not like this, Ottone. Indeed, I greatly dislike the way in which Ser Naldo looks at me."

"Neither do I," Ottone whispered back. "Were I Niccolo da Stresa again with a troop at my back, I would make sure that he would sing me quite another song. As it is, we must do as he says. I do not wish you less beautiful, Emilia, but were you not so, then you would not present such a temptation to every chance-met rogue between Verdato and Montefiore, and we should be the safer for it."

After a time Emilia began to think that she had

misjudged Naldo. His castle might not be as large or as imposing as that of Guido's, but it was more comfortable, and he not only made them welcome, but he placed good food and even better wine before them, and made no further attempt to distress Emilia by his bold looks. He was no fool, and asked Ottone some shrewd questions, and fortunate it was that he knew enough about the ways of merchants to give knowledgeable answers.

He possessed no wife, and the few women present, as they dined in his great hall before a huge fireplace, were the respectable wives of his courtiers and followers, and so all was decorous. He told them that his father had died when he was a boy, and an uncle, now also dead, had brought him up. Since his uncle's death he had been his own master.

The merchant, Ottone Rinieri, like his supposed wife, began to think that he might have misjudged the young lord before him, who was so busy ladling his charm over them both. He was not ill-looking, and only his arrogance prevented him from seeming to be as fair and pleasant a young man as either of them had ever met. Naldo rose when Ottone asked him if they might retire, explaining that his wife must be feeling weary after their long journey, and needed to rest, and, giving his grave consent, he watched them leave the room.

"We might, I hope, escape from here without harm." Ottone was seated on the great bed in their room, watching Emilia who was brushing her long hair. "But I do not like it that both Roberto and Pasquale have been lodged so far away from us. On the other hand, there is little enough that they could do to help us if things went wrong. Three men could not do much against Naldo's household.''

''We may be wronging him.'' Emilia sat on the bed beside Ottone as naturally as though she had shared a room with him all her life. ''He does not seem to be another Guido—and,'' slyly, ''he does not seem to possess a lady Isabella to pursue you!''

''To some extent,'' Ottone told her slowly, avoiding her eyes, ''all men in positions of power are likely to be Guidos. That is, they may use their position to gain the women they want! Oh, not invariably, but the temptation is there—which is why men guard their wives, their daughters and their mistresses so carefully.''

Emilia thought about what he had said, then conceded ruefully that there was truth in it, and told him so.

''And,'' pursued Ottone, continuing Emilia's education, ''there are women who will offer themselves to men of power.''

''Or even to a pedlar—if they catch their fancy,'' interrupted Emilia, a trifle pertly.

''True—and we have to hope that neither of us will become Naldo's victims.''

He had hardly finished speaking when there was a knock on the door, and before either of them could so much as answer it, the door opened, to reveal Naldo's major-domo, a middle aged man. Two large soldiers stood at his back.

The major-domo advanced into the bedroom, bowed low to them both and straightened up to announce, "The lord Reynaldo da Bisticci would have a private word with the merchant's lady this night. I am here to escort her to his room."

Ottone rose. He stood quite still and tense in the middle of the room as Emilia's hand flew to her mouth and her face turned as white as the snow which crowned the Appenines.

"And if *I* said that I do not wish my wife to have private words with the lord Reynaldo da Bisticci in his room at night—what then?"

The major-domo bowed low in what could only be understood as mockery.

"Why, Ser Ottone Rinieri, I have brought two of the lord's guard with me to persuade you to agree to what the lord wishes and I have several more down the corridor to assist them although I do not think that they will be needed. You are not armed, I see." And now the major-domo's mockery was plain.

Emilia said, standing up and walking to Ottone's side to take his hand, "And if I said that I do not wish to go to the lord's room, what then?"

"Then I shall give orders to the soldiers to carry you there." He bowed low again. "But I would prefer not to have to order them to do so."

Hysteria rose and bubbled in Emilia's throat. She had escaped both Gentile and Guido, only to fall prey to a spoiled boy who had taken a fancy to the merchant's wife—and this time, there was no-one to save her.

Ottone threw off Emilia's hand, and strode forward. "No!" burst from him. "You shall not take her, for you know as well as I what the lord wishes to do with her.''

"Merchant," said the major-domo, no whit abashed. "I have the lord's word that if you will go quietly on this matter, he will give you payment to the extent that the lady pleases him, so you see that you will not lose by this transaction. But if you try to oppose him by attacking us, then I fear that you will not simply lose the use of your wife for one night, but your life as well.''

Face livid, his hands fists, Ottone began to speak again. "I would be a cur to let her go to him without trying to prevent it—'' And he continued to advance on the major-domo so that the two soldiers moved into the room to come between them.

"No!" It was Emilia who spoke, and in tones of command such as she had never used even when she had been the lady of Novera.

"No, husband. You shall not needlessly give your life for me. For there is no way that we can successfully defy the lord, and your death would not save me from dishonour. Indeed, it would dishonour me further, and that I will not have.'' She turned towards the major-domo. "I shall go to your lord since I have no alternative, but not willingly, and he will have so little joy from me, that he shall pay my husband nothing. No, Ottone,'' she told him proudly, as he tried to stand between her and the soldiers. "You are not to stop me. I will not have you die for me, not after all that you have already done. And,'' she added meaningfully, "what you would once have done for me, I will do for you.''

Now Ottone turned away from the soldiers to take her in his arms, to look into her eyes, to say hoarsely, "You do not know what you are asking of yourself. It is not the same, and you know it."

The major-domo interrupted them to announce in a bored voice, "Come, cease this. The lord awaits the lady and will grow impatient if you haggle thus. It is not the end of the world if you share your lady with another."

For one dreadful moment Emilia thought that this insult might have Ottone throwing himself at the soldiers to die defending her. She clung to him, and almost shouted, "No," before releasing him as she felt him falter. "I will go with you, sir, and may you ask the Lord God's pardon for your part in this, for I cannot pardon you, or the man whom you serve." She was through the door, taking one last look at Ottone who had sunk down onto the bed, his hands over his eyes, before the major-domo closed the bedroom door behind her—and locked it.

Chapter Eleven

Braccio, Gentile and Guido were plotting together. Guido had allied himself to the lord of Verdato, after a good talking to from Isabella. She had ordered him to keep a close eye on Gentile whilst they were on the pedlar's trail for she did not trust him. Her last brisk words to him before he left her to join them had been, "Never forget, that if the man who took the lady of Novera from Gentile is the pedlar, and clever enough to deceive us all, he might change himself again, like the shape-changers who deceived the ancient Greek heroes."

Guido, being unlettered, knew little of what she was talking about, but he obeyed her all the same, and kept a keen eye on his fellows in villainy. He, Gentile and Braccio and their combined troops travelled swiftly along the road and learned from those they questioned that, yes, a pedlar had passed this way, and it was to be guessed that he was making for Burani. But once they had gone through Burani and were on the road north east again, all traces of the pedlar had disappeared. None they questioned in inn or farmhouse, had seen him, his doxy or his servant.

Like the man who had captured the lady of Novera he had gone from the face of the earth.

Guido remembered what Isabella had told him of the pedlar's cunning, but before he could speak of it to his unlikely allies, Braccio's sergeant rode up, pulled off his helm, saluted and said with as much deference as he could summon up, "Your pardon, lords, but would it not be wise to return at once to Burani? For since there can be little doubt that he reached Burani, then Burani he must have left. And since no-one has seen the pedlar *after* he left Burani, isn't it likely that he has altered his appearance again? Certes, if he could change himself and the lady once, he could do so again, The citizens there may know more than they think. They would bear questioning."

So they all trailed back to Burani, their tails between their legs, Guido, Gentile and Braccio all thinking up different and dreadful punishments for the devious swine who had them dancing to his tune.

More to the point, they searched the town, asking whether any strangers had been seen, and if so, of what kind they had been, and whither they were bound.

It was the sergeant, who was compelled to watch his inefficient superiors fail in their search for lack of imagination, who visited the stables and the saddlers. On his visit to the last saddler on his list he struck gold.

"Strangers, ser sergeant? We see few such in Burani. Nor have three resembling those you have described visited me. Now, had you asked about two strangers, then I might have been able to help you."

"Two strangers, then? Of what like were they?"

"The man was a merchant, rich, splendidly dressed, no pedlar he. His wife was young, blonde and as beautiful as an angel. Ailing, he said, expecting their first blessing. He bought several horses and hired my two sons to escort him to the north. He was passing rich, had letters from the Medici, they said, and was lodged with the goldsmith Farfalla. His name, I remember, was Rinieri, Ottone Rinieri."

Lodged with the goldsmith—and rich. It didn't sound very likely that he was the missing pedlar— and where was his fellow, who had accompanied him all the way from Verdato?

Nevertheless. "You are sure there was no other man with them?"

"Quite sure, your honour." The saddler thought a moment, then added as an afterthought, "He sold Alberto of the stables a mule."

"A mule!" The lady Isabella had said that the pedlar's man had ridden a mule. The goldsmith and Alberto of the stables would bear visiting.

But after he had talked to Farfalla and Alberto and told Gentile and Braccio of what he had learned from them, it was only to have them mock him. But Guido, who arrived late to their meeting—he had been scouring the taverns and was already a little merry—said roughly, "What better change of disguise to deceive us all than from ragged pedlar to merchant, travelling in state? And a blonde beauty with him. Was the lady of Novera a blonde beauty, Ser Gentile? The pedlar's woman was blonde, and pretty beneath the dirt.''

"Blonde and beautiful—beautiful as an angel. Perhaps Braccio's sergeant has smoked him out. The goldsmith is the man to visit.''

"No," said Farfalla brusquely, when they questioned him closely. "He could not possibly have been a pedlar. I have no doubt that my man was a merchant. He had letters of marque from the Medici Bank in the name of Rinieri—and he had the seal which sat beside theirs on the letters.''

Afterwards, sitting round a table in Burani's best inn, they had a conference. They argued and squabbled noisily about whether chasing a wealthy merchant of such credentials was a piece of arrant folly when they ought to be looking for a poor pedlar.

Guido rose at last. He had drunk well, and intended to eat well before he left Burani.

"You," he told Gentile and Braccio, "may do as you please, but I shall ask Braccio's sergeant to accompany me north after the merchant. I am sure that he has the right of it. My bones tell me so. I have a mind to capture the lady and offer her for ransom myself.''

"It's the drink telling you so," returned Gentile, but all the same, after hurried words with Braccio, he announced roughly that if Guido was determined on a wild goose chase, then he would accompany him. "For that is all we have to go on, and it is little enough. And if it prove that the lady is with this so-called merchant, then I do not want him killed when we take them. By the living God, I want him for my sport before I despatch him at the last!''

And so it was agreed. They would pursue the merchant who already had several days start on them, and hope to catch him before he reached Montefiore.

All unknowing that their enemies were in hot pursuit, and caring little had she known, for a greater danger stared her in the face, Emilia was hurried along the castle's narrow corridors to Naldo's bedroom.

Unreality walked with her. It could not be true that she was hastening towards the bed where she would be robbed of her virginity—she must be asleep back in Novera and this was all a nightmare. But no, this was all too dreadfully true and thinking so, she bitterly regretted that she had not offered her maidenhead to Ottone, for were she to lose it before she reached Montefiore then better with him than with some chance-met careless boy.

Naldo was eagerly awaiting her arrival and started up from a great carved chair to greet her when the soldiers and his major-domo escorted her into his room. The room was something of a surprise. Although what she had seen of the castle had been comfortable enough, it was nothing like the sumptuousness of Novera, but here all was luxury with a carpet and hangings brought from the East, with a large wooden bed, fantastically carved and painted. Its coverlet, embroidered in rich red and gold, showed the sun in splendour.

He wore a houppelande to match the coverlet, but was plainly naked beneath it, which almost brought on the shivers, but Emilia had told herself to be brave, not to show her fear and disgust of what was about to happen to her.

There was a fire in the hearth and thick candles in sconces. Once he had dismissed the major-domo and the soldiers, Naldo motioned to her to sit on a long settle, and then sat himself down again in his great chair, and chin in hand surveyed her as though he were looking at some beautiful thing brought in for his delectation. He was drinking in every aspect of her from the crown of her golden head to the tips of the elegant shoes which Ottone had bought for her in Burani before they left.

"You are beautiful, merchant's wife," he said at last. "A very princess. I like beautiful things."

Emilia tried to keep her voice steady. "You do not break beautiful things, I hope. So why break me?"

"To lie with me would break you?" His voice was offended.

"To lie with anyone other than my husband would break me."

"So virtuous, lady?" He leaned forward to inspect her the more closely, and broke into a knowing smile. "You know what they say? A slice off a cut loaf is never missed."

He rose to advance on her. His houppelande had fallen open and she could see the curling red hairs on his chest. He was smiling at her, ready now to take his pleasure. Emilia closed her eyes. I am not a cut loaf, she wanted to shriek at him. I am virgin, no one's wife, who is meant to be Leonardo di Montefiore's bride, but who would rather bed with Niccolo da Stresa, or whatever he is calling himself at the time! Not with you! Never with you!

But she said nothing.

His strong and urgent hands were around her waist now. If she opened her eyes she would look into his. Not Ottone's eyes. Never his. For if she became this selfish boy's trull she would offer herself to the Holy Mother afterwards and never hold a man in her arms again.

Emilia shivered.

He felt the shiver. "Open your eyes, lady," he whispered. "I do not wish to hurt you, only to give you pleasure."

"No," she told him, and though her voice was low he could hear the iron in it. "No, you may do as you will with me, but I shall not open my eyes whilst you are at your work."

He shook her and said roughly, "You must look at me. I would have you give yourself willingly, for I would rather not force you, that is never my way. But if you continue to refuse me, then force you I will."

Emilia opened her eyes and traded stare for stare with him; became again the lady of Novera. She gave him a distant icy smile. "Then force me," she told him proudly, "for I will never willingly surrender to you. You may break my body, but not my will," and she closed her eyes again.

She felt him shake against her. Naldo had never

been denied before, and told her so. "I will not be treated thus." He put her from him a little. "I may not be as large and splendid as your husband, for all that I am lord and he is merchant, but I am not ill-looking. Why fight me, lady? Why should not the nightingale sing for us? Why struggle against what will happen? Who is to know or care what delights we share tonight? A night of pleasure—and then, on your way."

"That is not my way, never my way." The pun was unintentional, but Naldo caught it. Why, she was a treasure, such looks, such spirit, and such wit when she was trembling before him like an animal caught in a snare—but she would not show her fear. Not she!

He drew in his breath, and seized her again by the waist. Then his hands roved her body, and what he would do next was his choice—never hers—she must endure it. And so they stood for a moment. He muttered, "Oh, lady, so soft, so fair. I would have you willing, but have you I will. Two can play at word games." He was kissing her, and now she was truly in the snare. Only the Lord God could help her, or His Mother, and she prayed silently to them, giving a great sob as her prayer ended, and he was leading her to his bed…to break her there…

But even as they reached it the door opened, and a child's voice said reproachfully, "Oh, Papa, you did not come to see me today, so I have come to you."

Naldo's eyes opened wide. He stepped back again, his seeking hands falling to his side.

"Sofia! What do you here? Where is your nurse?"

"I had not your nightly blessing, so I could not sleep. Give me your blessing."

The child walked further into the room until she stood in the light of the candle by the bed, her large eyes on her father and Emilia, who had been twined together and were now apart. Thus Emilia, opening her eyes, saw her for the first time. The voice, sexless because of its youth, was that of a girl child of some five years of age, a charming cherub clutching a rag doll to her breast.

Sofia looked up at them. "You have a pretty lady with you, Papa. Perhaps she could mend Lisetta for me. She has a poorly eye." She held the doll out to Emilia.

From being in the harem they were now in the nursery. High drama had declined into farce. Naldo's expression was one of mixed shame and pride. Shame at being interrupted in what was rape by his child, and pride in the child herself.

He muttered, "Sofia, you should not be here. I have told you before not to enter Papa's room without knocking." But there was no anger in his voice.

"You do not knock when you enter my room," she reproached him, adding, "If I had known that you had a pretty lady with you, I would have come before. Is the pretty lady to be my new mama now that my old one is in heaven?"

Emilia, avoiding Naldo's gaze, had taken the offered doll. The stitching of one of its eyes had worked loose and it hung down. She fell on her knees before the child, and said softly, "If you will find me a needle and thread, I will mend your doll for you, Sofia.''

"There is no need for that," interposed Naldo roughly. "Her nurse may do it for her in the morning."

"There is every need," Emilia told him, looking at him over the little girl's head. "What is broken must be mended as soon as possible, or life would become a chaos of shards and patches, without meaning."

She was speaking of more than the doll and the man before her knew it. His arousal had vanished. He could hardly look at the woman whom he had been about to ravish. His little daughter's arrival had changed everything, as though the Gods had thrown another dice, and a new game had begun. Sofia had made him man, not monster, had restored to him the humanity which he had been trying to deny by behaving like a brute beast.

Emilia rose, holding the doll. Sofia, clutching at her skirt, began to pull her to the door. Emilia said, before she left the room, with Naldo making no effort to detain her, "She is yours? Her mother is dead? You must have been very young when you were married."

"I was sixteen, and so was she," he told her roughly. "She died having Sofia. She was my only love. I want no other wife."

"So you take merchants' wives instead." This was said tonelessly, factually, and so he answered her.

"Not now. Mend Sofia's doll and get you to your man." He turned his back on her, and Emilia did as she was bid. He was not wicked, only weak, and the child's presence had shamed him, so the Lord God willing, he was not beyond salvation.

If Ottone had ever doubted that he was beginning to love Emilia as he had never loved a woman before, the feelings of anguish which overwhelmed him as he waited for her to return from Naldo da Bisticci's bed, finally revealed the depth of his love to him.

He lay down and tried to compose himself, for he was fearful that he would lose all self-control and begin to hammer on the locked door demanding her to be returned to him unharmed.

Which would be stupid and would merely serve to increase her shame and his. But lying there, he was doomed to endure the torments of his lively imagination. Writhing, he tried to banish the picture of Naldo and Emilia entwined—or else he saw her fiercely resisting her fate, and being compelled to suffer it...

No, the damned in Messer Dante's Hell had never endured such misery, and even as his fists clenched and his body tensed and he promised himself that when he reverted to his proper self he would bring a troop to the castle and hang Naldo from its highest battlement, he heard footsteps outside and voices. It was Emilia returning, and the night not yet a quarter over.

Unbelievably, Ottone experienced anger. Had she been so willing that he had joyed in her so rapidly and was sending her back with the payment which he had promised? Was she no more than any other trull who would lie with anyone if profit came from it? Oh, he was shamed to think such things, but even as the door opened, he started up to face her fiercely as she entered...

And she came in with such a holy calm written on her face, so coolly lovely, so untouched... How dare she look so untouched who had brought shame on them—for now Ottone was so beside himself that he almost believed that he was truly a merchant and this was truly his wife who had betrayed her marriage vows so lightly that she showed no ill effects from the rape she had suffered. He, *he* had been in Hell—and where had she been?

"So soon," he said bitterly. "So soon. I had thought that you would have pleasured the night away between you." He turned his face to the wall, for he loved her, and her shame was his.

Emilia was bewildered. She would have thought that he would be both pleased and relieved to see her back with him so early, and unharmed. But his words and his actions showed her that he thought that the worst had happened.

"Oh, no, Ottone," she told him earnestly, walking over to him to touch him on the shoulder and when he turned his ravaged face to her, to stroke it lovingly. "Oh, no. He never touched me. The Lord God sent me a miracle and I was spared," she whispered as low as she could. "I am maiden yet."

He stared at her, then said faintly, "You speak true?"

"Indeed, husband," for she thought it best to continue to dissemble, for who knew whether or no they were being spied on. "His little daughter burst in upon us even as he began his wicked work, and he was shamed by her presence and let me go, for he is not truly evil, only young and selfish."

Ottone bethought him of his own wicked thoughts of a moment ago, and said humbly, "As I am older and selfish. But, yes, the Lord God was with you. Oh, comfort me, Emilia, for I was so wracked by jealousy and shame that I thrust it all on you. I have been in Hell, forgetting what you might be suffering." Then he added anxiously, "You are sure that he has not hurt you?"

All unknowing of the mental hell through which Ottone had just passed, his self-reproach puzzled Emilia. To try to calm him, she held out her hands to him, and said, "I am unmarked, and I have spent my time away from you repairing his daughter's doll."

"I think that you had better try to repair me! Oh, Emilia." Now she had Ottone's arms around her, who had so recently nearly suffered at the hands of another man, and remembering that she held him away.

"He says that we may leave in the morning, but he will not bid us farewell. He does not want to see you, I think."

"I do not want to see him," returned Ottone savagely. "For although in the end he spared you, you must have suffered before he did. I am like to attack him if I see him again."

"Indeed." Now it was as though all the fear she

had suffered, and the strain of the long day fell upon Emilia at once. "Oh, Ottone, I feel so strange." The room darkened about her, and she fell into his arms, half-fainting with delayed shock.

"Battle weary. You are battle weary," said Ottone briskly, and he lifted her up to lie her on the bed. "And I am being careless of you, for one thing is certain. A woman who has so nearly been ravished by a man is likely to want to avoid all men for a space. Rest, my darling, and let sleep cure you."

Sleep she did, and Ottone sat all night in the chair by the bed, and watched over her. She was his first love, and would be his only love, that he knew—and that he must get her safe to Montefiore.

"I had not thought that he would truly let us go so easily."

It was Ottone speaking. They were sitting in the shade of a large tree having just eaten, the mountains above them and the road below. Neither of them had said anything to their two escorts of what had passed the previous night, but it was plain from the way in which Roberto and Pasquale looked at them that they had heard tell of the merchant's wife visiting the lord's bedroom and of her early return.

"I, too, was fearful, but it was as I said. He was weak not wicked." Emilia paused, began to speak again, but paused again. It was, Ottone knew, a habit of hers when she had something important to say to him.

"What is it, wife?" he asked her gently.

She looked at him, eyes almost blind.

"Nothing, no, that is not true. It is everything. You remember that we discussed whether one ever ought to do an ill thing that good might come?" She paused again. Ottone nodded, wondering what was coming.

"You said that it was easy to discuss such problems in the study, but that outside it was much harder when one was faced with a decision and no time to make it. I see now what you meant, and I also see how much I wronged you over Isabella." She fell silent, but, again, he did not answer her, for he could see that she was thinking, and that in some measure her thoughts were painful.

At last she looked frankly at him before she spoke, as though she had been another man, disputing with him in a discussion among students. "You see, I was prepared last night to save us by lying with Naldo—which was committing a sin to gain a good—when a priest would have said that I ought to have suffered both our deaths first. And what is more, and is a reproach to me, I understand now why you agreed to pleasure Isabella to save me, and that I was both wrong and cruel to hate you for doing so, and to be unkind to you."

"Oh, no!" He rose from where he was sitting and came swiftly over to her to take her hand and stroke it. "It was but natural for you to think and behave as you did, for when I thought of you with Naldo I behaved and thought exactly as you did when you resented me and Isabella! We are but poor weak creatures, Emilia, and the Lord God often asks too much of us. We must always pray that we bend and never break, and forgive one another, even as we wish to be forgiven.''

He had never in his life thought to make such a speech—and to a woman, too. But last night had proved to him how much he loved her and he did not want her to suffer by reproaching herself for the sin of being human.

''We are,'' he said, at last, ''what we are, with all our imperfections on us. If we love one another it is because we recognise that they exist, even as the Lord God loves us—despite our imperfections.''

Emilia acknowledged this with a grave nod of the head, and her hand tightened around his. Thus, barely touching, but together in silent communion they sat a while. She wished that this moment could last forever, but such a wish was futile for presently they would be on their way, and all too soon they would be in the busy corrupt world of men again. Alone here, among the mountains, fearsome and dangerous though they were, as all men and women knew, she was finding a peace which she had never known before.

Yes, all too soon after their rest, Ottone was saying that they must press on. They passed a farmhouse early in the afternoon and their escorts suggested that they spend the night there—which would mean that they would not reach Montefiore for another two days, so Ottone said them nay. Something was whispering in his ear that their luck was running out, had almost run out at Naldo's tower, and he had lived as long as he had done by not ignoring such whispers. The sooner they reached Montefiore city the better.

Emilia had decided that she never wanted to reach the city. For there she would have to say goodbye to Ottone, and she had no wish to do so. Satan was whispering dreadful things in her ear:

Item: that she should tell Ottone that she loved him.

Item: that because of this she would go with him wherever he wished to take her, as Ruth had followed Naomi in the Bible.

Item: that the lady of Novera should disappear, so that Leonardo di Montefiore might take another bride, and the lady become the wife, or the doxy, of the *condottiero*, Niccolo da Stresa.

The devil's voice grew louder with each passing mile, and that of the good angel, her conscience, grew softer. That told her that what she was contemplating was a sin, that her duty waited for her at Montefiore city. The lady of Novera had pledged herself long ago to carry out God's will, and the will of her uncle, and never to follow her own sinful desires.

Oh, how easy it had been for her to be good and true when she had no sinful desires!

But now she had them, and they all centred around the person of the man seated beside her in the cart whom she had come to love, not only because she desired his body, but because she also desired the mind and the companionship which he had given her, and which no-one had ever given her before.

He had taught her how to live, to fulfil herself, to endure without complaint, who had never endured before.

She was going to lose him, and her life would become a desert without him.

I would rather live with him as Angela, the pedlar's wife, than be the greatest lady between Milan and Florence, was her final thought, and the voice inside her was so strong that she was sure that he must hear it.

But he could not, and slowly the miles slipped behind them.

Behind them Gentile and his company followed in their tracks. They traced the merchant and his wife along the road to Montefiore and it became plain to them all that the man who had snatched her away from Gentile—if he were disguised as the merchant—was taking her to Montefiore whence she had originally been bound. Doubtless to claim the reward for rescuing her.

And because the cart slowed the merchant and his supposed wife down, with luck they would catch them up before they left Verdato. And if they did cross the border into Montefiore, why then, they would follow them and hope to capture them before they had travelled far into territory where Gentile's troops ought not to follow.

When they were only a day behind, although they were not to know that, like Ottone and Emilia, they came across Naldo and his men out on another day's hawking.

He stopped them, shouting, "The road to Montefiore grows busy these days."

"Why so?" queried Gentile pleasantly, for he

thought that he might be able to use the young man before him.

"Why, because you are the second party I shall have entertained this last few days—for night falls, and I crave company and you doubtless crave beds if you are travelling the road, Lord Gentile." He had recognised the badges on Gentile's pennons and on the jerkins of his men. Guido's he did not recognise.

"True," agreed Gentile, "but this first party of yours. Was it a merchant and his wife, together with two escorts?"

"You have the right of it, Lord Gentile. You know him?"

"I would know him," and Gentile's smile was wolfish. "I will tell you more later—when we have supped. You do intend to feed us, I trust."

Now this was not a request but a command from Naldo's liege lord, and as such was readily agreed to. Later when they had eaten and drunk, Gentile heard the story of the merchant and his wife, suitably edited.

"You say she was beautiful?" Guido asked, putting his oar in. He had no intention of letting Gentile do all the talking.

Naldo, flown with wine and the pleasure of being with such great men, exclaimed loudly, "Beautiful as an angel, beyond compare."

"And blonde?"

"As an angel, yes. The merchant is to be envied. They were most loving."

"Were they, indeed," snorted Gentile. "Yes, he is to be envied." Inside he was seething. So, the villain who had snatched his bride away had laid his foul hands on her and made her his doxy. No-one would envy him when Gentile and his torturers had done with him!

Fortunate it was for Naldo that he did not tell of his own designs on the virtue of the merchant's wife, but he was not proud of what he had tried to do, nor how it had ended. He said nothing, and sent Gentile on his way the following morning, blessing the Lord God that such a numerous troop was not billeted on him for more than a night, or the Lord God would soon see him bankrupted, like the Peruzzi who had been ruined by the late King Edward of England reneging on his debts.

They rode down the track which Ottone had followed, sure now that the merchant was their prey, and that he would soon be meat for the rack and the gallows.

Chapter Twelve

It was Ottone and Emilia's last evening together. They had crossed into Montefiore and driven by Morcote which stood a little off the road and which Ottone had pointed out to her in the distance the night before they had reached Naldo's castle. It had been another eventless day. Contrary to their earlier experiences they might have been the only people in the world travelling along the road. They had said little to one another until they had reached the spot where they intended to rest for the night, and were sitting before a fire in the cool of the evening.

Something seemed to be troubling Ottone. From the very moment in which they had crossed into Montefiore, driving the cart through a small stream, he had retreated into himself. Twice he had begun to speak, and then had stopped. Emilia decided to speak herself, to try to provoke him, to lighten his mood.

"And now we have reached Montefiore, will you hand me over to the Duke? Or shall we go on—to wherever you decide to take me?"

She said nothing of her own longing that he would not hand her over, but would instead simply continue on their journey until they reached Switzerland, or crossed into France, where they might disappear, never to be known to Italy again. The thought both excited and frightened her.

He said nothing. Which might mean anything.

Why would he not answer her? He was wearing a rapt expression now, as though he were looking into a far distance.

"Ottone?" Her voice was a query.

"Wife?"

For some reason this angered her. They were alone. There were no spectators for them to deceive. As usual, their two escorts were seated at some distance from them. So there was no need for him to pretend that she was his wife. She had told him so once before. Perhaps he called her wife because he proposed to make her so, by a forced marriage such as Gentile had embarked on.

Except that he did not need to force her. Did he know that? A thought struck her, sent by Satan, no doubt. If he did marry her by force, then no one could reproach her for not marrying Leonardo! Oh, yes, this was the devil talking, was it not? For she loved Ottone and wanted him most desperately, but perversely and impossibly she wanted him with her honour intact. But the Lord God, or her conscience, told her that she could not have it both ways. Oh, if only Leonardo di Montefiore were not waiting for her at her journey's end, expecting his bride to be a virgin, untouched! But even if he weren't, she would never be allowed to marry a nobody of a landless *condottiero*.

Oh, it was all too much for her, and she gave a great sigh, so that Ottone, alarmed, swung his head around and forgetting all pretence for once called her by her true name, exclaiming, "Marina! What is it? What troubles you? You are not truly ailing?" For during the last few days they had made some decorous jokes about her supposed pregnancy.

"No, I am not ill. It is only that I wish…that I wish…that this journey could go on forever, you and I together roving the roads, and that honour and duty do not demand that I should return to being Novera's lady and the bride of Montefiore. I have been so happy on the road with you."

There it was, out at last in plain language. She might not have used the exact words, but she had told him that she loved him and wished to be with him. And she had done it without sighs and dropped eyes and false modesty.

Ottone moved towards her. Emilia's words had affected him more than he could say. No woman had ever told him before so sweetly and simply how much he meant to her.

"Oh, my dearest heart," he murmured gently into her ear as he put an arm around her shoulders. "That would be to wish to live in one of Messer Boccaccio's fairy tales. You would soon discover if you were to live it for very long that the life of the roads is hard and cruel. It is summer now, and living in the open is easy. It is playing at life—but think of the cruelties of winter. And besides, you are only enjoying yourself so much because before, in your old life, you were so restricted that the freedom which you are experiencing now is pleasing to you. But you were meant and trained for more than this. And even if it were possible that we could disappear from the life which we lived before I snatched you from Gentile's side, and forget the duties which we owe to ourselves and to others, how long should we remain happy knowing that we have betrayed everything which we have been taught to respect?''

Emilia stared blindly into the growing dark. She knew that everything which Ottone had just said to her was no less than the truth. More, he had told her something else—that in his own life he, too, had duties. She wondered what they were. Another thing also puzzled her, and she must question him about that before their inevitable parting. From everything he had said and was now saying, he was going to return her to her future husband, and to the life which she had almost forgotten how to live in the few weeks of freedom which she had spent with him.

And she had never known how much she had been in chains.

So she asked him her question, for she was sure that he would give her a true answer, whereas when she was princess again she could never be sure that what was said to her was simply what would please her, and not the truth.

''Why did you treat me so harshly when we first met?''

She felt him stiffen, but the kind and loving arm remained around her shoulder. ''Why, I knew you only by reputation. That you were as beautiful as an angel, but also that you were proud and haughty; were cold and cruel in dismissing those who came to you as suitors. I treated you as the selfish creature that I thought you were, God forgive me. For I soon came to see that all that icy hauteur was put on to protect you, that beneath it was a shy, vulnerable woman. And once you were tried and tested when you were compelled to become Angela, the pedlar's wife, I found that not only were you brave and true, but that you put honour and duty first—even when you were treating with poor peasants. A woman who did as I bid her—not always, I admit, with the best of grace—but then how gracious would *I* have been, had I had to undergo what you did? Beppo told me not to hurt you before he left, and God forgive me, I know that I often have.''

"You have made me love you," Emilia told him simply. "Is that to hurt me?"

His arm tightened around her, but he made no move to make love to her, only his voice was loving, if a little sad. "I don't know yet."

Something was troubling him. In the close proximity in which they had been living, she had come to know him in all his moods, as well as to love him in all of them. Like herself, he could be proud, haughty, brave, aye and cruel, as well as kind, compassionate, loving and tender—for were not God and the devil mixed in all men? Father Anselmo had said that belief might dub him heretic, but his experience of life had taught him that it was true.

Also like all men, he could be fearful, and he could

be distressed, but being the man he was, he rarely made his fear or his distress overt.

The look which she turned on Ottone as she thought this was so tender and loving that it quite undid him.

He gave a kind of groan and pulled her to him, to place his lips on hers, his hands behind her head so that she was cradled there, returning the kiss he gave her with such passion that he was further lost to everything but the willing and loving woman in his arms.

His mouth still on hers, his tongue saluting hers, he dropped his hands so that one of them cupped her firm right breast, and the other slid down her back so that she was tightly pressed against him as though he were trying to make her one with him, even before they were truly united.

Emilia, who was Marina, who was Angela, was in a delirium of joy and pleasure such as she had never experienced before, and which she could never have believed it possible that she could experience. All her fear of men, of making love, had vanished as she returned the love of the one man who had pierced through the chilly armour which she had always worn to find the tender heart which beat beneath it. Broken words of love, caressing hands in which neither was the leader, but in which both met as equals were all that could be heard in the glade of the forest which had, by the end of their journey, seen the birth of their love.

For if Ottone had needed to strip Emilia of her defensive armour, she had, albeit unknowingly, stripped him of the armour of cynicism which he had worn since he was a boy. The nightingale had begun its song for them, and they were hearing it, not with their bodily ears, but with their inmost spirit, the spirit which told them both that here, at last, was their one true love.

And so, inevitably, as he bore her to the ground, they were both about to celebrate the liberation which they had together discovered after the fashion of which the poets sang, and of which Messer Boccaccio had written. They had forgotten both honour and duty, for these were but words, and they were beyond words. All that remained to them was to seal their love in bodily and spiritual union, for great love demands both, since without the spirit being involved, love is mere lust.

They were saved, if that were the correct word to use of the end to their loving, almost immediately before consummation of it by the busy world, whose demands would not let them rest.

Roberto came crashing through the trees towards them, shouting, "Messer Ottone, where are you? There is a mountain cat prowling about, and you and your lady should not stray far from the camp."

He stopped shouting on seeing them, but their moment out of time was over. Ottone sighed, pulled his arm away, and helped Emilia to stand. They were both panting in the aftermath of frustrated desire, staring at one another, their faces soft, their eyes glowing, mouths swollen and parted. Ottone muttered, "Oh, lady, forgive me for what I so nearly did. I should not have touched you, even lightly in friendship, for to do so is to start the flames of desire burning, and I must not take you, here in the forest, like a brute beast.''

"No," whispered Emilia. "I must take the blame as well. I forgot that I was promised to the lord Leonardo, and that my duty is to him." She saw Ottone's face change as she spoke, and asked urgently, "What is it, my love, which troubles you so?"

His answer was to take her gently by the shoulders again, and turn her worried face towards him. "Look at me, my darling, there is something which I should have told you before—" But he got no further for Roberto was calling again.

"Messer Ottone, for your lady's sake, do not delay."

There was no helping it. Ottone sighed again, and muttered, "That must wait for a better time. There's no use in posting sentries if we ignore what they tell us. Let us find this cat and despatch it. Would that all our problems could be so easily solved!"

But they never found the cat, and Ottone never finished the sentence he had begun. Emilia could not help wondering what was so urgent with him that it troubled him so, but which he was having difficulty in telling her.

She was still puzzling over this problem when kind sleep took her.

But it was long before Ottone slept, and when he did so his dreams were troubled.

It was a brilliant morning. The sun shone on them all. On the troops of Noverans and Montefiorans; on

Gentile, Guido and Braccio; on Niccolo and Marina pretending to be Ottone and Emilia.

Emilia awoke early. The camp was asleep. Pasquale, who was supposed to be playing sentry, had succumbed to temptation and was sitting propped up against a tree trunk, snoring heavily. Ottone was asleep too, and for a moment Emilia studied the face which after today she might never see again. He needed to shave, his beard was dark on the strong lines of his chin and jaw, but far from detracting from his beauty, it seeemed to enhance it. Emilia yearned over him before making her way into the trees. The humble necessities of living over, she walked towards the sound of falling water, to discover a large cascade dropping into a boiling pool.

It was a place where the nymphs and satyrs of legend might sport, and she had the odd notion that if she only stood still and quiet enough, they would emerge from the shadows to enjoy themselves before her.

Her delightful solitude was broken by the sound of someone walking towards her. It was Ottone. He came to stand beside her, and to say in a hushed voice, "The Gods might disport themselves here, lady. Had we but time, we might imitate them and bathe in the pure waters below us."

The mere idea was exciting. To stand naked before him, man and woman, Adam and Eve, Mars and Venus... But he had the right of it, they must away, and taking one last regretful look at this vision from Arcady, they turned away, hand in hand, Adam and Eve driven out of Paradise.

After that, to up camp was an anticlimax. They were setting off earlier than usual and Montefiore loomed ever nearer. They would not see it properly until the road bent sharply to the right some miles away.

Pasquale, now unashamedly awake, informed them, "It is a fair sight, Messer Ottone, if you have never seen it before. Not Florence nor Milan, but a jewel of a city with a good Duke, they say, who does not oppress his people."

Well, that was something, thought Emilia dismally, for she must think of herself as Emilia until this masquerade was over. Perhaps Leonardo was like his father, and would also be good. Oh, she did hope so, for otherwise life would not be bearable.

Ottone, after their early morning walk, was strangely silent. The odd humour which she had sensed in him yesterday was still on him, and when they stopped in the heat of the day to eat among the trees, and rest until it cooled, it was with him still.

His mood matched her own. For each yard they travelled brought them nearer and nearer to parting. Silently they ate, and silently they set off again. Since they had left Naldo's castle they had encountered few on the road, nor had they seen or heard anything of Gentile's soldiery. Perhaps he had given up searching for her, was reconciled to her loss.

She said so to Ottone. His answer was sceptical. "Pray God you are right. I shall not count us safe until we are inside Montefiore's walls. To be taken now would be the unkindest blow which the Lord God could deal us, so near we are to sanctuary."

They had been travelling for about an hour after their siesta, when they passed the bend in the road where Montefiore came into view. Shortly afterwards, the road began to run downhill into a valley where a river shone in the sunlight. Because of the steepness of the gradient the speed of the cart was slowed to a walking pace, which caused Ottone to fret further at the delay it was imposing on them. The nearer they grew to their destination, the more the shortness of his temper increased. They had almost reached the bottom of the slope where the road began to rise again—which would delay them even further—when they heard a great noise behind them. Pasquale, who had been riding well to the rear of the cart, rode up to report that a large party of armed men on horseback was approaching them at speed.

"Best pull over to the side of the road, and allow them passage," he urged, but he was too late, the troop was almost upon them. Ottone and Emilia saw, with sinking hearts, that the banners it was carrying were those of Gentile da Cortona and Guido Orsini. No chance that they would pass them by once they realised that the lost lady of Novera was riding in the cart!

And so Emilia thought. Eyes wild, she clutched at Ottone's arm. "May the Lord God be with us," she breathed, "for no-one else can save us."

Ottone said nothing, pleased only that now that the dread moment was on them, Emilia had not taken refuge in hysterics. He released her arm gently and swung the cart round to face the oncoming troops. To Pasquale and Roberto he shouted, "Ride, both of you, ride. This quarrel is none of yours—save yourselves if salvation be possible.''

Neither of them stayed to argue with him, but at his bidding put spurs to horse and were away, climbing the hill, perchance to reach safety. One of them, Pasquale, stopped as they neared the summit to look back, to see that the leading horsemen of the troop had slowed their company to a trot, and had ridden forward to speak to the two in the cart, keeping the rest of their company at a little distance. The sight had him urging his horse on again, for it was plain by their behaviour, as well as Ottone's, that the newcomers meant no good to the merchant Rinieri, or any with him.

Once he had swung the cart round, Ottone had leaned into it to pull out his huge broadsword which had been hidden by a blanket, and a long slim dagger with a beautifully ornate sheath. Placing the dagger on the seat beside Emilia, he said urgently, before leaping out of the cart to face his enemies, ''Hold the horse for me, wife, and pray to St Michael and all his angels that Gentile will see reason. He will not attack us for fear that you are hurt in the ensuing mêlée, and of all things he will not want that. I will try to parley with him.''

Now, Ottone said this merely to give Emilia hope, and not because he believed a word of it—other than that a brute attack was unlikely for the reason he had given—and for another reason which he had not told Emilia. He was under no illusions as to what would happen to him once he was captured. He was sure that they wished to capture, rather than kill him, so that he might provide sport for them in the torture chamber.

By now Gentile and Guido had ridden forward, ahead of their men, leaving Braccio in charge of them. A small group of men-at-arms dismounted and followed them, to stand quiet and steady until they were needed to lead the merchant away.

The expression on Gentile's face was exultant as he looked down at Ottone, who was now leaning on his broadsword, facing them as calmly as though he were going into battle with an army at his back, instead of standing before his enemies cornered and defenceless.

"So!" Gentile exclaimed. "We meet at last, soldier, pedlar, merchant, who treated me as though I were filth to be flung into the dirt, and took my bride from me. A pretty dance you have led us, lady," he added, looking over to where Emilia sat, the reins in her hands. "Shall I still call you lady now that you have graced this villain's bed?"

To answer him in kind, or at all, would be but to play his game. Emilia stared at him proudly.

"What silent, ser, and silent, your leman, too?" He was enjoying himself, no doubt of it, even though their refusal to return his insults irked him.

He swung his head towards Ottone again. "See how merciful I may be, ser kidnapper. For I am minded to tell you that if you surrender yourself and the lady of Novera to me humbly, I shall spare your miserable life, though little you deserve it. There, there is my noble offer, accept it, and live, where others might have cut you down on the spot."

Guido chose at this moment to stifle a guffaw. Gentile had spent the last few days detailing what he would do to the villain who had taken the lady Marina from him, and he, and the whole world, knew how worthless Gentile da Cortona's word was.

For a moment Emilia was taken in by him, was minded to shout to Ottone to surrender them both forthwith. Then her commonsense, and what she had learned of the world on her travels, took over, and she was fearful of one thing, and one thing only. That Ottone *would* surrender, and that Gentile would then break his word. But there was one way of testing the fell man before her, and before Ottone could check her she was speaking.

"Noble Lord Gentile, if you be so minded, then let me surrender, but only after you have allowed Messer Ottone to take horse and ride safely to Montefiore city in the wake of our escorts. Then, and only then, shall I know that you mean what you say."

Gentile's smile was ugly and he gave Emilia the answer which Ottone, staring long drawn out death in the face, expected.

"Why, lady, was he so potent a bed-mate that you wish to save him further trouble? No, you must accept my word. He will return with us to Verdato, and after several days...entertainment...he shall leave my castle."

Emilia shook her head, and would have answered him, but that Ottone forestalled her. Still leaning on his sword, and knowing now that Emilia understood what Gentile's plan was, he was plain in his speech. "He palters with us, lady. He does not wish to kill me immediately, for he intends me to suffer a slow death by torture for thwarting him and causing him trouble. Is not that so, Gentile? I shall be carried out of your castle at the end of your entertainment, a helpless, mindless cripple, to die in the ditch there.''

Gentile applauded him, clapping mailed hands together.

"Oh, brave. And how shall you stop me then?''

Ottone walked forward, the broadsword hefted in his hands. "With this, for if I have to die I shall die in a manner of my own choosing, as a man, and not as a drooling thing, begging for mercy.'' And now he lifted the broadsword and continued his walk towards Gentile and the men-at-arms behind him.

Inside Emilia something shrieked in anguish. He was going to die here, in front of her, and she could not say him nay for the very reason he had given. And if he died, either here before her, or later, in agony, then she might as well die too, for she had no wish to live without him to become Gentile's thing. And she knew what she had to do, and by the living God she would do it!

"Wait," she cried as loudly as she could, seeing that Gentile was giving the signal to his men-at-arms to cut his losses and strike Ottone down. "Wait! I have a message for you, Lord Gentile.''

The heads of all of them, Gentile, Guido, Ottone, and Gentile's men-at-arms all turned towards her. So engrossed were they that the distant sound of other men approaching on horseback behind the brow of the hill, whence Pasquale and Roberto had fled, went unnoticed. Only Braccio's sergeant, always alert, rode forward to check what the untoward noise was.

Emilia took no note of him, or of anyone. She was entranced. Unseen by them all whilst Ottone and Gentile had been parlaying, she had picked up Ottone's long dagger and drawn it from its sheath, in order to hold Gentile and his men at bay for a little when they came to take her. But this was not now her intent.

Instead she stood up, held the point of the dagger to her bosom and shouted, with all the power and strength that she, as the lady of Novera, could call on.

"It is this, Lord Gentile. If you kill Ottone, then I shall kill myself, for I shall have nothing to live for and will rather risk purgatory and hell than continue to live without him! Choose, Lord Gentile, choose whether I live or die!"

For a moment, time stood still. Stasis reigned—to be followed by confusion. Ottone, turning to her, lowered his broadsword, crying desperately, "No, Emilia, no!"

Gentile, stunned by this untoward turn, bellowed at his men-at-arms who had begun to advance on Ottone. "Stop, in the name of God, stop! The bitch means it." Emilia wore an expression of such dedication that he could not doubt that she meant what she said.

Guido Orsini, delighted by the stalemate which the pedlar's supposed wife had created, and the discomfort which it was causing Gentile, shouted, "No bitch, Gentile, but a gallant lady. If you do not want her, then you may have Isabella in exchange. Her nagging would keep even you in order!''

His words were lost in the din. And what Gentile might have said or done, or Ottone, or even Emilia herself, became irrelevant, because Braccio's sergeant, who had mounted the hill to gaze towards the north-east from whence the sound of horsemen came, was riding towards them in a mad gallop, shouting.

So urgent was he that Gentile, for the moment forgetting Ottone and Emilia, rode towards him in anger.

''What the devil is it, man, that you should disrupt our counsels so rudely?''

The sergeant skidded to a stop. ''Noble lord, it is right that you should know at once that a great host, many times larger than ours and sporting the banners of Montefiore is advancing on us at speed—and we in their territory, unasked and unpermitted.''

Even Gentile could not ignore this warning. He swore an oath so ugly that Emilia blenched at it, before she shouted, the dagger still held at her bosom, ''Let us go free, Gentile, for you cannot wish to fight a pitched battle against superior forces.''

''No!'' Gentile raised his voice to shout. ''Cut him down, and the bitch may die as well, if I may not have her.''

Emilia's wail of agony was unnecessary, for even as Gentile spoke, Guido Orsini, his face white, and in no mind to die a needless death, had drawn his sword, and lifting it, shouted to the men-at-arms who were once more advancing on Ottone. ''Cut the mer-

chant down, and I shall cut the lord Gentile down!''
The unlikely allies had become enemies again.

Gentile glared at Guido, and shouted, his voice
now hoarse between baffled rage and fury at being
baulked of his victims, ''Do as he says. I shall deal
with him later. Let the merchant live.''

It was as well that he had given such an order, for
now the forces of Montefiore were pouring down the
hill, banners flying, led by a young captain who was
a cousin of Leonardo di Montefiore, and whose reputation as a *condottiere* was as great as Leonardo's.
After him streamed his captains, and over twice as
many lances as Guido and Gentile commanded together. There would be no battle, for Gentile's position was too unequal. Neither did Montefiore wish
a battle, for to fight against Verdato would weaken
them both in their attempts to keep themselves free
from being conquered by Milan or Florence.

There was to be no sacrifice. Emilia lowered her
dagger as Gentile surrendered to the inevitable. The
after-effects of her courage and of her dreadful decision to die with Ottone were upon her. Her legs
were shaking and she felt sick and ill. She hardly
dared to look at Ottone, who had lowered his broadsword and was himself a trifle dazed by the speed of
recent events.

She saw Panfilo di Montefiore dismount and walk
towards him and Gentile, and begin to speak to them.
Unsteady though she was, when Panfilo looked towards her, she felt it to be her duty as the lady of
Novera to go to him to welcome him and to thank
him for his timely arrival, but her legs would not

permit her to do any such thing. She had enough sense left to see that Gentile was trying to make the best of things, for there was still the matter of his kidnapping her, and the slaying of her escort when he did so, as well as trying to marry her, to be taken into consideration.

All in all, although she ought, as the lady of Novera, to be wondering what dispositions and decisions were being made as they spoke together, she was too shaken to care greatly for anything other than that Ottone was safe—and might go on his way. Whilst she, she would have to go to Montefiore to do her duty. This knowledge only added to Emilia's distress. She might as well have thrust the dagger into her bosom.

Why did Ottone not come over to her? Perhaps it was because she was princess again, he but the lowly man who had rescued her, and their difference in rank divided them. And why should he, who had so narrowly escaped slaughter, seem so anxious when he ought to be looking happy? She was not destined to wonder for long. Panfilo, having finished his business with Gentile, Guido and Braccio—who began to argue furiously among themselves when he left them—walked over to her, Ottone a little behind him.

Panfilo bowed low to her, and took the hand which had held the dagger to her bosom, to say gravely, "Oh, lady Marina, it seems that I arrived but in the nick of time, and it is well that I did. A pity it were that my cousin, having almost got you safely home, should fall prey to Gentile at the last moment."

Emilia saw Ottone close his eyes in pain, and answered Panfilo dazedly, "Your cousin?"

Panfilo smiled, and when he did so she saw his likeness to Ottone. "Why, who but my cousin, Leonardo, who has brought you safe to Montefiore."

Ottone was Leonardo di Montefiore! No, it could not be, and Emilia, to whom so much had happened in the last month, overwhelmed not only by that, but by the knowledge that the man with whom she had fallen so desperately in love, was also the man whom she had so often said that she did not wish to marry, felt her failing senses leave her. Her last sight was of Ottone, his face ghastly, reaching out to catch her as she fell.

Chapter Thirteen

The window of Marina's bedroom opened on to a covered, open-sided corridor, much like a cloister, which ran round a quadrangle in the centre of Duke Theodore di Montefiore's splendid palace. The quadrangle was filled with a large green lawn surrounded by beds of flowers. In its centre was a lemon tree.

Inside the bedroom everything, as elsewhere in the palace, was of the most splendid. There were carpets on the floor and a fresco on the wall opposite to Marina's bed, showing the Gods disporting themselves on Olympus. Jove, a thunderbolt in his hand, had his wife Hera by his side, and in the background, Venus, the goddess of love, and Mars, the god of war, were making sheep's eyes at one another. Cupid, the little god of love, having transfixed their hearts with one of his arrows, was flying overhead, and laughing at their torments.

Worse than that, he had, down on earth, transfixed the heart of Marina Bordoni with one of his arrows and made her love someone whom she was now sure did not love her, and she could not forgive boy Cupid for that. She could hardly bear to look at the fresco, for Niccolo, Gianni, Ottone, who was really Leonardo di Montefiore, and who had lied to her so repeatedly, might have sat as a model for Mars, he was so like him in appearance.

On the wall beside her bed hung an oval Venetian mirror, set in an ornate gold frame. At her bed's end stood a painted *cassone*, a chest for holding clothes, which was so lovely that Emilia had never seen its like. She had thought that her home at Novera was sumptuous, but it could not hold a candle to Montefiore's glories.

Not that she had seen many of them, since she had not left her bedroom after she had been carried into it, semi-conscious. She had no memory of the last stage of her journey to Montefiore city, did not know that Ottone, his face white, had picked her up and carried her to the cart, to be driven straight to the palace.

But Lucia, her waiting woman, had hardly drawn breath since Marina had recovered consciousness, as she reported to her mistress the wonders of the state, of which, if she married Leonardo, she would one day be Duchess. She had travelled with Ugo as part of his train to be ready to serve Marina when she was rescued and brought to Montefiore.

"And the lord Leonardo, so handsome, so brave! And to think that he rescued you from that wicked man, and brought you safe home into Montefiore itself! Why, it is like something that the old troubadours made songs of, and one will surely be made of your adventure!''

Whilst she chattered on, Lucia was not idle. She was busy fetching clothing out of the *cassone* and holding up a series of magnificent dresses for Marina's inspection. She, who had once been Angela, and then Emilia, had turned herself into Marina again the very moment that she had learned of Leonardo's lies, and she intended never to be anyone else. Angela and Emilia were dead and gone, particularly Angela, who had so enjoyed being the wife of Gianni of the roads, the unconsidered pedlar.

''Come, lady, tell me which of these you would prefer to wear when you meet the lord Leonardo after noon has passed. His lady mother, they say, chose them especially for her son's bride. Seeing that you had no clothing with you, other than the one worn gown which you had on when you were rescued, she sent them for you to wear. It is most gracious of her to take such trouble for you.''

''None of them—or any of them. You choose. I really don't care which.'' Marina was still sunk listlessly back against the pillows. Her hair had grown again whilst she was playing at being Emilia, and was streaming, a golden glory, down her back. Lucia had spent the best part of the last three days since Marina's arrival in Montefiore lamenting over the state she was in, and washing and brushing her gilded mane until it was as lustrous as it had been before she left Novera.

Lucia dropped the dress she was holding and put

her hands on her hips to scold Marina as she had used to do when she had been a naughty little girl.

"I am sure that I don't know what has come over you since the lord Leonardo carried you in. You won't consent to see him, or the lord Ugo, or the Duke. You are scarcely civil to me, your faithful servant. Are you still ill, since you mope so? The physician said that you were recovered, and that being so, lady, you should not give way to foolish whim-whams and grievings. I would have thought that you would be offering thanks to the Lord God that you no longer needed to travel the roads dressed as a beggar!"

How to say, I wish that I *were* travelling the roads, a beggar, with Gianni by my side.

Instead Marina sprang out of bed, and tired of moping, as Lucia called it, exclaimed fiercely, "Go to, Lucia! I will not listen to your reproaches. If you cannot speak to your lady after a proper fashion, then I shall have you sent back to Novera and ask my uncle, or the Duke Theodore, to find me a new woman. Give me any of the dresses from the chest, never mind which, tire me, and do not say another word. And why I choose to receive, or not receive, the lord Leonardo is my business, and no-one else's."

Lucia's hands dropped from her hips. Her mouth dropped open. Never, in all her years with her lady, had she been spoken to so firmly. Marina had been so sweet-natured that, privately, Lucia had sometimes feared for her, since husbands frequently took advantage of a woman's gentleness. Whatever had happened to her since that monster had kidnapped her to change her so? There was a fire about her which had never been there before. It would be wise not to cross her. But it would be easy to respect her.

So she was unaccustomedly silent as she helped Marina out of her nightrail and into the most beautiful gown of all of those which the Duchess had sent to her. It was of blue and silver, the colour which suited her blonde beauty the most, and for Marina's hair there was a matching rouleau of blue and white silk flowers to match, as well as a fan which consisted of blue and silver feathers at the end of a black and silver rod. Attired thus, the lady Marina looked a proper princess most fit for the heir to Montefiore to marry. Lucia was already a little in love with the handsome Leonardo

"Yes, lady. As you wish, lady," she muttered submissively, below her breath, every few moments. She was so unaccustomedly submissive that Marina inwardly reproached herself for being so harsh with her. But to have Leonardo, his father, his mother, and his palace constantly held up to her to be admired was almost too much.

May the wretch burn in hell for having made her love him, when all he had done was rescue the woman who was to be his bride in order to marry her purely as a duty. Of course, he did not love her, for had he done so he would have told her the truth about himself the moment that she had betrayed to him the love she felt for him.

How he must have laughed at her! Particularly when she had spoken to him so frankly about Leonardo di Montefiore, telling him that she thought of her marriage to him as a hateful duty. Marina writhed at the memory of how naïve she had been.

Of course, she owed him a debt of gratitude for having rescued her—well, almost rescued her. It had needed Panfilo and the Montefiorean army to do *that*. Now this was hardly fair to Leonardo, when she remembered the dangers which he had run on her behalf, once he had decided to disguise himself and rescue her without using an army.

She could only wonder why he had chosen to do so. There was perhaps some good reason why he had, and one day he might choose to tell her why. But, in the meantime, there was the distasteful business of meeting him again, knowing how much she had betrayed of herself, and how little he had betrayed of himself.

Such deceit!

For there were a thousand occasions upon which he could have enlightened her—and he had chosen not do so.

And she thought of the times when she had almost given herself to him, and thanks be to the Lord God that she had not surrendered to the demands of her body. Had she done so, he must have dubbed her no better than a wanton, seeing that she was promised to another...

Oh, if only Lucia would leave her alone for a moment! But the lady of Novera was never left alone. Oh, if only she were, then she could cry for her lost love, and perhaps purge herself of it. And how could she go to confession? How could she say, Oh, father, forgive me, for I wished to lie with a man I could not marry, which was a great sin. And then I found out that he was the man I was to marry, and now I do not know what to think, for I feel so betrayed.

And then, But I love him so, still. Which was the worst thing of all, and she must never let him know. He must think that her love had dropped stone dead at the moment that she had discovered who he was, and so they would go to their marriage as equals in despite, if in nothing else.

So it was that when Marina entered the great hall of Duke Theodore's palace, she appeared so coldly beautiful that she took away the breath of all those present: the Duke, Ugo, Leonardo and Panfilo, as well as the assembled courtiers and servants. Lucia had already told her that the Duchess kept to her own quarters so Marina was not surprised by her absence. What did surprise her was that Gentile da Cortona and Guido Orsini were present.

She tried not to look at Leonardo, as the major-domo—who had escorted her in with such courtly grace, quite unlike the manner in which Naldo da Bisticci's man had behaved—presented her to the company. He insisted on calling her "The most noble lady of Novera, the Princess Marina Bordoni." Which magnificence made her feel less like the late Angela of the roads than ever.

And now it was her turn to curtsey to the Duke, who put out a shapely hand to lift her. He was sombre in black and silver, and when she looked at him, she could see how like Leonardo was to his father.

"Welcome at last, my soon-to-be daughter," he

greeted her, in his courtly fashion. "Although he needs no introduction to you, it pleases me to present him to you in proper form. I give you my beloved son, Leonardo di Montefiore, who not only desired to marry you, but made certain that he did so by rescuing you from those who sought to prevent your nuptials."

After which splendid speech, he first took her hand and then Leonardo's and joined them together, exactly as the priest would do when they were married. Perforce, Marina was compelled to look at *him*, and he was even more beautiful than she could have imagined him to be, tricked out in scarlet and gold. She had always wondered what Gianni/Ottone would look like if he were dressed like Leonardo, and now she was finding out.

The splendours of the merchant Ottone were as nothing to those of a prince of the house of Montefiore. He had bathed, his hair had been washed and cut and clung round his shapely head in a mass of dark waves, enhancing the deep blue of his eyes. He was newly shaven, too, the line of his jaw, stronger than ever, not blurred with an incipient beard.

His clothes were magnificent in their simplicity, but the chain around his neck was of gold set with rubies and pearls, and the belt around his waist was gold, too, and set with more of the same gems. His long legs showed to advantage in hose which clung to them like a second skin, one leg being scarlet and the other gold. The scarlet one had a garter around it, just below the knee, inlaid with more pearls and rubies.

There was nothing about him to remind her of Gianni of the roads, and Marina had never felt so desolate, so lost.

His face bore the impersonal imprint of his station. He was a living icon, meet to be worshipped by a kneeling populace, or ready to lead an army into battle once he had donned helmet and breast plate. In her desolation, Marina forgot that she bore the same stamp of pride and authority; that she was also sharing in a ritual designed to set them apart from those whom they were to rule.

But beneath the clothes they were as human as their subjects—as Marina had found on her long journey to safety with him.

"Lady Marina," he murmured, and lifted her hand to his lips to kiss it. "I am pleased to be able to welcome you to Montefiore at last."

"As I am pleased to be here," she answered him, but the words were a lie, and he knew it, for her voice was as cold as a mountain stream, and as impersonal as that of a judge passing sentence. The light in Leonardo's eyes which had been there from the moment in which she had walked in, died at the sound. He had been ready to smile at her, to hold her hand tenderly, to remind her that, despite all that they had endured during their time together, they had come to love one another. That she had been willing to die for and with him.

Alas! She had turned into the princess of whom he had been told. Who froze men with a look and who had made it plain that although she might marry, it was her body which she was offering to her husband, never her soul. She was quite other than the brave companion whom he had come to know on their travels—and whom he had partly created.

The devil of it was that he knew why—and that he would have to woo her all over again. This time he was not sure that he could win her, for she felt herself betrayed.

Leonardo could not but admire the way in which Marina played the part of a great princess, who had been carefully trained to obey all the precepts in those manuals written to ensure that young women were modest in all things, and would consequently arrive chaste and untouched at their marriage ceremony.

Everything which she did was perfect. She smiled as she sat beside him at the great banquet put on to celebrate her safe arrival and her coming marriage to him. She spoke to his father after a manner which suggested her admiration for him, as well as her deference to his superior station. She was perfect with Ugo, and with Panfilo, too.

She had even been perfect when Gentile and Guido had been dealt with, showing no unseemly emotion.

"Daughter," the Duke had said, turning to her immediately after her arrival and after he had insisted that she sit by him on his right, with Leonardo on his left. "It is only meet and proper that you are present when justice is done to those who ravished you away, and would have forced you into an unwanted marriage."

Marina had bowed her agreement, as did Ugo, who

was seated on a chair of state a little to the right of the Duke's party.

"Indeed, lord Duke," she replied, her voice calm, "I will defer to your judgment, as I am sure that my uncle will do—whatever that judgment may be."

The Duke rose. His voice as stern as he could make it, he announced what he had decided.

"If all men had their deserts," he announced, "then I should consign you, Gentile da Cortona, and you Guido Orsini, who bears a name which is not yours, to the dungeons, the torturers and finally the headsman, for what you attempted with Montefiore's bride. Furthermore, you compounded your offence by invading my territory and seeking to murder my son—no matter that you did not know that he was my son." He said this last as both men opened their mouths to remonstrate with him.

"Murder is murder," he continued, "whoever the victim is, and my son was but seeking to recover that which was stolen from Montefiore and Novera." He paused, to allow Gentile and Guido to stare at him ashen-faced, before going on to say with great deliberation, "Nevertheless, bearing in mind the threat which all three of our states, Montefiore, Novera, and Verdato, faces from our powerful neighbours, to begin a war between us which might give them the opportunity to intervene and take us all up, would be worse than foolish.

"That being so, I shall spare you to return to your own states, after you have ordered your citizenry to raise and pay a ransom which I shall name, and after you have gone on to your knees before me to swear fealty to me in the cathedral at Montefiore, before the High altar there. To break that oath would be to risk excommunication by the Holy Father himself.

"Furthermore, you Gentile, having no son or heir of your own, will swear to me that the state of Verdato will revert to Montefiore on your death. You understand, both of you, that if you refuse these terms, the rack and the executioner's block await you. This is the mercy that I offer you."

Gentile began to protest. The Duke raised a hand to silence him, and said, his voice like stone, "Many would have executed you the moment you were brought here, after your troops had surrendered to mine. You should be grateful that I am sparing you, even if am doing so only as a matter of statesmanlike policy which benefits all of us, not only myself. Although, as is proper, I am the greatest gainer in this.

"Decide quickly what your answer will be. I will not palter with you long."

Guido jumped foward to kneel before, not the Duke, but Marina.

"Forgive me, lady, for what I tried to do to you. Praise God, I failed. I will be your servant, lord Duke, and accept the generous terms which you offer, as will my overlord, the lord Gentile, once he has come to terms with your magnanimity." He kissed the toe of Marina's slipper, disregarding the shudder of distaste which she had given when she saw him kneeling so near to her.

And so it was decided. Gentile, when push came to shove, had no mind to die an ignominious death when a way out was offered to him. He and Guido

were led away to quarters, which, if not as sumptuous as those which housed the Duke and his family,
were rather better than the damp dungeons which
might have been their due!

Marina's only display of emotion had been to
shiver when Gentile, having knelt to the Duke, gave
her and Leonardo a baleful stare before the man-at-
arms took him by the shoulder to urge him on his
way so that the ducal party might process to their
banquet. After that she was impassivity itself, her
cold smile never reaching her eyes.

If the Duke and Ugo noticed how withdrawn she
was, neither of them said anything. To Ugo, indeed,
Marina was as she had always been, and as he had
described her to the Duke, so he was not surprised
by her manner. Only Leonardo tried to revive the
lively and loving woman who had sat beside him in
the forest, had eaten the rabbit which Beppo had
cooked them, had offered up her flowers to God at
Ostuna, and shared in the simple pleasures and sor-
rows of its citizens.

A great silver platter of beautifully cooked food
was placed before them, to be served by the pages
who ran everywhere to do their masters' bidding.

"This is a little different from our fare in the forest, is it not, lady?" he whispered to her, to have her
offer him her shoulder and say coldly.

"Indeed, ser Leonardo, very different," with no
warmth in her tone.

The only time her perfect control faltered was
when he caught her looking around the table, and at

the men-at-arms who lined the walls, there for their protection.

"What is it, lady?" he asked her. "What do you seek?"

She turned her beautiful face towards him, but to Leonardo she was not as beautiful as she had been as dirty Angela, because Angela had been warm and human, and this woman was as cold as ice. "I but wondered whether Beppo, I mean Marco, was present tonight, and if not, where he was."

This gave Leonardo hope. He replied eagerly, "Why, lady, he is at present on an errand for my father at the court of Milan, given him when he reached here after he left us."

"I had hoped to see him," was all she said to that.

The beautiful food was dust and ashes in her mouth, as it was in Leonardo's. He wished most passionately that he might speak to her alone, but that privilege was denied to him. For the moment they were on public display, surrounded by the many friends and relatives of the Montefiore family, as well as the most rich merchants in the duchy, who were responsible for its ever-increasing wealth.

Tomorrow! Yes, he would see her alone tomorrow, when all those around them were about their own business, and try to repair the breach which her discovery of his deception of her had created.

But tomorrow was no better. He had asked if he might wait upon her in the morning, and she had inclined her head and answered coolly, "Of course, my lord of Montefiore." But when he arrived in her

living chamber next to her bedroom, she had her
waiting woman with her, who looked at him with
great greedy eyes, and was certain to listen avidly to
every word he said to her mistress.

Marina looked lovelier than ever. She was in a
cream silk gown decorated with scarlet carnations,
and the scarlet was repeated in the velvet of the sash
which bound her tiny waist. She was wearing one of
the new headdresses which had come from France,
a tall conical cap from which a veil of the finest
gauze depended.

He was dismally aware that his own splendour
matched hers, and he wondered if she was as miserable behind it as he was behind his. If so, nothing
showed: she was as great a dissembler as he was.

"You look well, lady," he told her, to such ba-
nalities was he reduced.

Marina inclined her head as graciously as she
could. She could hardly bear to look on him. Today
he was favouring a suit of black and silver similar to
the one which his father had worn the evening before, and its sombre glory suited him even more than
the scarlet and gold he had worn for the banquet.

He wanted to take her in his arms, to kiss her, to
remind her of the times when they had laughed and
talked together, had confessed their love not only in
words, but in exchanges of glances, sighs and secret
understandings.

But not only was the waiting woman there, presently Marina summoned a page who brought in wine
and little cakes and pastries, and set them out on a
small inlaid table which had come from Constanti-

nople. There were goblets of silver, and a tall jug. The page hovered about them, awaiting further orders.

A plague on them all! He would have none of this! As Marina put out a hand to offer him the plate of pastries after the page had poured him wine from the jug, Leonardo seized her slender wrist, and exclaimed urgently, "Lady! I would speak with you privately. No offence to those who serve you, but I bid you send them away. We are affianced now, and may most properly be left alone."

He saw her tremble, saw her lip quiver and the colour mount in her face, but she could not gainsay him because he had the right of it. It would be most unnatural of her to refuse such a reasonable wish on the part of an eager future husband.

Marina waved Lucia and the page away. What could he have to say to her? And did he know that every time she looked at him her heart melted within her, and all that she wanted was to be in his arms again! Oh, how weak she was, to love him still. He who was simply taking part in a dynastic marriage, made for political gain. She would not wait for him to speak, she would attack first.

"What have you to say to me, Lord Leonardo, that may not wait until our marriage vows are made?"

"This," he said roughly, and putting out his hands, seized her shoulders roughly, and pulled her to her feet with such power that she felt the brute strength of him for the first time since he had freed her from Gentile's clutches. "Why are you treating me so coldly, so cruelly, now that we are at my father's court? This is not how you were wont to behave when you were Emilia and I was Ottone. Whence comes this change? Why have you transformed yourself into a cold princess again? Is this the woman who wished to die by my side and so threatened Gentile?''

"Why, ser Leonardo!" she told him, trying to preserve her lovely calm even as she trembled at his touch, and wished to lean forward to kiss the mouth which was so near to her own. "You know as well as I why I have done so. This is the woman whom you are contracted to marry, the lady of Novera. The woman whom you deceived from the moment you seized her at the altar, to the moment when the forces of Montefiore arrived and compelled you to acknowledge your trickery. Think you that I could ever trust a word which such a one as you have proved to be said? I was Angela who loved Gianni, Emilia who loved Ottone. But they were phantoms. You lied to me. Compelled me to love a man who did not exist. Humiliated me, because you even made me want to cancel all the vows of chastity which I had taken. Made me fearful that I might betray the man to whom I was promised—who was you! And never once did you so much as hint to me the truth of yourself.

"I will marry you because the reasons of state which made my uncle and your father agree to this match are all-compelling—and for no other reason.''

"No!" he exclaimed hoarsely, holding her still against him. "I regret that I never told you who I was when once I began to love you, as I have never

loved another woman. But I—rightly as I now see—
was fearful of how you would behave when once you
knew the truth of me. Your safety was always my
concern, the more so as the days passed and our mutual passion grew. Do not shake your head. Remember your behaviour at Burani, and later, in the woods,
as we drew near to Montefiore.''

His grip on her had slackened for a moment, and
Marina pulled herself free, to retreat to the far end
of the room, to stare at him with tear-filled eyes.

"Oh, do not remind me of my shame. Leave me
only with the memory that, for whatever reason, you
saved me from Gentile, and for that also I will marry
you. But do not pretend that you loved me. If you
had, you would have told me the truth, and not
waited for me to discover it from another's lips."

He was across the room, to throw himself on his
knees before her. "Nay, no pretence, Marina. I love
you more than I would have once thought possible.
It breaks my heart to see you reject me, even though
I understand why you do."

She made him no answer, but turned her head
away, and put out a hand as though to ward him off.

"Nay, my heart, my life," he cried, "do but listen
to me. It is true that before I met you, marriage to
you was but a duty which I did not particularly want.
But once we were on the road together, and I came
to know the true lady of Novera, not the one of legend and rumour, I came to love you. There were
good reasons why I dared not tell you who I was. It
was best that you did not know so that you could not
by accident betray my true identity if we were

caught—giving Gentile and later, Guido, a hostage to bargain with. Better that they thought me naught but a lowly mercenary—which I once was, before my brother died.

"And later, when I could have told you, we were so happy together that I was fearful to spoil what we had come to share—and, if you would but listen to me, could share again." He picked up the skirt of her gown to hide his face in, before looking up at her to say with passion, "What oath can I swear to prove that what I am saying to you is true? Tell me, and I will swear it. Do but remember that you loved Ottone so dearly that you were ready to die with him. I am that Ottone, Marina. I and none other."

Oh, if she could but believe him. If only she could recapture what she had felt when she had faced Gentile and Guido with the dagger in her hand. She had been ready to sacrifice her life, as she had been ready to escape being the Noveran princess, to be lost, never to be found again, in order to live with the man whom she had come to love.

She, who never cried, was weeping. Weeping for the past, for the woman who had travelled the roads and found love, but now dare not trust that love. So many of her kind married for convenience, as an act of state, that she could not believe that he was telling her the truth. On the road everything had seemed simple, but now nothing was simple.

Something of her torment, her anguish, touched the man kneeling before her.

"Trust me," he said, abandoning justification,

abandoning explanation. "Angela trusted Gianni, Emilia trusted Ottone."

"But we are neither," she whispered through her tears. "I will marry you, Leonardo—but you must be patient with me." Her sobs renewed as she remembered the camaraderie of the road, the laughter, and the loving—and the fear, which had served only to bind them together, as high state and comfort never could.

Leonardo slowly rose. He recognised exhaustion when he saw it, and for the moment he must be content. The tears which his dear love was shedding told him that she was human still, not cold goddess.

Be patient, she had said, and so he would be.

He took her hand, so cold, so icy cold, and kissed it.

"Farewell," he said. "Patience shall be my mistress—if you will allow mercy to be yours."

Chapter Fourteen

"So, we surrender completely and you go home, not only empty-handed, but heavily in debt to Montefiore. A fine end to our expedition! And all done without exchanging so much as a blow. That is not how I thought Gentile da Cortona ordered matters. So much for reputations!"

Gentile was confronting an angry Braccio after telling him of the Duke's decision.

"Be reasonable, man," Gentile said wearily. "This pains me even more than it does you—you merely go to serve another master if you are discontent with me. But I, I have to pay the ransom, and sign my lands away. No!" He held up his hand as Braccio began to speak. "I had hoped to wed the lady before Montefiore and Novera's forces arrived to stop me. Once wedded there was nothing Ugo Bordoni or any other man could have done. But once I was in Montefiore and my gambler's throw had failed, and I was confronted by a host better armed and twice as large as mine, it would have been throwing all our lives away to have offered battle. This way I at least live to fight another day."

"And Leo di Montefiore lives not only to mock us, but to make us the laughing-stock of all Italy. Snatching the lady away at the altar, humiliating us all, disguising himself and her, and achieving refuge just as his cousin's army arrived to save him: it is a song fit for a troubadour to sing—and bring us further mock."

Gentile's smile was nasty. "Well, you may thank your own lack of judgment, Braccio, for losing us this throw. After all, you had him and the lady in your hands at Ostuna, and let them go. I owe you no thanks, and another lord would not have given you your pay before turning you off, after you had caused him such grief."

Braccio made no answer to that: there was none to make. His hatred of Leonardo was a living thing which gnawed at his vitals. He had spent more than one happy hour plotting what he would do to him once they had captured him and taken him back to Verdato's dungeons. All to no avail.

He looked at the moth-eaten old man who stood before him whining about his losses. And who now took the opportunity to jeer at him further. "I hear your sergeant, the only one with any brains in your troop, has asked Panfilo di Montefiore to hire him to serve in his band, having no mind to serve further such a one as you. Do as he does, and as I am doing. Cut your losses. Forget this and resolve to be a little more careful in future as to whom you allow to escape from your clutches."

Yes, every cruel word was like a white hot sword twisting in Braccio's guts. Oh, he could not have his revenge on Gentile—no point in that—but he was suddenly resolved that before he left Montefiore Messer Leonardo should pay for all his deceits.

He said nothing further. Best let the old fool before him think that he had swallowed all the insults which he had put upon him. What he had decided to do must be done secretly if it were to succeed—and if it did, why, then, Messer Leonardo might not think himself so clever after all!

The preparations for the wedding went ahead with speed. Now that the lady of Novera was safe, and her future husband with her, the Duke felt that it was imperative that nothing should stand in the way of the alliance which would benefit both states so signally. The splendour of the celebrations would show to all the world the power and the might which Montefiore would command when Leonardo inherited Novera.

This did not mean that he saw Marina merely as a pawn in a diplomatic game. He was pleased by both her beauty and the cool control which she had displayed from the first moment in which she had walked into his presence. His son was acquiring a wife who would do him and Montefiore justice, and so he told his wife, singing her praises so much that the Duchess decided to delay no longer in meeting her son's bride.

She had been ill again with a complaint which no doctor could identify, beyond the belief that the humours of her body were not in agreement, and there was little that they could do to help her—except dose her with strong medicine which made her feel worse.

Marina was seated in her room, trying to read when the Duchess's woman arrived to tell her that her mistress wished to see her on the instant—if that were agreeable to her.

It was not agreeable to Marina. It was not long after Leonardo had left her and she was still inwardly shaking from her encounter with him. Could she believe him? The words ran through her head again and again, preventing her from reading the book which she had taken up.

Nevertheless her strong sense of duty had her agreeing to visit the Duchess Caterina at once. She was pleased that she had done so when the waiting-woman told her hesitantly, "I must inform you, Madonna, that the Duchess is very weak, and finds it difficult to talk overmuch. If I am to be honest with you, I must also tell you that she lives only to know that Leonardo is married."

So Marina was not surprised when she entered the pretty room, where flowers blossomed in every corner, and which overlooked the park at the back of the palace, to find the Duchess reclining on a daybed in the loggia which adjoined the room. She was swathed in shawls, although the day was warm. She possessed the remains of great beauty, but there was a transparent look about her, which told of suffering, long endured. Her voice was still strong, however, when she welcomed her future daughter-in-law.

"Come, let me see you, child! Yes, you are as

lovely as Theodore and Leonardo said you were. Sorry I am that I have been too ill to welcome you to Montefiore before. Sit beside me, and we will talk of what women love—of men and gardens and books and the children that we have borne—and will bear.''

Marina needed no second invitation. Wine was brought in, and cakes and sweets, and as the Duchess had said, they talked of women's things. But, slowly and discreetly, the Duchess questioned her about her recent adventures with Leonardo and Marina answered her as honestly as she could.

She looked beyond the Duchess to the bright scene in the park outside. A serving maid was running along the path, a young man chasing her, and their distant laughter floated into the quiet room. How to speak truthfully, how to say, I wish I were that girl, and Leonardo the boy who pursues her?

She said at last, the Duchess watching her keenly as she hesitated, ''It was like one of Messer Boccaccio's tales, where a lady of high degree is disguised and performs tasks and duties which she has never dreamed of—and finds herself to be quite another person.''

''I see,'' but what the Duchess saw was not immediately plain. She continued, ''And Leonardo? Was he kind? I have always found him kind, although some, I know, find him severe.''

So she could be truthful. ''Yes, he was severe with me, a little, at first. Which was a good thing I now see, for I had to do so much that was foreign to me, and it was important that I did not give him away.''

Could she be completely truthful? Perhaps she

could. "The only thing which I do not understand is why he came himself to rescue me. It was such a dangerous thing to do. I quite see why the Duke and my uncle did not want to send an army after me, and provoke a war with Verdato, but there must have been others who could have been sent to save me."

"His father told me," the Duchess said slowly, "that Leonardo asked to go because he knew that he could trust himself to care for you properly, and see you safe into Montefiore. You understand me, I am sure."

She knew from Marina's expression and manner that there was something wrong, but what it was, she was not quite sure. Perhaps nothing more than the reaction of a young and innocent woman to the dangers which she had passed, and to the realities of the life of the helpless among whom she had briefly lived.

"My son is a good man, and will try to see you happy. He did not wish to be his father's heir, for he liked a roving life. He also loved his elder brother dearly, and was greatly distressed by his death."

Marina nodded her head gravely. "I know. He told me so, once, when we were talking. I did not know then that he was speaking of the heir to a duchy, nor that he was Leonardo, the man I was to marry." There was pain in her voice when she spoke, and the Duchess's intuition told her what the trouble was.

"And when did he tell you, child?"

"He never told me. His cousin Panfilo did at the very moment when he rescued us from Gentile. Oh, lady," she burst out. "Why did he not tell me? I...I said so much to him that was wrong. That I was marrying out of duty only…things I would not have said had I known who he was.''

Here, then, was the meat of it. The Duchess took Marina's hand which lay lax in her lap. ''Do you love my son, Marina?''

Oh, to say it at last! ''Yes, yes, I do, but does he love me? Why not tell me the truth?''

''If it will help you, I will tell you the truth I know. From the way in which he speaks of you, I think that my son loves you, and that he did not tell you who he was in order to protect you both. He is a man of honour, and I do not say that simply because he is my son, but because all Montefiore, and those for whom he worked when he was a roving *condottiero*, know it to be so.''

Marina kissed the Duchess's frail hand. ''If I could but believe that…''

''Believe it…have pity on him…and now, drink your wine and we will talk of other things. I may not go to your wedding, the doctors will not allow me such excitement, but afterwards you shall tell me of it.''

Could she believe the Duchess? She would try to. Leonardo had asked her for mercy and the Duchess had told her to show pity.

They were both attributes of which the Lord God approved, and she took the memory of her meeting with Leonardo's mother to bed with her that night. Could she, as the Duchess had told her, trust him?

She fell into an uneasy sleep, and somewhere towards the dawn she began to dream. She was lost in a forest at night. But she was not alone. Her hand was in someone else's. A man's hand. Large and strong and warm. He was urging her along, almost running her through the trees. What man was this? Why was he being so urgent with her? There had been other men with them once, but they had been sent away some days ago. How did she know that? Did she know the man whose hand she held, or more accurately, whose hand grasped hers? More importantly, did she trust him?

She stopped suddenly, so suddenly that he stopped, too, and spoke to her.

For some reason she could not see his face, but she could hear his voice.

"Do you trust me, Marina?" he asked her urgently.

"With my life," she told him. "With my life."

Even as she said the last words everything swirled away into the dark: the moon, the forest and the man, and she was awake again, remembering everything which had happened to her since the morning when her uncle had sent for her, to end forever the peaceful life which she had been living as Novera's lady...

Marina sat up in her bed in Montefiore city. What a strange dream! She might have thought that all she was doing was remembering the past—but although many strange and exciting things had happened to her on her long journey with Leonardo, what had happened in her dream was not one of them. Nevertheless the dream was trying to tell her something and that something was that she could trust Leonardo. Her deepest self was telling her so. Many believed that dreams told true, and perhaps this dream had been sent as a sign.

If it were a sign, then she must speak to him alone, and soon. Perhaps then she might discover whether the dream—and the Duchess—did speak true.

But privacy was hard to find in the world in which Leonardo and Marina lived. Gianni and Angela had found it easy to be private, but they were simple people, not great persons of state surrounded by courtiers with many duties imposed on them. That afternoon Leonardo went hawking with some of the envoys from Florence, Milan, Mantua, and other great cities, who had arrived for the wedding. There were meetings to be attended where business was done. Merchants came to the palace, not only to buy and sell, but to consult the Duke and his counsellors. Scribes ran importantly about. Marina had thought Novera a busy state, but it was as nothing to Montefiore.

It was not until late on the following afternoon after yet another banquet that Marina was able to speak to Leonardo at all. He had been cool towards her as they sat together, as cool as she had been to him, and she supposed that she deserved it. Looking at his imperious profile, for the first time she felt a little afraid of him—which made her wish more than ever that she was simple Angela again.

She touched him on his sleeve as the meal drew near to its end. He was looking particularly handsome in a short tunic whose colour was a deep burnt sienna. His long legs were clad in hose striped in sienna and gold. For once he was armed; the dagger with which she had threatened to take her life was at his waist. His tunic was decorated with narrow bands of some golden fur. Each day seemed to take him further and further away from the man who had been Gianni. Was this grave creature the pedlar who had laughed and sung in the square, who had joked with the peasants who came to buy the wares he carried in his cart?

"I would speak with you, alone," she whispered.

His eyes shone a deeper blue at her words. It was the first time since she had discovered who he was that she had started a dialogue with him. Before she had responded only to what he said to her.

"I will come to your room—but only if you send your dragon away as soon as you return there. Is she the know-all nurse with whom you belaboured me on the road?"

For the first time since she had arrived at Duke Theodore's court Marina gave a genuine laugh. Her uncle smiled at the sound, and Leonardo's eyes grew bluer still.

"I am pleased to hear you happy," he told her, and lifted his goblet of wine to her in salution, so that, perforce, she was compelled to imitate him. Before she could stop him he leaned forward as she lifted her own to drink from it, looking deep into her eyes.

"Bravo," someone shouted, to celebrate the first time that the affianced pair had shown any emotion before others. Blushing, Marina ducked her head, for Leonardo to chuck her beneath the chin, as he would have done Angela.

"Courage," he told her. "There will be more than that to endure when we are wedded, and then bedded, so that all may know that we are truly man and wife."

Which made her wish more than ever that they were back in the forest again.

Something of this showed on her face, so that Leonardo, emboldened by her changed manner to him, whispered in her ear, "At least we do not have to seal the marriage in public as our ancestors did—we are spared that." And when her face flamed scarlet at the very thought, he added, "Until later, then."

It was very much later because Panfilo, flown with wine, shouted, "Let the coming bridegroom sing and play for us. Have the servants bring you your lute, Leo—and does your lady sing? Is her voice as beautiful as her face?"

"Go to," began the Duke, but then, as several of the younger men hammered on the table in support of Panfilo, "Oh, very well, but one song only, mind."

"But only if my bride will consent to sing with me. And it shall be *The Blackbird's Song* or nothing."

It was almost like being on the road again. To Ugo's surprise his shy niece, who had always avoided such exhibitions, rose to stand beside Leonardo when his lute had been handed to him and he had tuned it, betraying none of the embarrassment which he had expected. Nor was she overset when her pure voice soared into the Duke's newly painted ceiling, showing the Nine Muses celebrating on Mount Olympus.

The company cheered when the song ended, and Leonardo, compounding his naughtiness, asked Marina in a voice which none but she could hear, "Now shall we entertain them with *The Englishman and the Venetian Tart*?" bringing back memories of their evening with Isabella and Guido.

But he was only teasing her, they were let off after singing their one song, and more than one of the half-cut diners envied the heir of Montefiore his pretty bride.

"Not so cold, eh?" being the universal agreement of them all, "nor so haughty," for her coolness towards Leonardo had not escaped notice.

But Marina was not cool as she waited for him in her room. She had done as he bade her, and had sent Lucia away. She had taken off her grand clothing and wore instead a linen chemise with a *gamurra*, a simple wool tunic, over it. She had no idea of what she would say to him, nor had she even made up her mind as to whether she believed what he and his mother had both told her: that he loved her.

At his knock on the door she jumped fearfully before she walked over to let him in. Like her he had left off his garments of state and was wearing a simple brown woollen tunic over plain hose. When he saw her he pulled off his hat, a large one made of black felt, with a narrow brim and the top of it puffed out like a huge plum pudding.

He smiled when he saw her looking at it. "The latest thing from Paris, they tell me. I thought that we might walk in the park—the evening is warm and the air is full of the scents of flowers. I see that you have sent the dragon away.''

Unspoken was his thought that out in the open again, among the trees and shrubs, they might imagine that they were on the road, and the constraints of living as prince and princess might disappear.

Marina nodded, and took the hand he held out to her, after she had picked up her straw hat from a shelf by her bed. Leonardo put on his hat again, and they set off together, without courtiers, pages, waiting women, footmen, or men-at-arms to follow them and bow them on their way.

A sleepy man-at-arms, his falchion at the ready, watched them incuriously. It was not for him to question what the great ones of his world might do. Outside it was as pleasant as Leonardo had told her it would be. He said nothing to her as they walked along, only led her into the park towards a great pool of water where fish swam, gold and silver in the moonlight.

There was a stone bench in front of the pool, and he bowed her on to it, to sit beside her himself. Beyond the pool, dim in the half dark, was a statue of Apollo, ready to loose an arrow from his outsize bow. The bow which only a god from Olympus could carry. They removed their hats in homage to the God, and the warm night.

"What is it, Marina? What is it that you wish to say to me?"

His voice was gentle. He was neither Gianni nor Leonardo, but someone whom she did not know.

The world swam before her eyes. Apollo first faded, and then re-appeared. Amazingly, tears were not far away.

At last she said, "I saw your mother today."

"I am glad of that," he replied. "She is not long for this world, as you must have seen, and she is a woman worth knowing."

"Yes," said Marina, stricken by the desolation in his voice. "She explained a little why you acted as you did." She went on, "Perhaps I was thoughtless to reproach you for deceiving me."

His answer was an unexpected one. "No, you were right. I was a coward. After Burani, once I thought that we were safe away, and almost home— although I was wrong there—I should have told you. Several times I began to do so, but I could not go on. The last time was on the night before Gentile caught up with us. But I could not bear to think of you turning away from me. How strange, that in battle I never need to remind myself to be brave, but there on the road with you, I needed that reminder, and there was no-one to give it to me. Can you forgive me?"

Of course she could forgive him. He was speaking like the man whom she had come to love on the road. She could forgive that man anything.

"There is nothing to forgive," she said huskily. "It is only that I do not know myself now that I am once more the lady of Novera. Oh, how I wish that we could be Gianni and Angela again, and ride the roads forever. That I had never learned who you are.

Everything was so simple then. Is that stupid of me?''

"No, not stupid. But that is not our life. This is our life. We have duties and responsibilities that we may not shed. I never wanted them. I was happy to be Niccolo da Stresa, which was the name I took when I became a soldier, because I did not wish to feel that I owed any advancement I might gain simply because I was a son of Montefiore. But once I inherited my brother's life, that simple life was lost to me.

"I must be honest with you. I did not wish to marry you, for the same reasons that you told me when you were Angela and Emilia, that you did not wish to marry me. A marriage out of duty to a woman I had never met was distasteful to me. Those beneath us might marry out of love, or friendship, but that was to be denied to me, as it was to you. And then..."

He fell silent, and in the end Marina murmured hesitantly, "And then?"

"And then..." His smile was brilliant. "But you know the rest, my lady. We shared danger, and those who do so frequently find that a bond grows between them, which those who have only known a life of ease and safety cannot experience. And that bond blossomed into love: a mutual love, I thought. Was it love, Marina?" He looked deep into her eyes as he spoke. "Was it a mutual love or was I deceived? Did the first difference which came between us destroy that love? For if it did, it was not love, but love's counterfeit. Tell me that it was love, Marina.

For if it be so, then the life of duty to which we are both pledged will be the easier to endure in the knowledge that another loves us and will share our burdens.''

So speaking, he took her in his arms, for he saw by the brilliance of her look, the very quiver of her mouth that she was willing to be his, that the love which they had found in danger and hardship, was not to be lost to them in easy prosperity. No words were needed, for those who love deeply share a common self which goes beyond the normal bounds of living, as though they also share a soul, even though they may only briefly be one body.

Marina had come home again. What she had temporarily lost had been found.

''You asked me for mercy, and your mother asked me for pity,'' she whispered into his chest, ''and I grant you both of them, on condition that you show them to me for having doubted you—which was ungrateful of me after you had risked your life to save me from Gentile's clutches.''

''Granted,'' he murmured, savouring the scent of her, the feel of her soft and warm against him, the only woman he had ever loved, or would love. Beautiful she might be, but he loved her for more than that, for the courage she had shown on more than one occasion, and for her compassion, freely granted.

Suddenly passion, long repressed, seized them both in its grip! One moment they were quiet and gentle in one another's arms, and in the next they were lovers who wanted nothing but the one true end of loving. Leonardo gave a groan as his mouth found

Marina's to discover that what he wanted, she wanted also. To be one, not two, was their only desire. There, alone beneath the moon in the beautiful garden, they had found their Eden.

Such sweet sensation! Such bodily joy! In the few short passages of love which she had shared with him before they reached Montefiore Marina had not experienced such unbounded pleasure. For a moment she thought that she was like to faint, as his hands and body taught her what true love can mean.

The nightingale had begun its song in earnest. But it was not to finish it that night. At the last moment, when consummation was upon them, the reality of what they were doing struck them both at once. The duty to which they had bound themselves called to them—and was heard.

Leonardo lifted his head from Marina's breast, and stared blankly into her blank eyes, to hear her say faintly, "Our vows, Leonardo, our vows. Those we are to make in the cathedral. I am meant to come to you before all men a virgin, or else the ceremony will be a mock. We must not begin with a lie."

To lift himself from her arms was an agony. It was he, this time, not she, who had begun their meeting with lofty talk of duty, and here he was, ravishing his love before the priest had said the proper words over them, before her uncle had handed her into his keeping. He was shaming himself before God and man if he could not wait the few hours left to them before he might lawfully lie with her.

Nevertheless Leonardo was shuddering with love denied when he said to Marina as, with shaking hands, she tied the strings of the chemise which he had loosened to find her breasts, "Forgive me. I was a brute beast to set upon you here in the open, before the priest had said the words which bind us as man and wife."

Marina put her hands over his mouth. "Do not say so. For you did nothing which I did not wish you to do. The shame, if there be any, is mine as well as yours." She looked at him, and saw the marks of passion on his face. Knowing how ravaged she felt, she said, "Let us walk a little in the park before we return to the palace, lest our faces betray us to any we meet. Whatever else, we must contain ourselves publicly before the world."

"Oh, wise child," he muttered, and taking her hand, he added, "There is something I must show you. It is but a short walk away, through the trees, and the moon will only add to its beauty. Come."

Hand in hand they walked, as though they were the first man and woman, alone in Eden. A bird was singing, but it was not Boccaccio's nightingale. That they must wait for. At the end of an alley they came into an open space, and there Marina saw what Leonardo had promised her.

Before them, silver in the moonlight, water cascaded down a gently sloping hillside in a giant fall to end in a basin even larger than the one before which they had been sitting. Seated by the edge of the pool was a marble statue of Narcissus, frozen as he stared into the troubled waters to find his beautiful face. Around the pool stood a circle of marble statues, each statue showing a satyr balanced on a pedestal, with a nymph leaning against the pedestal. Each satyr caressed his nymph after a different fashion, and their faces were like the faces which Leonardo and Marina had worn when they were making love.

"See," whispered Leonardo. "This place is dedicated to all lovers, and on the night we marry, I shall bring you here, to love you in the open, as Gianni would have loved Angela. This I promise you."

"Oh," breathed Marina. It was all that she could say.

They stood there for some time, watching the changing patterns of the water, until, as the night grew colder, Leo whispered, "We must be away before someone misses us."

Hand in hand again they walked back towards the world of duty—and the world of danger. Leonardo felt as though he were walking on air after having walked in mud ever since he had arrived home. They were entering the long alley beyond the pool where they had earlier sat, and were in the dark again. To the left there were lights coming from a small building which housed the pages of the court and their lieutenants. Before them, in the distance, were the lights of the palace, their future home.

Leonardo, anticipating their future life together, looked with affection at the sweet face of his true love, sure now that she would be not only a loving helpmeet but a brave one. Her character had been forged like strong steel in the troubles she had faced since Gentile had reft her away from safety, and from all the comforts of a life which had known only roses, never thorns.

Well, she had survived that nobly, and had captured his heart into the bargain, and when he uttered his wedding vows before the priest, it would be in a very different temper from the one which he had thought to bring to the altar. Oh, he was doubly blessed—as his mother had told him, after she had seen and spoken to Marina.

Even as he thought this, there were rapid footsteps behind him, and before he could turn to see who was coming he was seized around the neck from behind by strong and strangling hands. He had been caught, unwarned, around the throat, exactly as he had caught Gentile, and was consequently as helpless as Gentile had been.

Blinded, his consciousness already affected by his inability to breathe properly, he was only able to croak something unintelligible at Marina, in an effort to warn her.

He felt himself dragged backwards, losing her hand which had lain so trustingly in his. She gave a sudden cry even as Leonardo's hand left hers, and he felt the prick of a dagger at his throat. She saw how he had been trapped, and heard the man who had trapped him shout savagely, "Make a noise, lady, or run for help, and I shall cut your paramour's throat on the instant. I would prefer him to die slowly for the trouble he has caused me, but if needs be, I shall finish him off quickly—and then take my fill of you!"

Impossible to tell who it was who was speaking,

whether it be Gentile, Guido, or Braccio, and what mattered who it was, if he intended but to kill Leonardo, quickly or slowly. Under the strong hands which pinioned him and cut off his ability to breath, Leonardo felt his consciousness ebbing quickly, and cruel it was that just as he and Marina had reached haven, he should be snatched from her and from life. Desperate, he tried one last throw, brought up his right foot to stamp it down as hard as he could on his assailant's, either right or left, he did not know, nor did it matter which.

Dimly, as in the distance, he heard Marina's sobbing cry, even as the man holding him loosened his death-grip round his throat, under the impact of a blow which might not have been severe, but had been enough to surprise his assailant. This allowed Leonardo to swivel around, gasping for breath, sucking in air, and try to catch at the hand which held the dagger, ready to deal him a death blow.

By St Michael and all the archangels he would not go meekly to his death, but would die fighting, if die he must!

Leonardo's hand—his strength renewed a little with each breath, air had never tasted so sweet— grasped his attacker's wrist, even as the dagger sought to find his spine, to deal him a killing blow. He was at a disadvantage, having left off his own dagger which he had earlier worn as an ornament. Fool! Fool! I should have expected this, humiliated men will always take their revenge. What price my cunning now—that I, unarmed, fight an armed man, in the dark, and I am already weakened.

Their struggle had turned into a wrestling match, and the man who was now opposite to him was testing the wrist which held his. Slowly, slowly, he drove the dagger point forward towards Leonardo's ribs, there, where the heart beat, and was on the point of success when Leonardo, his strength still returning, caught him behind the knee with his foot, using a wrestling trick which the acrobatic Marco had taught him. This had the effect of causing the dagger to fall away as his attacker lost his balance, but before Leonardo could disengage himself, his opponent caught him round the waist so that they fell to the ground together.

At some point during the last few hectic moments they were both aware of Marina shouting, and of her shouts growing more distant. She was running for succour, having doubtless decided that to try to help him might hinder him. God grant that she found it in time!

His attacker swore, and came at him again, hissing in his direction, "Prepare yourself for death. The bitch cannot save you. You shall be a dead man when she returns."

He made no answer. He needed all his breath, all his wits, to save himself, to try to snatch the dagger away and use it on the man who would have used it on him. Once, the dagger caught him on the arm, tearing a great rip on his sleeve, as well as a shallow wound on the arm itself. The struggle grew more savage. For a moment he was on top, and then his attacker was above him, trying to manoeuvre in order to give him the *coup de grâce*.

He lifted his hand with the dagger in it, for Leonardo to catch his wrist again, and begin to twist it. His enemy's riposte was to try another wrestling trick, which had Leonardo letting go of the wrist, but succeeding in pulling the other man away so that he was unable to use the dagger as he wished. As was common in such struggles, both men were becoming exhausted—something which those who had not engaged in a fight to the death never realised until they were in one. Luck, more than strength or skill, might decide who survived. But luck is usually on the side of the better armed—and that was not Leonardo.

His wound had begun to bleed where the dagger had nicked it, making his left hand sticky—which made grasping anything difficult. His opponent gave one last thrust, pushing Leonardo on to his back in such a position as made it difficult for him to move— and prepared to finish him off...

When the murderer's attention was diverted from Marina as Leonardo began to struggle with him in earnest, once he was no longer held prisoner, she realised that there was little that she could do to assist the man she loved. To try to help Leonardo might make matters worse, given her inexperience. Instead, she picked up her skirts and began to run towards the pages' lodgings, shouting at the top of her voice—it was that which the struggling men had heard.

No one answered her. Light there might be, but the pages had not returned from their revels in city to which they had repaired as soon as the at the banquet were over. Gasping and sobbing, almost falling, looking back once to see the two men still struggling, Marina made instead for the palace along the pathway which she had so recently taken, beyond the pool where she and Leonardo had been reconciled.

To see a man running towards her. It was Marco whom she had thought at Milan! He had a long sword in his hand and was dressed in half-armour. "God aid me," she gasped. "Leonardo, unarmed, is fighting for his life. We were ambushed in the park."

"Fools," snarled Marco. "Fools not to have you both guarded until after the wedding." He broke into a run with Marina staggering along behind him, out of breath, fearful, but determined to stay with Leonardo to the end.

Which was, she saw, as she stumbled into the clearing, almost imminent. Hampered by his lack of a weapon and the earlier damage to his throat which made breathing painful, Leonardo was losing the unequal battle. Marco said afterwards that it was a miracle that he had survived for so long—a tribute to his basic strength. The pair of them were on the ground, rolling over and over, until the murderer, with Leonardo pinned beneath him, raised his dagger to strike the fatal blow, precisely at the moment when Marco came upon them...

Without the slightest hesitation, or word of warning, Marco thrust his long sword into the back of Leonardo's would-be murderer, who tried to raise himself, then fell forward across Leonardo. Leonardo, expecting death at any moment, did not at first understand exactly what had happened, and could scarce credit that, at the last gasp of all, he had been saved.

He looked up, to see Marco throw his sword from him, after looking around to see whether any others waited to attack them. But all was silent, so he knelt by Leonardo who was trying to rise. Still wordless, Marco rolled the dead man over, to show his white face to the moon. It was Braccio degli Uberti, whom all men thought had left Montefiore after Gentile's failed coup to find new employment.

No, he had not forgotten the vow he had made to himself to teach Leonardo a lasting lesson. He had hidden himself away, waited for a suitable opportunity, had scaled the wall of the park, and prayed for his victim to appear. It was afterwards discovered that this was the third night on which he had looked for revenge on the man who had made fools of them all, and had almost found it.

Marina also knelt by Leonardo who was now sitting up, feeling his damaged throat. She threw her arms around him. "The Lord God be praised that Marco was here to save you. Ah, God, Leo, I thought that I had lost you, even as I thought all danger past," she cried. "Tell me that you are not hurt!"

Leonardo returned her embrace, then looked over her head at his faithful friend, and said hoarsely, "My thanks to you, Marco, for saving me when I thought all was lost. No, I am not seriously hurt, my love. Only a small scratch and some bad bruises. Speaking will be painful for a time. My pride is the most damaged, that I should so nearly fall a victim to the oldest stratagem of all!''

''A small scratch!'' exclaimed Marina, examining the blood on his hand, and trying not to look at the dead Braccio.

Marco shook his head, and said soberly, as he and Marina helped Leonardo to rise, ''Thank your lady, Leo, for running for salvation instead of fainting and wringing her hands. She behaved as Angela would have done, not some pampered princess. But what possessed you both to walk in the open, unguarded, when such creatures as this foul the earth?'' He stirred Braccio's body with his foot. ''Fortunate it was that I came early back from my mission, to ask for you and learn that you were in the park with your lady! I came a-running on the instant, without waiting for help, to find your lady doing the same thing!''

Leonardo's smile was wry. ''Why, I think that we thought that we were Gianni and Angela, and that my father's park was safer than the forests between Verdato and Montefiore! But you have the right of it.''

He looked at Marina's white face. She was clinging to him as though she never wished to let him go, lest danger strike again. All the doubts as to their future happiness had disappeared from both their minds—peril shared had revealed to them the strength of their love. Leonardo bent his head to kiss her warm cheek which was pressed against his breast. ''And thank you, lady, for keeping a steady head. Now you may be Angela again for a short time and help me back to the palace. I thought that you might have forgotten what you had learned on our travels, but I see that I was wrong."

Marco listened to them approvingly, and nodded when Marina replied, still shuddering a little, "I shall never forget Angela, but I will also remember that first of all, I am Marina, now the lady of Novera, who is to be the lady of Montefiore."

"Who has helped to save Montefiore's future lord. Something, Leo, which you must never forget," Marco added.

Nor did he. A week later they were married amid all the pomp and circumstance which Montefiore could provide, and when they had been publicly bedded after being lighted to their room with music and with torches, Leonardo took Marina to the circle of satyrs in the park, which Marco had arranged to be guarded, so that none might try Braccio's trick again.

There, on a carpet of silk, brought from Constantinople's fall, Leonardo and Marina heard the nightingale sing, and she learned at last that when one loves truly it matters not whether a man be lord or peasant.

And the nightingale sang for them for the rest of their lives together, and for their children also when their time came.

* * * * *

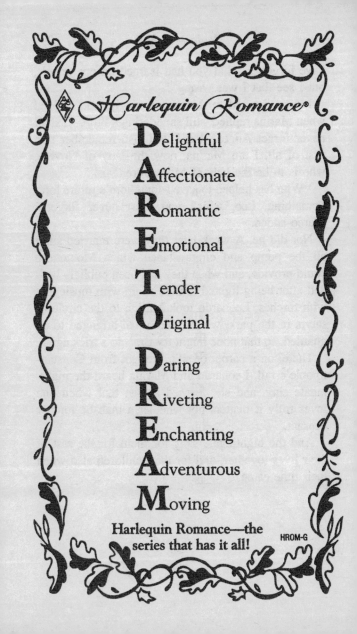

Harlequin Romance®

Delightful

Affectionate

Romantic

Emotional

Tender

Original

Daring

Riveting

Enchanting

Adventurous

Moving

Harlequin Romance—the
series that has it all!

HROM-G

HARLEQUIN  PRESENTS®

HARLEQUIN PRESENTS
men you won't be able to resist
falling in love with...

HARLEQUIN PRESENTS
women who have feelings
just like your own...

HARLEQUIN PRESENTS
powerful passion in
exotic international settings...

HARLEQUIN PRESENTS
intense, dramatic stories that will keep you
turning to the very last page...

HARLEQUIN PRESENTS
The world's bestselling romance series!

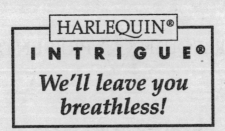

LOOK FOR OUR FOUR FABULOUS MEN!

Each month some of today's bestselling authors bring
four new fabulous men to Harlequin American Romance.
Whether they're rebel ranchers, millionaire power brokers
or sexy single dads, they're all gallant princes—and
they're all ready to sweep you into lighthearted fantasies
and contemporary fairy tales where anything is possible
and where all your dreams come true!

You don't even have to make a wish...
Harlequin American Romance will grant your every desire!

Look for Harlequin American Romance
wherever Harlequin books are sold!